Erle Stanley Gardner and The Murder Room

>>> This title is part of The Murder Room, our series dedicated to making available out-of-print or hard-to-find titles by classic crime writers.

Crime fiction has always held up a mirror to society. The Victorians were fascinated by sensational murder and the emerging science of detection; now we are obsessed with the forensic detail of violent death. And no other genre has so captivated and enthralled readers.

Vast troves of classic crime writing have for a long time been unavailable to all but the most dedicated frequenters of second-hand bookshops. The advent of digital publishing means that we are now able to bring you the backlists of a huge range of titles by classic and contemporary crime writers, some of which have been out of print for decades.

From the genteel amateur private eyes of the Golden Age and the femmes fatales of pulp fiction, to the morally ambiguous hard-boiled detectives of mid twentieth-century America and their descendants who walk our twenty-first century streets, The Murder Room has it all. >>>

The Murder Room
Where Criminal Minds Meet

themurderroom.com

T0352402

Erle Stanley Gardner (1889–1970)

Born in Malden, Massachusetts, Erle Stanley Gardner left school in 1909 and attended Valparaiso University School of Law in Indiana for just one month before he was suspended for focusing more on his hobby of boxing that his academic studies. Soon after, he settled in California, where he taught himself the law and passed the state bar exam in 1911. The practise of law never held much interest for him, however, apart from as it pertained to trial strategy, and in his spare time he began to write for the pulp magazines that gave Dashiell Hammett and Raymond Chandler their start. Not long after the publication of his first novel, *The Case of the Velvet Claws*, featuring Perry Mason, he gave up his legal practice to write full time. He had one daughter, Grace, with his first wife, Natalie, from whom he later separated. In 1968 Gardner married his long-term secretary, Agnes Jean Bethell, whom he professed to be the real 'Della Street', Perry Mason's sole (although unacknowledged) love interest. He was one of the most successful authors of all time and at the time of his death, in Temecula, California in 1970, is said to have had 135 million copies of his books in print in America alone.

By Erle Stanley Gardner
(titles below include only those
published in the Murder Room)

Perry Mason series

The Case of the Sulky Girl
  (1933)
The Case of the Baited Hook
  (1940)
The Case of the Borrowed
  Brunette (1946)
The Case of the Lonely
  Heiress (1948)
The Case of the Negligent
  Nymph (1950)
The Case of the Moth-Eaten
  Mink (1952)
The Case of the Glamorous
  Ghost (1955)
The Case of the Terrified
  Typist (1956)
The Case of the Gilded Lily
  (1956)
The Case of the Lucky Loser
  (1957)
The Case of the Long-Legged
  Models (1958)
The Case of the Deadly Toy
  (1959)
The Case of the Singing Skirt
  (1959)

The Case of the Duplicate
  Daughter (1960)
The Case of the Blonde
  Bonanza (1962)

Cool and Lam series

The Bigger They Come (1939)
Turn on the Heat (1940)
Gold Comes in Bricks (1940)
Spill the Jackpot (1941)
Double or Quits (1941)
Owls Don't Blink (1942)
Bats Fly at Dusk (1942)
Cats Prowl at Night (1943)
Crows Can't Count (1946)
Fools Die on Friday (1947)
Bedrooms Have Windows
  (1949)
Some Women Won't Wait (1953)
Beware the Curves (1956)
You Can Die Laughing (1957)
Some Slips Don't Show (1957)
The Count of Nine (1958)
Pass the Gravy (1959)
Kept Women Can't Quit (1960)
Bachelors Get Lonely (1961)
Shills Can't Count Chips (1961)

Try Anything Once (1962)
Fish or Cut Bait (1963)
Up For Grabs (1964)
Cut Thin to Win (1965)
Widows Wear Weeds (1966)
Traps Need Fresh Bait (1967)

Doug Selby D.A. series

The D.A. Calls it Murder (1937)
The D.A. Holds a Candle (1938)
The D.A. Draws a Circle (1939)
The D.A. Goes to Trial (1940)
The D.A. Cooks a Goose (1942)
The D.A. Calls a Turn (1944)
The D.A. Takes a Chance (1946)
The D.A. Breaks an Egg (1949)

Terry Clane series

Murder Up My Sleeve (1937)
The Case of the Backward
  Mule (1946)

Gramp Wiggins series

The Case of the Turning Tide
  (1941)
The Case of the Smoking
  Chimney (1943)

Two Clues (two novellas) (1947)

Some Women Won't Wait

Erle Stanley Gardner

An Orion book

Copyright © The Erle Stanley Gardner Trust 1953

The right of Erle Stanley Gardner to be identified as the author of this work has been asserted in accordance with the Copyright, Designs and Patents Act 1988.

This edition published by
The Orion Publishing Group Ltd
Orion House
5 Upper St Martin's Lane
London WC2H 9EA

An Hachette UK company
A CIP catalogue record for this book is available from the British Library

ISBN 978 1 4719 0898 9

www.orionbooks.co.uk

FOREWORD

MY FRIEND, Tom Sidlo, is in his quiet way doing a job of great importance to the country generally and to you readers of mystery stories who are interested in justice.

I want to tell you a little about that job in this short foreword.

Today there are dangerous forces at work undermining our whole concept of justice. Some of these forces have a tendency to lessen respect for the organized bar of this country.

Too few of us realize what the organized bar really is, or appreciate the work it is doing.

Individual lawyers are, of course, retained to represent individual clients. Whenever one side wins a lawsuit it follows that the other side loses. It is only natural for the loser to cuss the lawyer on the other side (sometimes the lawyers on both sides).

But lawyers *as a group* are constantly fighting for *you*, to protect *your* legal rights, to safeguard *your* constitutional liberties.

The organized bar accepts that as an obligation of the profession. The organized bar asks for nothing in return. It is constantly trying to secure better justice.

People generally know far too little about this work of the organized bar. They know far too little about the activity of the "office lawyer" whose function it is not to win lawsuits after a brilliant trial, but to handle affairs so as to avoid lawsuits in the first place.

These men are entitled to the one thing that you and I can give them—a measure of increased respect.

Two classes of people have poor public relations—mothers-in-law and attorneys at law.

The mother-in-law soon becomes "grandmaw" and grandmothers have excellent public relations.

Too frequently the lawyer remains behind the eight ball.

This is a bad thing for your freedom and for mine. It is time some of us called attention to the work being done by the organized bar and by those lawyers who specialize in what is known as "Preventive Law." (See *A Manual of Preventive Law,* by Louis M. Brown—Prentice Hall, 1950.)

Tom Sidlo is Chairman of the Public Relations Committee of the American Bar Association. For years he has devoted the biggest part of his time and energy toward helping the general public learn about the organized bar and what it means to all of us.

He's entitled to the thanks of the public and to some expression of appreciation for the work he is doing.

So I dedicate this book to my friend,

THOMAS L. SIDLO

Chairman of the Committee on Public
Relations of the American Bar Association.

A. A. Fair
Erle Stanley Gardner

1

I WAS HALF AN HOUR LATE getting to the office. Anyone would have thought I'd embezzled a hundred thousand dollars.

The elevator man said, "Bertha Cool was looking for you, Mr. Lam."

"Thanks," I told him.

"I think it's important."

"Thanks."

We rode up the rest of the way in silence. He opened the door, and I walked down the corridor to the door that bore the legend on the frosted glass: *Cool & Lam, Investigators.*

I opened the door, and the receptionist, who was frantically plugging in telephone lines, said, "Oh, *there* you are! Bertha Cool wants you at once."

"She alone?" I asked.

"No. Mr. Bicknell is with her."

"Who's Bicknell?"

"Someone new."

I said, "Give Bertha a ring. Tell her I'm here and that I'll be in in a minute."

I walked into my own office, and Elsie Brand, my secretary, said, "Gosh, Donald. Bertha's having kittens all over the place. Have you seen her?"

"Not yet."

Elsie was quivering with excitement. "Donald, do you know what?"

"What?"

"You're going to Honolulu."

"That's nice."

"Aren't you excited?"

"I'll wait for confirmation," I told her.

"No, you're going tomorrow. On the *Lurline.*"

"You don't just sail on the *Lurline* on twenty-four hours'

notice," I said.

She looked at her watch. "You'll have a little more than twenty-four hours."

"What's it all about?"

"I don't know," she said. "I'm giving you scuttlebutt. Bertha has been wringing her hands trying to find you. She put through a call to the Matson Navigation Company. She had the file clerk running in with some papers on an old case, and this man Bicknell was begging her to go to Honolulu. She said nothing doing, that you were going and—"

The knob on the door of my private office twisted as though someone were trying to wrench the brass apart. The door burst open. Bertha Cool stood on the threshold, a hundred and sixty-five pounds of greedy-eyed, money-hungry anger.

"Where the hell have *you* been?"

"Out," I said.

"Well, I'd certainly say so! I've been raising the roof trying to get you for half an hour. Here we have a client who's a gold mine and we can't locate you. This man wants what he wants when he wants it, and he wants it now."

"What does he want?"

"He wants you to go to Honolulu."

"Let him tell me so, then."

"He's talking to me."

I said, "Then it's you he wants to go to Honolulu."

"What he wants and what he gets are two different things."

I said, "All right, let's go talk with him."

"Now wait a minute," Bertha said, closing the door and glaring at Elsie Brand as though resenting her presence. "Let me tell you something about this fellow."

"Go ahead."

"He's a fragile little pipsqueak," Bertha said, "and when you shake hands with him just give him a token shake. If you squeeze the least bit you'll hurt his arthritis, but don't let him know you look on him as anything other than a

2

big he-man."

"What's the case?" I asked.

"Time for that after you get in there," she said. "I'm only wising you up now. I don't like to leave a prospect alone. A client is a funny fish. You have to dominate the situation. Leave him alone too long and he gets ideas. I just wanted you to know how to make the initial approach. I'm going back there. You give me about ten seconds and then come in. Make a stall about having been working on a case. I don't want him thinking this is an office where a partner comes drifting in any old time he pleases."

"How did he happen to come to us?" I asked.

"He's known about us for a long time."

"He knew you were a woman?"

"Certainly he knew it."

"Well, that helps," I said.

Bertha Cool had herself listed on the door as *B. Cool*, and, as senior partner, it sometimes made for embarrassment. Clients would want to see the head of the organization, and when they found out the B stood for Bertha, it was sometimes hard to hold them in line—not that Bertha couldn't do it, but every once in a while it took time. Bertha was hard as a spool of barbed wire and by the time she got done with a client there was never any question about her being soft because she was a woman. Sometimes it took a little while to get the idea across.

"As a matter of fact," Bertha said, "Mr. Bicknell *wants* a woman. He feels that this is a case that calls for the feminine touch."

Knowing that Bertha's feminine touch was a steam roller of ruthlessness, I couldn't help grinning.

"Who's Bicknell?"

"Bicknell has orange groves, gold mines, and oil wells."

"If he wants anyone to go to Honolulu on short notice it'll have to be by air," I said. "You can't just walk on the *Lurline* and—"

"Don't kid yourself," Bertha interrupted. "He's got bookings for half a dozen people. He's going over himself, and—"

"And wants you to go and do the job," I said as she hesitated.

"Well, yes."

"Why don't you go?"

Bertha said, "I don't like to travel. I don't like to climb stairs. My God, look at my feet!"

She pulled up her skirt and thrust out a leg that was still shapely but would have graced a football player. It tapered down to a trim ankle and a foot that had a high instep, neat lines, and shouldn't have been called on to support more than ninety pounds.

"Here I am," Bertha said, "with feet that go with an antelope, and a fanny that's like the differential on a truck!"

Elsie and I knew she was inordinately proud of her feet, so we looked at the smooth-fitting expensive shoe.

I nodded and said, "There are elevators on the boat."

Bertha said, "There are elevators on the boat and they're crowded. There are hills and mountains all over Honolulu. I've seen pictures of it. The whole damned Island is uphill. It gets hot. If I tried to lug myself around Honolulu I'd sweat and I'd swear. What's more, you can put up with this guy and I can't. I hate sickness and I hate people who are sick."

"What's the matter with Bicknell?"

"He's all gummed up with arthritis. If I went on a boat with him and had to listen to the sonofabitch creak I'd throw him overboard. Now don't let on I've told you anything about him. Give me about ten seconds, then come in and make a stall about having been working on a case."

Bertha turned, jerked the door open, slammed it shut behind her, and walked across to her own office.

"Gosh, Donald," Elsie said, "it would be wonderful if it should turn out to be a big case, and *I* had to catch a plane over there to do shadow work or something. Think of it! Honolulu! Diamond Head! Waikiki Beach! Leis! Luau! Poi!"

"And raw fish," I said.

She wrinkled her nose. "They say it's delightful."

I said, "Well, don't get your hopes up. If we needed any confidential work done on the Island, Bertha would hire someone by the hour or the day. The very idea of sending a secretary from the mainland would give her a heart attack."

"I know," Elsie said, "but I can build air castles, can't I?"

"Sure," I said, adjusted my tie, and walked across into the office that said, *B. Cool, Private.*

Bertha's smile was simperingly sweet. "Mr. Bicknell, Donald," she said, and then beamed at Bicknell and said, "This is Donald Lam, my partner."

I crossed over quickly to him, said, "No, no, don't get up," and extended my hand.

He gave me the tips of his fingers and was drawing his hand away even before I touched it.

"Careful," he said, "my hand's a little sore—just a touch of rheumatism."

"I'm sorry," I told him.

I looked at my watch and said, "Well, we've got that case all cleaned up, Bertha. The one you were worrying about last night."

"Oh, is *that* where you've been, Donald?"

I drew up a chair and sat down.

Bertha said, "Mr. Bicknell has a problem he wants us to work on."

"What is it?" I asked.

"He'll tell you," she said, and then added, "You'll have to go to Honolulu, Donald."

"How come?"

"That's where the case is. You're to sail on the *Lurline* tomorrow."

I said, "Call up the Matson people and they'll tell you that the *Lurline* is booked solid for—"

"You're sailing tomorrow," Bertha interrupted firmly. "Mr. Bicknell has everything all arranged and they're making out the tickets right now."

I turned to Bicknell and gave him a good once-over.

He was around forty-five. A good wind would have blown him away. He had bushy eyebrows, penetrating gray eyes, high cheekbones, and stringy dark hair. There was a waxy look about his skin that made him look unhealthy. He wore a tailored suit of clothes that must have cost over two hundred and fifty dollars, shoes that were polished so they fairly glittered, a hand-painted twenty-five-dollar necktie, a shirt with French cuffs, and cuff links of emeralds set in gold. His bony hands were wrapped around the knobby head of a sturdy cane. He was trying to be the big executive, but his face was drawn with anxiety as though he might be afraid of something—perhaps that we'd turn him down, perhaps that somebody would ask the wrong questions.

"How long have you had reservations on the *Lurline?*" I asked.

"Quite a while."

"You knew the case was coming up in advance, then?"

"No."

"Intended to take someone else along, then?"

Bertha said, "For God's sake, Donald, let Mr. Bicknell tell this in his own way. Don't cross-examine him. You're going to get things all balled up."

"I was trying to get it straightened out."

"Well, you're getting the cart before the horse, putting the horse in the shafts backward and facing in the wrong direction."

I grinned and asked, "Who's the horse?"

Bertha's eyes glittered with concentrated anger. "You are," she said, and then suddenly she was all smiles as she looked at Bicknell and said, "Donald loves to kid. You mustn't pay any attention to him. He's brainy as they come and he'll get the answer to your problem."

"I hope he does," Bicknell said. "I'd feel a lot better if you'd go along, Mrs. Cool. Not that I underestimate you at all, Mr. Lam," he assured me.

Bertha said hastily, "Well, we'll talk about that later on, but we can't both of us be away, and as it happens Donald can leave on short notice and I can't. Now, Mr. Bicknell, if you'll just go over the details once more. Just hit the high spots. I have some notes and I can fill Donald in on the details, but I want him to hear about the thing from you. I want him to get it firsthand."

Bicknell folded his bony, warped hands over the head of the cane, leaned forward so that his skinny shoulders pushed up as he put part of his weight on the cane. "There really aren't any details," he said. "You'll have to uncover the details."

"Well, you want a woman protected," Bertha said. "You think it's a blackmailing-racket."

"Exactly," Bicknell said. "I want Mira protected—and I don't want her to know that she's being protected. That's why I was anxious to have a woman on the job. I would *much* prefer a woman, Mrs. Cool."

"I know," Bertha told him, "but after all what you want is results, isn't that right?"

"That's right."

"And Donald is the brainy little devil who'll get them for you. Donald is young and full of pep and—"

"And that may not be an advantage," Bicknell said irritably.

"Why not?" Bertha asked.

"Mira is—well, I don't want to have the situation complicated."

"You mean Mira is susceptible?" Bertha asked, her voice showing sudden realization of a new angle.

"Well, Mira is unpredictable. Let's put it that way."

"You don't need to worry about Donald," Bertha said, all too vehemently. "Donald is all business once he gets on the job."

Bicknell looked at me dubiously. So did Bertha!

"Perhaps I can run over a little later on," Bertha said, and then with her greedy little eyes appraising him she added, "if the job is big enough."

7

"The job is big enough," Bicknell said. "It's big enough to warrant the greatest effort. Understand, now, I'm not an easy mark, Mrs. Cool. I don't want to be stuck. But I am willing to pay for what I get."

"Well, we're the ones that'll give you what you pay for," Bertha said, beaming all over her face. "Now tell us some more about Mira."

"Mira," Bicknell said, "has wired me that she's in serious trouble. She needs money. That's all I know."

"Now Mira is Miriam Woodford?" Bertha prompted, looking at me.

"That's right."

Bertha looked at her notes. "She married your partner, Ezra P. Woodford, and Woodford died and left her a pile of money."

"That's substantially correct. Ezra was fabulously wealthy. He had no living relative other than Mira."

"How long ago did he die?" I asked.

"Three months."

"How long ago was he married?"

"Nine months."

Bertha said, "Ezra Woodford was sixty-nine. Is that right, Mr. Bicknell?"

"That's right. Sixty-nine when he died. He was sixty-eight when he married."

"And Mira?" I asked. "How old is she?"

"Twenty-seven."

I said nothing.

"All right," Bicknell said, glaring at me. "It was a marriage of convenience, but Ezra wanted her. Mira didn't throw herself at him. Mira is a swell girl. Ezra didn't have anyone else to leave his money to other than Mira and me. He loved Mira. He liked to be around her. Once you see her you'll realize exactly what I mean. She radiates life, youth, laughter, activity. She somehow makes you realize that there's more to life than just the ordinary routine of living. She makes you laugh. She makes you feel good. She's like a breath of fresh air, a drink of wine. She—"

8

"Yes, yes," Bertha interrupted. "The girl is good! Now, Donald, Mr. Bicknell was in partnership with Ezra Woodford. There was a partnership agreement that if either partner died while unmarried all of the partnership property went to the survivor. If either party left a widow, then the widow was to get half.

"Well, Ezra Woodford married, and in accordance with the partnership agreement promptly changed his will. Under that new will Ezra left his property in two parts. Part of it went outright to Mr. Bicknell, and the other part went to Mira in trust."

"With you the trustee?" I asked Bicknell.

"That's right. I'm discretionary trustee. I invest the money and turn over the income. In addition to that I have the right to turn over such amounts of the principal as I think may be required. That, however, is only in the event of an emergency."

"How long does the trust continue?"

"For five years."

"Then what?"

"Then Mira gets the principal provided that during that time she has not become involved in any scandal that in my opinion would cheapen or besmirch the name of her dead husband."

"And if that should happen, what becomes of the trust?"

"That won't happen."

"But suppose it does?"

"Then the money would go to several charitable institutions."

I said, "That trust may be subject to question. What state was it in?"

"Colorado."

"Have you looked it up?"

"The attorneys seem to feel that the way the will is drawn it's quite all right."

I said, "To put it on a cash basis, your partner's marriage cost you quite a sum of money."

"As it turned out, yes."

"Knowing it might turn out that way, didn't you oppose the marriage?"

"I misunderstood Mira's motives at first."

"And opposed the marriage?"

"Not in the way you mean. Ezra was old enough to reach his own decisions."

"They cost you half a fortune."

He laughed. "I had plenty. I can't possibly spend all I've got. However, I thought at first Ezra was making a fool of himself."

"Later?"

"Later on I realized he had done a wonderful thing. He had achieved happiness."

"Now, then," Bertha said, "let's get down to brass tacks. Mira has wired you that she's in trouble; that she needs a substantial amount of money in addition to the income; that it's an emergency."

"That's right," Bicknell said.

"How much?" I asked.

"Ten thousand dollars," Bicknell said.

"And," Bertha said, "Mr. Bicknell believes it's blackmail. He thinks that someone is putting the squeeze on Mira."

I looked at Bicknell.

Bicknell met my eyes and nodded. He said, "After all, the estate is very large. The amount of money involved isn't particularly important. It's the principle of the thing. Once you pay blackmail you have to keep on paying blackmail. I want to protect Mira fully. She can't be protected by paying money."

"Who's trying to get the money out of her?"

"I don't know. I'm not absolutely certain anyone is."

I said, "Let's be frank about this, Bicknell. Miriam Woodford is evidently a live wire."

"She is."

"She's twenty-seven."

"That's right."

"She married a little over nine months ago."

He nodded.

"Her husband's dead and she's wealthy. Now who's going to blackmail her over what? Quite obviously some indiscretion that she may have committed isn't going to bother her very much—not ten thousand dollars' worth."

"Well, of course, Mira is a nice girl. She is well thought of and—well, of course, if it's a scandal within the meaning of the trust—you see my position, Mr. Lam."

"Where did Ezra Woodford live?"

"Denver."

"Mira was a Denver girl?"

"No, New York."

"How long had she known Ezra before they were married?"

"Three or four months."

"How did Ezra meet her?"

"On a cruise."

"How long had you known her?"

"I met her after Ezra did."

"You're fond of her?"

"She's a very charming young woman."

"What was the idea in making the will so that she had to avoid scandal for five years or lose all of that money? That was just an invitation for blackmailers to move in."

"I never discussed the matter with Ezra. I assume, however, he knew Mira was impetuous and he wanted to protect the name he had given her in marriage."

"Just what do *you* want?" I asked.

"I want to surround Mira with a wall of safety. I feel that something has happened, that she is in danger. I want her to be protected."

"That's going to be difficult without letting on that we're looking out for—"

"That is the one thing I do *not* want her to know. I feel that she would be indignant if she felt I had communicated her troubles to anyone."

"Just what *do* you want us to do?"

"That," Bicknell said, "is why I preferred to have a

woman on the job. I came here because of my knowledge that Mrs. Cool was a very competent, very determined, very resourceful woman, and that she was hard as nails. I felt that she could casually meet Mira, could cultivate her friendship, find out the danger, and forestall it."

"Suppose she's being blackmailed?"

"I think she is."

"What kind of protection do you want her to have? Do you want the blackmailer arrested?"

"Good heavens, no. I just want him—well, I just want him eliminated. Removed from the picture."

"How?"

He said, "I don't care how, Mr. Lam."

"Why don't I fly over?" I asked. "If Mrs. Woodford is in danger it seems to me I'd be wasting a lot of time—"

"I want you to go on the boat because there'll be an opportunity for you to make a contact on the boat."

"Yes?"

"Norma Radcliff is a friend of Mira's. She's sailing to-morrow to join Mira. I felt that there would be an opportunity on the boat to build up an acquaintance with Norma Radcliff, and through Norma a contact could be made with Mira."

"I see. What do you know about Norma Radcliff?"

"Very little."

"Do you know her personally?"

"No, I've never met her."

"She's not from Denver?"

"No, she's a New York girl. She's been a friend of Mira's for years."

"In the meantime, what have you told Mira? She's wired you asking for money."

"I've told her that I was arriving on the *Lurline*."

"Oh, you're sailing tomorrow yourself?"

"Yes."

"And she knows you're coming?"

"She does by this time."

"Well," Bertha said, "I guess that's it, Donald."

Bicknell said, "I will be willing to add substantially to the agreed rate of remuneration if you will go yourself, Mrs. Cool."

"I'd be lost," Bertha said. "I can't run around. I can't do the leg work."

"I would *much* perfer a woman," Bicknell said.

Bertha looked at her wrist watch, at the stack of stuff on her desk.

"And, of course," Bicknell said, "I shan't be niggardly about expenses, Mrs. Cool. I know that it costs money to travel to the Islands—"

Bertha glanced at me. "Why not?" I asked, grinning.

Bertha glared and said angrily, "Because I hate boats. I hate travel. I hate climbing. I hate these overrated tropical paradises of the Pacific. I hate to hear tourists gush ga-ga. I don't like Hawaiian music. I don't like to leave the office. I want to be where I can keep an eye on what's going on. I—"

Bicknell slid one hand into his breast pocket, significantly pulled out a checkbook, opened it, and waited.

Bertha broke off talking as the checkbook came into sight. Her greedy little eyes were riveted on it.

There was silence for several seconds.

"All right," Bertha said angrily. "I'm headed for Honolulu. Give him your fountain pen, Donald."

I grinned at Bicknell. "If Bertha is going you won't need me?"

"That's right."

Bertha sputtered, "Why damn it, *I* need him. I can't get around the way *he* can. I can't—"

"Oh, yes, you can," Bicknell said in his dry, dispassionate, husky voice. "You can do everything that needs to be done, Mrs. Cool. I'll feel much better if you handle it. In fact, the understanding is that you are to handle this personally, otherwise we'll just call it off."

There was a period of silence.

I handed Bicknell my fountain pen. "It's all right," I said. "She'll go."

2

BICKNELL HOBBLED from the office with his peculiar shuffling gait. His gray face was twisted into a triumphant smile.

I saw him as far as the elevator, then came back to talk with Bertha.

Bertha had already placed a phone call to the Denver bank. She was talking as I came in.

"This is Bertha Cool of Cool & Lam. We hold a check for three thousand dollars payable to us, signed by Stephenson D. Bicknell. Is it good? . . . You're certain? . . . I'm putting it through my bank tonight. . . . You're certain about it? . . . Because we're going to have to incur some expenses. . . . All right, thank you."

Bertha banged up the telephone, said to me, "The guy didn't even stop to look at a ledger. Just said the check was good as gold."

I said, "While you're at it, wire our correspondent in Denver. Tell him we want to know everything we can find out on short notice about Miriam Woodford, about Ezra P. Woodford, and Stephenson D. Bicknell."

"Our client might not like that," she said.

I said, "Okay, go it blind if you want to. I have a hunch you'll be sorry."

"Why?"

I said, "He tries to tell us this is an emergency. He wants us to go by boat. He insists that we go by boat. You could take a plane and be there tomorrow."

"He's explained that. He wants us to make a build-up through this Norma Radcliff."

"Sure," I said. "That's a good way to get acquainted, but it means a delay of five days. Why should a contact be worth that much time? Why not have you go by boat and let me go by air?"

Bertha blinked her eyes at me. "What do *you* think?"

"I think Mira's 'trouble' is a lot more serious than the

14

routine job Bicknell tries to make us believe."

"Why?"

I said, "He's sending you over to the Hawaiian Islands by de luxe transportation. He isn't doing that just because he thinks you need a little surf-bathing on the beach at Waikiki."

"Bathing!" Bertha snorted. "Hell's bells, I look like a sack of potatoes in a bathing-suit, and I blister the minute the sun touches me. I hate Hawaii. What the hell did I ever agree to go over there for?"

"Money," I said.

Bertha looked at the check. "You said it, Donald."

I said, "All right. Now wire our Denver correspondent."

Bertha demurred, but finally sent the wire through.

At four-thirty that afternoon we had the answer.

MIRIAM WOODFORD MARRIED EZRA P. WOODFORD NINE MONTHS AGO. SIX MONTHS LATER EZRA DIED LEAVING HUGE FORTUNE HALF TO STEPHENSON BICKNELL HALF TO WIDOW. MIRIAM WOODFORD REPORTED IN HONOLULU. DETECTIVE EDGAR B. LARSON OF DENVER HOMICIDE SAILING TOMORROW FOR HONOLULU ON LURLINE OSTENSIBLY ON VACATION. BICKNELL LEFT DENVER TEN DAYS AGO WHEREABOUTS UNKNOWN. SUGGEST EXERCISE EXTREME CARE. WIDOW MAY BE GOLD DIGGER WHO WOULDN'T WAIT FOR NATURE TO TAKE ITS COURSE. POLICE ARE QUIETLY INVESTIGATING.

I said to Bertha, "Well, that's more like it. From what I gathered about Mira's character anyone could dig an episode from her purple past and she wouldn't even turn a hair. Murder is a different matter."

"Fry me for an oyster!" Bertha said under her breath, then added, "But the widow only got half. Bicknell also inherited."

"Don't go overboard on that line of thinking," I told her. "Bicknell was a full partner. He's rich in his own right. Moreover, if he'd planned on getting rid of his partner he'd have done it *before* the marriage, not afterward."

"Why?" Bertha asked, and then, before I could answer, said hurriedly, "Oh, yes, I get you. It would make a fifty-percent difference."

I nodded.

"He seems to like her," Bertha said.

"He does now."

"What are you getting at?"

"When Miriam married Ezra Woodford," I pointed out, "Bicknell must have hated her. Now he sings her praises all over the place. Perhaps after Mira realized he was going to be custodian of her money for five years she decided to cultivate him. If she made that much change in that short time she must be a fast and willing worker.

"Perhaps her wire about trouble was just to get Bicknell over to Honolulu where he'd be under her influence without having all of Denver society watching developments."

Bertha looked owlishly at me.

"And," I went on, "Bicknell is carrying the torch for Miriam Woodford. He wants her protected but he wants to be damned certain it's a woman who furnishes the protection. He didn't like the idea of a man entering the picture. But does he *really* want her protected, or does he want evidence that would enable him to declare she'd forfeited her interest in the trust?"

"Mash me for a potato and dish me up with parsley!" Bertha exclaimed. "This could develop into one hell of a mess!"

"Do you," I asked, "want to give him his money back?"

"Do what?" Bertha screamed.

"Give him his money back," I said.

"Do you think I'm crazy?" she yelled.

"Well," I said, "have a nice trip on the boat, Bertha. Maybe you'll have a chance to strike up an acquaintance with Edgar B. Larson. Or, on the other hand, he might be the one who takes the initiative. He might want to know what you're going to the Islands for."

With that I walked out, stopped by my own office, and said to Elsie, "Ring up one of those companies that makes a specialty of packing junk in baskets covered with cellophane, tied up with ribbons, and with a lot of 'Bon Voyage' wishes stuck all over them. Send a big basket to Bertha Cool, care of the *Lurline*."

"Who pays for it?" she asked.

"The office does," I told her, "and we put it on the expense account in the Bicknell case."

"She'll be mad as hops," Elsie warned.

"I know she will," I told her. "I just want her to be in a good mood to meet a fellow passenger."

"Who?"

"You wouldn't know him," I said. "His name is Larson. He's on the Denver police force. We'll put a card on the basket, 'Compliments of The Denver Police Force."

"Good Lord, Bertha will froth like a broken champagne bottle!"

I said, "Bertha needs something to take her mind off of the office problems. This will do it."

3

I WAS BUSY all Friday morning. I telephoned the office a little before noon. Bertha was out. I telephoned at twelve-thirty. She hadn't come in.

I had to search some records at the county clerk's office. The job proved more complicated than I had expected. I didn't finish until a little after two o'clock.

I telephoned the office.

"Bertha in?" I asked.

"No. Is this you, Mr. Lam?"

"Yes."

"Bertha left a message that you were to see her before she leaves. It's an absolute necessity."

"I want to see her," I said, "but the way things look now I'll have to go down to see her at the boat. Let me talk with Elsie."

The operator switched me over to Elsie Brand.

Elsie said, "Donald, are you going down to see Bertha

off?"

"I suppose I'll have to."

"Could I go? I'm crazy about ships and—and about Honolulu. Oh, Don, *why* didn't you go?"

"Because our client thought I had wolfish tendencies," I said, "and under the circumstances Bertha was the logical person."

"Well, I'd certainly like to go to the boat with you. Don't you suppose there'll be some last-minute conferences and stuff with Bertha that you'd want your secretary to take down?"

"Probably," I said. "I'll pick you up in about twenty minutes. I'll be finished here then."

"The boat sails at four o'clock," she said.

"I know," I told her, "but we'll make it."

"Be sure you do. Bertha is *really* having kittens. She left word all around the office for you to get in touch with her."

"I've been trying to get in touch with her," I said. "Damn that woman, I can't carry on business and trail her around, too. What's she been doing?"

"What do you think she's been doing?" Elsie said. "She's been shopping, getting her hair done, getting some clothes to wear on the ship."

"Bertha!" I exclaimed.

"Bertha," Elsie told me. "After all, she's a woman, you know."

"You could have fooled me," I told her and hung up.

Twenty minutes later I stopped by the office and gave Elsie a ring. I thought under the circumstances it would be better not to go in, so I had Elsie come down to join me. I had the car at the curb and opened the door as Elsie came running out.

She jumped in and said, "Donald, you're going to have to drive like everything to make it."

"I know," I told her. "Just hang on."

We barely managed to squeeze through the traffic signal at the corner, fought our way to the freeway, and made time.

"I have a map showing where the ship is berthed," Elsie said.

"It's okay," I told her. "I know how to get there."

We violated a few speed limits, took a chance on a signal, and suddenly found ourselves at the pier with the *Lurline* looming high above us, buff-and-blue smokestacks outlined against the clear sky.

A whistle was bellowing.

"Oh, I'll bet it's too late for visitors," Elsie said in dismay.

"We'll make it," I told her.

"But there isn't a parking-space within miles. We—"

Just as she spoke a car pulled out of a parking-space that was almost opposite the entrance to the gangway.

I backed my car into the vacant parking-space.

"It's an omen," Elsie said.

I grabbed her arm and we hurried through the big covered shed at the pier, up to the gangway.

Bertha was standing there, tight-lipped with indignation.

"Well," she said, "it's about time!"

"I called the office four or five times this morning," I said. "You were out shopping."

"Well, why not? My God, I can't walk around that boat without anything on," Bertha said. "I didn't have a thing to wear. You don't realize what it means to try and get ready on short notice, to—"

"Well, you're here," I said. "Anything on your mind that you want to discuss before you shove off?"

Elsie Brand opened her purse and whipped out a notebook.

Bertha said, "Elsie, you wait there. Donald, you come with me. I have something to tell you."

"If you want any notes," Elsie said, "I—"

"No. Donald, come with me."

Bertha opened her purse, handed Elsie Brand a folded envelope, and said, "Those are instructions for you. Read them."

I started to follow Bertha up the gangplank.

A big guard said, "No more visitors permitted. The boat sails in a few minutes and—"

"Shut up," Bertha told him. "We're passengers."

She led the way across the gangplank, up into the lobby.

"You've got to see Stephenson Bicknell," she said.

"I haven't time," I told her. "He's way up on A deck and—"

"You've got time," Bertha said. "You come with me."

Bertha started punching at the elevator button.

I said, "Have a heart, Bertha. This is sailing-time and—"

Miraculously the elevator seemed to appear from nowhere. The attendant opened the door.

"A deck," Bertha said.

We went up, got out of the elevator, and I started for the door leading out to the deck.

"We'll never find him in this mob, Bertha," I said, looking at my watch.

"This way," Bertha said.

I followed her down A deck to a line of single staterooms near the front part of the boat. Bertha fitted a key to the lock, jerked open the door, and said, "Hurry, Donald! We're going to have to cut it fine because the boat sails in ten minutes."

I stepped inside and looked around the spacious, single-occupancy cabin.

I heard the slam of the door and the click of the lock being turned from the outside.

I flung myself at the door.

It was locked.

"Bertha!" I yelled.

There was silence from the other side of the door.

I looked around the room. A suitcase under the bed looked familiar. I jerked it out. It was my suitcase. Another one was there. That, too, was my suitcase.

I opened the door of the closet. A bunch of my clothes were neatly arrayed on hangers.

I moved over and looked out of the porthole. Music was blaring over the loud-speakers. Paper streamers were festooned along the side of the ship. The crowd far down below was looking up, smiling and waving.

I tried the telephone. It seemed to have been disconnected. I tried the door again. It was locked.

To hell with it. If they wanted to play jokes it was all right with me. I stretched out on the davenport, pulled a pillow under my head, and lit a cigarette.

A long, bellowing whistle reverberated through the ship, echoing back from the dock.

I knew the answer by this time. I was going to Honolulu.

4

IT WAS AFTER FIVE-THIRTY and the ship was nodding and swaying in the channel out beyond the breakwater when I heard the sound of a key in the lock.

The door opened and big Bertha stood there on the threshold glaring at me.

I was lying on the davenport which would make up into a bed at night, pillows propped behind my head.

"Hello," I said.

"Go on and say it," Bertha demanded. "Get it off your chest."

"Get what off my chest?"

"The whole business. Let's have it over with."

I said, "There's nothing on my chest. Sit down, Bertha. You look tired."

"Damn it, Donald," she said. "Don't ever tell a woman she looks tired. I don't care if she looks like a sack of wheat with a busted seam. *Don't* tell her she looks tired."

"I've never seen you looking better, Bertha," I said. "Sit down."

She kicked the door shut, sat down, and heaved a long, weary sigh. She kicked her shoes off, massaged her feet.

There was silence for several seconds, broken only by the slow creaking sound made by a ship at sea.

"Listen to it," Bertha said.

"All ships do that," I told her. "It's normal."

"It may be normal for ships," Bertha said, "but it isn't for human beings. That client of ours is going to drive me nuts. Have you heard him creak?"

"No."

"His knees creak."

"He probably doesn't like it any better than you do."

"You aren't sore at me, Donald?"

"Why should I be sore at you?"

"Kidnaping you."

"I hope," I said, "you made arrangements for Elsie Brand to get back to town. I have the keys to the car, you know."

"Don't worry. I sent her a note of instructions with a duplicate car key. I thought of everything. I'll say one thing for myself, Donald—when I go all out on something I make a damn good job of it."

I nodded.

"That's why I couldn't see you in the office," she said. "I was afraid I'd let the cat out of the bag. My God, the time I had! I had to go out to your place and pack up all that junk. Donald, you leave that apartment of yours in a hell of a mess. There's no system to it. Why do you keep your pleated dress shirts in with your colored shirts and your ordinary everyday white shirts?"

"Because there isn't enough drawer space."

"It's the worst place I've ever seen. I never did find cuff links. You can buy some aboard. I think I got all the rest of the stuff."

"What's Bicknell going to say about this?" I asked.

"It's all right with Bicknell," she said. "I told him I had to have you. I have an understanding with him that I'm to be the only one to make the contact with Miriam Woodford and be in charge of things over there—that you're going to work on the boat, making a build-up with Norma Radcliff. You're acting as my assistant."

"Then why all the cloak-and-dagger stuff?" I asked.

"Why didn't you simply tell me to come along?"

"Because I knew damn well you wouldn't have done it," Bertha said. "You'd have said it was my party, that Bicknell really didn't want you messing around in the thing, and that you weren't going over there and take orders from me."

"I still feel that way."

"All right, then," Bertha said, flaring at me, "jump the hell overboard and swim back."

I looked out of the window and estimated the distance.

"Don't be a fool," Bertha said, suddenly apprehensive.

I said, "Before you get done this is going to cost you your friendship with Bicknell."

"No, it isn't," Bertha said. "I told him that when you were working on a case you were all business, and I'm going to be along to see that you *are* all business. If you so much as look twice at that girl I'll break your neck personally."

I grinned at her. "Suppose she makes a pass at me?"

Bertha snorted.

"Suppose she does?"

"She isn't going to," Bertha said. "You aren't going to get near her. I'm going to handle the contact, and, believe me, I've sketched you as being utterly oblivious to feminine charms unless it was in the line of duty. I told Bicknell that when you were on a job you got so wrapped up in the business part that you wouldn't see a girl even if she walked nude along the promenade deck."

"That makes me seem a hell of a detective."

"You know what I meant, Donald."

"I don't, but Bicknell probably did."

Bertha fished in her pocket, pulled out a green slip, said, "Here's your ticket." She slammed down a yellow slip. "There's your table reservation—and if you don't think I had one hell of a time getting you at the same table with Norma Radcliff you're nuts. I even had to tip a couple of stewards. Think of it! Laying good money out on the line and—"

"You put it on the expense account, didn't you?"

"Well, I hope to tell the cockeyed world I put it on the expense account," Bertha said. "Do you see me laying out money on a case without putting it on an expense account?"

"Then what are you crabbing about? Bicknell will pay it."

"It's just such a whacking **extravagance**," Bertha said. "This guy Bicknell is a card, Donald. He's carrying a torch for Mira Woodford. He thinks nobody knows it. He's as obvious as a two-month-old puppy. And that's all about him that's puppy. Just puppy love. For the rest of it, he's an old dog with rheumatism."

"He isn't so old," I said. "His arthritis bothers him and makes him seem older."

"He's old," she said. "Worn out. Burned out."

Suddenly she said, "Well, maybe he *is* around my age, but the way he hobbles around—he doesn't dare to get in a crowd. He's in his stateroom and he's going to stay shut in his stateroom until all the excitement has died down. He's so damned afraid someone will bump into him."

"If you had arthritis you'd be afraid someone would bump into you."

Bertha squared her shoulders. "That's one thing about me," she said. "Let 'em bump. All they've got to do is to bump into me right hard and they'll bounce back against the rail."

"Well," I told her, "it's your party. When are you going to serve the refreshments?"

"You're at the second sitting, Donald," she said. "You go into the Waikiki dining-room at seven-thirty—my God, how I hate the idea of eating on a boat for five days."

"Why?" I asked. "The cuisine of the Matson Line is considered tops."

She glared at me.

"Well, what's wrong?"

"You know perfectly well I'll eat the stuff."

"That's what it's there for."

"And I'll get fat."

"Don't eat it, then."

Bertha said, "Are you nuts? There's all that food on the menu. I've paid for it. I'm not going to let any old steamship company cheat me out of eating food I've bought and paid for. I get hungry on the ocean, and sitting there with my appetite and that feeling of not letting the steamship company get away with anything is just too much for me. I'll eat like a horse."

"Well, that's fine," I said. "Who's at your table, Bertha?"

"I don't know yet. I felt that you were the one to make the play for Norma Radcliff. That's the way I sold Stephenson Bicknell on boosting the ante to have you come along. Now don't be too obvious about it. Just take it easy, lover. We don't want her to get suspicious. Just drift along and take things as they come. And it'll probably be better if you and I pretend we don't have anything in common. We can act like steamship acquaintances."

"Where's your stateroom?" I asked.

"About thirty feet down the line," Bertha said. "My gosh, I guess Stephenson Bicknell must have reserved about all of the single staterooms on the ship. And that took a little doing. This ship is supposed to be sold out for about ten months in advance. Of course, they have cancellations as long as your arm."

"Do you suppose Bicknell planned all this exodus to Honolulu that far in advance?"

"I don't know *what* he planned," she said. "Now I'm going to tell you something about him, Donald. Whenever you question him it makes him nervous as the devil. He doesn't like to be questioned. He wants to tell you things and the minute you start anything that sounds like a cross-examination he gets mad. That's one of the things you did that got you in bad with him. You started cross-examining him."

"I didn't cross-examine him," I said. "I just tried to find out about certain things."

"Well, he doesn't like it. There's something about Mira

that he's trying to cover up. He's just like a hen with one chick. He thinks his sole reason for existence is to be around to protect Mira.

"What a babe she must be! Think of changing a crabby old fool like Bicknell from a deadly enemy into a guy who's ga-ga, and doing it all in three months!"

I said, "Bicknell is going to have to get accustomed to questions. I don't like playing things blind. I already have a few lined up for him to answer."

"Now, Donald, don't be like that! You've just got to curb that impatience of yours. As long as he's paying salary and expenses he's a client. Now you get all prettied up and fix it so Norma Radcliff looks you over. Be just a little bit shy. On a ship of this kind there aren't too many eligible men. If Norma Radcliff is the kind of a girl I think she is, she'll know all about that.

"You're going to be a prize catch, and if Norma lets you go wandering around for as much as thirty seconds without having her brand on you some other girl is going to throw her hooks into you and have you all hog-tied. Norma will know that, so don't start making any plays. Just be shy and diffident and let her carry the play."

"Suppose she doesn't do it?" I asked.

"Don't be silly. This is a boat, Donald. You might have halitosis and dandruff and all the other things you read about in the advertisements, but any decently ambitious girl will throw her hooks into you just the same. Not that it means she gives a damn about you personally. It's a distinct feminine achievement to be able to grab off an eligible male early on a cruise and wear him around like new clothes."

Bertha twisted the doorknob, jerked the door open, stepped out into the corridor, and a room steward said, "Are you Mrs. Cool?"

"Yes. Why?"

"There's a package for you."

"What is it?"

The man indicated the huge basket piled high with

26

fruit, candy, and all wrapped around with yellow cellophane.

"I'll take it down to your stateroom if you wish," the room steward said.

Bertha grabbed up the envelope that was dangling from the handle of the basket, jerked it off, opened it, pulled out the card, glanced at it for a minute, then said hurriedly, "Leave it here for the present. You can take it down later."

Bertha slammed the door. "Donald," she said, "we're in a spot."

"What's the matter?"

She handed me the card. *Compliments of The Denver Police Force.*

I tried to keep expression from my face, but there was something in my manner, or perhaps something in the utter incongruity of the situation which dawned on Bertha and gave her the idea.

"Donald!" she screamed at me. "This is another of your crazy-fool jokes. You—" She picked up the ornamental basket, started to swing it as though about to smash the whole thing over the floor of my stateroom.

"That cost twenty-four dollars and seventeen cents, including the tax," I said.

Bertha stopped her swing, glared at me, then at the basket. "You and your practical jokes!"

"Well," I told her, "the stuff is still edible."

Bertha jerked the yellow cellophane off the basket, started pulling out fruit, candy, nuts, jars of marmalade.

"Don't unpack it in here," I told her. "It's yours."

Bertha kept on unpacking.

I said, "I won't eat the stuff. It'll just be thrown out."

Bertha kept on unpacking.

"All that money going to waste," I said. "Perfectly good fruit that cost money. Candy that—"

Bertha heaved a sigh, slammed the wrappings down on the floor, put the fruit and candy back in the basket, and started back to her own stateroom.

"Donald," she said, "you know good and well that I can't stand by and let this go to waste. I'll eat it."

"Give it away," I told her.

"Who to?"

"Anybody who looks hungry."

"Nobody's going to look hungry on this ship," she said, and then added, "Besides, who the hell do I know well enough to give away twenty-four dollars and seventeen cents' worth of goodies to?"

"That Denver policeman," I said, "Edgar Larson. You might lay the foundations for a beautiful friendship."

Bertha glared at me and lugged the heavy basket to her own stateroom.

5

I WAS PURPOSELY A LITTLE LATE getting down to dinner and found that I was at a table for six. Four were already there.

There was evidence of the constraint which grips people during the first few hours of a sea voyage. They want to be friendly but they don't know just how to go about it. Each one clothes himself with an air of reserve and waits for the other fellow to make the first move.

"Good evening," I said, seating myself. "My name is Lam. I guess we're going to be together for several days."

Norma Radcliff was the redhead on my left, a girl with dancing, mischievous blue eyes, somewhere around twenty-seven, who looked as though she had heard all of the questions and knew most of the answers.

There was another girl on my right who gave her name as Phyllis Eaton. She was blond and hard to figure. Looking at her you'd say she certainly must have been designed to cause palpitations of the masculine heart, but she kept her eyes lowered demurely and her voice so low and softly modulated that it required a little effort to hear what she was saying.

Directly across from me was a man who gave his name

as Sidney Selma, a complete phony, three-dollar-bill type of individual who obviously assayed fourteen-carat brass.

I gathered that the young woman seated next to him, Rosa Flaxton, had probably been first at the table. Selma had arrived second and had naturally seated himself next to her. She was a little on the fleshy side, in the early thirties, but a friendly, good-natured type of gal who had a roving eye with a twinkle.

A moment later the last occupant of the table, Edgar Larson, came in.

He was a tight-lipped, wiry individual, around forty. He had a high forehead, gimlet eyes, and was wearing a gray suit and a gray tie. He looked as though he might be trying to be inconspicuous, but, by the studied nature of the attempt, he had made himself more conspicuous than ever.

As soon as I saw him I knew that his being seated at that table was a matter of influence. A good steward wouldn't have seated him there unless there had been a specific request backed either by a financial inducement or some insignia of authority.

I couldn't have had a better setup for the type of game I was playing. This guy, Selma, was so eagerly wolfish that all I had to do was to sit back and let him carry the ball.

He ran on at considerable length about himself, about his background, his worldly wisdom. No one asked him what he did for a living, and he didn't volunteer that information. He was so typically a spoiled son of a rich family that, looking at him a second time, I wondered if this wasn't a front for something else. He could be the come-on guy for a gambling setup—or a pimp. I decided that Sidney Selma would make himself something of a nuisance before the voyage was over.

Detective Larson did most of his listening with his eyes. Whenever anyone spoke he'd raise his gray eyes, watch attentively, then lower his eyes to his plate. Sometimes he smiled rather vaguely. He probably didn't say more than ten words all during the meal.

Afterward we went out on deck and wandered around a little, but the decks weren't too comfortable. Rather a chill wind was blowing. There was a chop which was rapidly building up, and the passengers, not knowing exactly what to do with themselves, tired from packing and the farewell parties, gradually melted away.

I decided Bertha had been one-hundred-percent wrong in suggesting that Norma Radcliff would latch onto me so that someone else wouldn't grab me.

The waiter had served the meal so that we were all ready to leave the table at about the same time, but Norma Radcliff had announced she was going to unpack, then take a turn around the deck and go to bed.

I loafed around deck for a little while, waiting for her to show up. Then because it was chilly, I went to my cabin, adjusted the automatic heat control so that I could be comfortable sitting in the chair reading.

Bertha's heavy knuckles pounded on the door about nine o'clock.

"Come in," I invited.

Bertha pushed her way in and banged the door shut.

"What are you doing here?"

"Reading."

"You're supposed to be making goo-goo eyes at Norma Radcliff."

"You told me she'd take the initiative," I said.

"Well, what the hell do you want her to do?" Bertha said. "Come down here, jerk the door off its hinges, grab you by the coat collar, and drag you into her stateroom so she can put one of her baggage labels *Wanted in Stateroom* on you?"

I said wearily, "Well, I did just what you told me to do. Frankly, she didn't *seem* particularly interested."

Bertha said, "A smart girl doesn't play things that way."

"What makes you think she would be interested?"

"Get out and look this tub over," Bertha said. "People are going over to the Islands for pleasure. That means you have a few highly paid secretaries who have saved their money for a boat trip. You have some young widows. You have a sprinkling of married women whose husbands are holding their noses to the grindstone and sending their wives over on a vacation. You have a bunch of people who have started to crowd seventy, who wonder what good it is to save their money so the government can collect an inheritance tax when they die. They've decided to retire and obey that impulse. The trouble is, they aren't impulsive any more. They're just going to Honolulu.

"Now then, all of those younger women are looking around for eligible males. How many eligible males do you find on a boat these days?"

I kept on acting dumb.

"Don't kid yourself," Bertha said. "By the time a young man gets out of college, gets out of the army, tries to get himself established in business, he doesn't have any money to take three weeks off, loafing over to Honolulu on a luxury liner. You have a few rich brats and a few traveling salesmen who are trying to pretend they're rich brats. Women want someone to squire them around on the voyage. They want a dancing-partner. They want to parade around the decks showing that they have what it takes to capture some young male."

"I think a fellow by the name of Sidney Selma is the guy she's going for," I said.

"Sure she is," Bertha told me, "if you don't get on up there."

"You mean she's up on deck?"

"Walking around the deck," Bertha said.

"She mentioned something about going to unpack for a while and then take a turn around deck before she went to bed."

Bertha groaned. "Good Lord, she told you where she'd be and when she'd be there. Come on, snap out of it! Get the hell up on deck and at least give the girl a chance."

I picked up a cap, switched out my lights, and went out on deck.

There was no trace of Norma Radcliff. Sidney Selma

was walking the deck with three women—Rosa Flaxton, Phyllis Eaton, and some woman I hadn't met. They all seemed happy.

I started back down, then decided to make one more complete turn.

That time I noticed a huddled figure in a fur coat standing in the shadows.

I gave her a quick once-over. It was Norma Radcliff.

"You look as though you're hiding," I said.

She laughed. "Just keeping out of the wind and getting a little fresh air before I turn in."

"I suppose it's quite a job getting clothes on hangers and all of that," I said, making the inane, getting-acquainted preliminaries.

"It is."

"And you still look as though you're hiding."

"All right. I am."

I raised my eyebrows.

"The wolf," she said.

The quartet came walking around the deck again. The motion of the boat was giving Selma an opportunity to lurch against the women, to slip a steadying arm around their waists, then withdrawing it so that his hand slid smoothly across their hips.

"Rather a fast worker," I observed.

She nodded, started to say something, changed her mind.

A few of the older people were around on the deck. Two or three married couples, and four or five pairs of women in the early thirties apparently walking the decks, not because of any urgent need of fresh air, but to look the situation over and size up the ship and the passengers.

Abruptly Norma Radcliff said, "Well, I've had my air and I think I'll go to bed. Good night, Mr. Lam."

"Good night," I told her.

She moved toward the door. I held the door open for her.

"Going to stay out in the fresh air?" she asked.

I suddenly changed my mind and said, "No, I'll turn in,

32

too."

"Good night," she said and smiled a friendly smile.

I went back to my cabin on A deck.

Bertha had her door open so that as I walked past she saw me and motioned me to step into her cabin.

"How did you do?" she asked.

I shook my head.

"Didn't you find her?"

"Oh, I found her," I said. "She was bundled up in a fur coat, standing in the shadows where she was hard to see."

"But you saw her?"

"I saw her," I said. "I guess she moved or something. She had on a dark fur coat and it wasn't easy to see her."

"All alone?" Bertha asked.

I nodded.

"You stopped and talked with her?"

"Yes."

"What did she say?"

"Said she was going to turn in," I told Bertha.

"Anything else?"

"I told her she acted as though she was hiding, and she said she was. Something about the wolf."

"You mean that eager beaver who was walking around the deck with three babes, sliding his hand over their fannies every time he got a chance?"

"That's the one."

Bertha snorted. "My God, he's going to be a pest! They'll put up with him though, because he hasn't any particular competition. Unless they can get their hands on you, Donald. You're playing it smart now. And so's Norma."

"Norma isn't playing anything," I said. "She just wanted a breath of air, and then almost as soon as I showed up she decided she was tired and was going to roll in."

"You held the heavy door open for her? The one from the deck?"

I nodded.

Bertha smiled. A wise, enigmatic smile.

"You're doing all right," she said.

I went back to my stateroom, then after ten or fifteen minutes became obsessed with curiosity and wondered just what was happening to Selma and his three women.

I went back up on deck. Nearly everyone else had left, but Selma and his trio were walking around and around.

Rosa Flaxton was on the outside. When she saw me she said, "Perhaps we can persuade Mr. Lam to take a turn with us. Come on, Mr. Lam. We're doing a mile."

She dropped away from the four-abreast group and extended her hand.

I took it and tucked my arm through hers.

Selma turned back and looked at me, a look that was far from cordial. Then he devoted his attention to the two girls. By this time he had an arm around each waist every time the boat rolled, then as the ship righted he would take his arms away.

I noticed that the girl who was on his left had evidently indicated some displeasure at his familiarity, but Phyllis Eaton, who was on his right, made no protest. She looked as demure and virginal as ever, but by some subtle process of telepathy Selma had found he wasn't going to get slapped. He was following up the advantage.

Rosa Flaxton carried me around the deck for two more laps, then she said, "That's it, Mr. Lam. That's my mile. I've done my duty. Good night."

She turned abruptly toward the heavy door, pushed her weight against it, and struggled.

"Permit me," I said.

I got the door open, and she slipped inside.

"Good night," she said, her eyes laughing into mine. "I'll be seeing you."

I didn't know whether she had used me as an excuse to break away from Selma, or whether she had really completed her mile.

I decided I wouldn't tell Bertha anything about going up on deck that last time.

34

6

On SHIPBOARD it is all right to say good morning to fellow passengers, to stand by the rail and engage in conversations, and, if it seems desirable, to exchange introductions. This is utterly foreign to the conventions ashore, where people plod along in their own grooves of habit, never acknowledging the presence of other human beings who are also plodding along in parallel grooves.

On a ship, however, the situation is different, and people adjust themselves to it in different ways.

There are always the snobs who don't want to be spoken to and try to see that fellow passengers have that impression given them at once. There are eager beavers who are running around altogether too anxious to make shipboard acquaintances.

There are people who are escaping for perhaps the first time in their lives the humdrum routine of everyday existence, and who would like to add cruise acquaintances to their otherwise drab and uninspired friends.

There are people who want to enjoy the cruise and meet people, but who are too shy to act friendly. There are hordes of normal people who are perfectly willing to get acquainted with others who have similar backgrounds and congenial tastes, but who are amply supplied with friends at home and not unduly anxious to add to the list.

All in all, it makes a peculiar combination of human nature and personalities, milling around on the first day out, getting the feel of the ship, adjusting themselves to a new way of life.

By the second day things change. People have somehow classified themselves. The tension of business life ashore has relaxed, and passengers begin to be human beings. It is on the second day and the third day that most shipboard friendships are formed.

It was interesting to watch the various people work. Sidney Selma met with several rebuffs on the morning of the first day. By afternoon, when the girls had sized up the possibilities of the ship, Sidney Selma began to look a lot better to them, and by afternoon of the second day he was going like a house afire.

Norma Radcliff, however, continued to avoid him, and trying to escape Selma, she tended more and more to gravitate toward me for protection.

"I can't stand him," she told me. "It's not that I'm particularly narrow-minded, and I am wearing a sweater that isn't exactly a sack, but after all, personality counts for *something,* and you like to feel that people care for you as an individual.

"Now that Selma person is different. He's interested in only one thing. All a girl needs to appeal to him is a full complement of anatomical equipment."

Bertha Cool was more direct about it. "Look at the guy screening them out," she said.

"How come?" I asked.

"He might just as well put a tag around their necks for all the passengers to see."

"What do you mean?"

"Look at him. He picks up some girl and gives her a great rush. She looks the ship over, sees that he's one of the few available possibilities, decides to make the best of what's at hand. She wants to enjoy the cruise so she gives him a tumble. They go around thick as thieves for a while, and then suddenly she draws back into her shell and he drops her like a hot potato.

"Then with some of these girls he keeps getting more and more friendly—hell's bells, he might just as well label them."

I laughed. "I hadn't thought of it that way," I said.

"If you were a woman you would," Bertha snorted. "Every pair of feminine eyes on the ship is sizing up that demure little blonde that's sticking with him so close. Her face says she's a sweetly virtuous little babe. Her figure says she's a human being, and Sidney Selma's label says she's a pushover."

And Bertha, who didn't want to be seen talking with me except casually, moved away, walking down the deck, adjusting herself to the roll of the vessel, and hating every minute of it.

Stephenson Bicknell had a deck chair fixed up in a sunny corner. Moreover, he had the deck steward piling blankets around him whenever there was the least bit of chill in the air. He had arranged to have Bertha's deck chair alongside and he wanted her near him at all times.

Bertha had other ideas.

In desperation Bicknell turned to me, but it had been agreed that I wasn't to be too friendly with Bicknell—just a casual, chatty, shipboard friendship.

I dropped into Bertha's vacant chair and said, "Good morning, Bicknell. How are you coming?"

"I ache."

"That's too bad."

"The motion of the ship throws me off balance every once in a while, and if I hit against something it's like pounding an aching tooth."

"That's a shame."

"How are you getting along with Norma Radcliff?"

"Oh, I talk with her once in a while."

"She seems to be with you a lot."

"She's dodging the wolves," I said.

"I see," he commented dryly, and then, looking me over, said, "You have a way with women."

"I do?" I registered surprise.

"Yes, you."

"It's news to me."

"And I'm damned if I know what it is," Bicknell went on. "There's nothing tall and handsome about you. You don't have that God's-gift-to-women physique, and you don't seem to run after them, but for some reason I can't understand, *they* seem to run after *you*."

"You've got me all wrong," I told him.

"No, I haven't got you wrong. Now I want you to understand this. Mira is a rather unpredictable young woman. You can't tell what she'll do, and I don't want any trouble."

"What do you mean?"

"I don't want the situation complicated."

"What do you mean, complicated?"

"Well, I don't want—I think it would be better if you let Bertha Cool get acquainted with Mira and have Mira confide in Bertha. Then you can be there to help Mrs. Cool."

"That was my understanding of the way you wanted it played," I told him.

"Just so you understand it," he said, and put back his head with a tremulous sigh and closed his eyes.

I got up and walked around the deck.

I went over to my own deck chair and settled down. A few minutes later Norma Radcliff came out and eased into the chair next to mine.

"I hope you don't mind, Donald."

"What?"

"I bribed the deck steward."

"How come?"

"To put my chair next to yours—and whenever that Sidney Selma person shows up, would you mind looking at me very attentively and listening raptly to what I'm saying?"

"What will you be saying?"

"Anything," she said. "I may be talking about the weather in a low voice, or I may be asking you what you had for breakfast, but it will help a lot if we can be too engrossed in each other to know that Selma is alive."

"You don't like him," I said.

"Like him!" she said. "I grit my teeth every time he talks to me until I'm grinding all the enamel into powder. I'd like to throw the guy overboard."

Against this background Edgar Larson, the Denver detective, moved as quietly as a mouse slipping through a house after the lights have been turned out and the family gone to bed.

He'd turn up at unexpected hours on the deck, in the cocktail lounge. He'd be at the shipboard horse races, playing Keno, standing by the door when the motion picture shows were on. The man seemed to be everywhere. Completely unobtrusive, yet always in some strategic location, watching, listening, observing.

And in his quiet sort of way he made a lot of headway. People confided in Larson. All he had to do was turn those quiet gray eyes on a person, bend his head slightly forward in a listening position, and that person seemed under some compulsory obligation to bare every secret in his life.

So the big luxury liner knifed its way through the blue waters of the Pacific. The third day out the weather underwent a significant change. The cold winds gave way to balmy tropical breezes. The sun began to pack a terrific wallop. The swimming-pool was filled. Girls who lay around on the sun deck began to brown like bread in an electric toaster.

The passengers were well acquainted by now. The dinner hour in the dining-salon was punctuated by a background of continuous chatter. The cocktail lounge was crowded before dinner, and after dinner groups gathered around over liqueurs discussing politics, taxes, and surfboarding.

The Hawaiian cruise director had his classes in the hula dance well under way, and it was surprising to find the number of women who wanted to learn the genuine Hawaiian hula dance, and were willing to stand up in front of a room full of people, self-conscious as they went through the first awkward stages until gradually the rhythm and swing that is so much a part of the beauty of the Island dancers began to make itself manifest.

As these people learned that the grace of the Hawaiian dancer was no mere haphazard combination of extemporaneous motions, but followed tradition, with the body gracefully portraying the forces of nature, the rainbow in the sky, the falling of rain, the sunlight, the waving of the palm fronds, the restless rhythmic surge of the ocean, they began to study the dances with a new-found concentration. What had started out to be a gag became a serious study.

It was surprising the extent to which a few hours of practice could develop a rhythmic grace of motion, and naturally as the passengers themselves realized what was taking place there was a new-found respect for the beauty of the Islands.

Sidney Selma continued to strut his stuff. He had his harem down to four or five now—girls who seemed perfectly content with his idea of companionship.

Then suddenly came the night when Norma Radcliff was no longer in the deck chair by my side but was promenading the deck with Sidney Selma, looking into his eyes, listening intently to his conversation, his remarks with their obvious double meaning, his raucous risqué stories.

Bertha heaved herself into the chair alongside of me.

"What've you done, Donald, what's going on here?"

"What?" I asked.

"Don't try to be so wide-eyed. What did you do to that girl?"

"What girl?"

"Norma Radcliff."

"Nothing."

"What did you try to do to her?"

"Nothing."

"Dammit," Bertha said, "that's no way to get along with women. They have to feel they're on the defensive. You don't need to be offensive about your offensive, but you have to let them feel that you're alive; that they do things to you; that you're human after all.

"Now get cracking and make a play for that girl. Beat that oaf's time."

"Somehow, Bertha, I think that would be a mistake."

"*You* think it would be a mistake," Bertha said. "What the hell do *you* know about women?"

"Nothing."

Bertha said, "Sidney Selma is too aggressive. Everybody

knows what he's after. You're too damned retiring. Your little wren has decided to see if she can't stir up a spark of jealousy and get you to come to life. Probably you've been treating her like a cold plaster saint.

"Now get out of that deck chair, walk around, and keep your eye on Norma Radcliff. When you find her separated from Sidney Selma grab her again."

Bertha heaved herself up out of the chair and walked down the swaying deck, her shoulders set rigid with indignation, her eyes snapping, her lips pressed tightly together.

I continued to sit in the deck chair.

The night was warm and moonlit. I was watching the reflection of the moon on the waters when Norma Radcliff slipped into the chair at my side.

"Donald, may I ask you something?"

"What?"

"Advice."

"Go ahead."

"I'm in trouble."

I turned and raised my eyebrows.

"Not that kind of trouble," she said.

"What?"

"I'm being blackmailed."

"Over what?"

"Over some letters."

"What kind of letters?"

"Not the kind you'd like to have read in court."

"Don't you know better than to write letters of that sort?"

"I do now. I didn't then."

"Who's the blackmailer?"

"Our very dear mutual friend," she said, with hatred dripping from the words.

"You don't mean Sidney Selma?"

She nodded.

"I thought you'd taken a great and sudden interest in him," I said.

"I tried playing up to him when I found out what I was

up against. I didn't know what he wanted."

"What does he want?"

She shrugged her shoulders.

"When did you find out he had the letters?"

"This morning."

"Had you known him before you got aboard?"

She shook her head.

"You mean you have no idea what he wants?"

"He wants my beautiful brown body, if that's what you're driving at. But that isn't all he wants."

"Is it brown?"

"You mean you didn't see me out by the pool in my elastic swim suit?"

"I guess I missed it. I was reading."

She sighed. "If you weren't so lovable you'd be impossible. I was hoping you'd join me."

"I don't like small ships' pools."

"There's the scenery."

"Yes, of course. You say it's blackmail?"

"Yes."

"Then he's told you you'll have to buy the letters?"

"It amounts to that."

"But he's fixed no price."

"No."

"He's sounding you out. The price will come later."

"I suppose so."

"I can't give you very much advice."

"I thought you could."

"What made you think so?"

"Because you give me the impression of being sort of— well, brainy and knowing your way around. What do you do for a living, Donald?"

"You'd be surprised," I told her.

"Are you a lawyer?"

"Not exactly."

"What do you mean by that?"

"Nothing."

She let her face show exasperation.

I said, "Suppose you let me ask a few questions. When did you decide to go to Honolulu?"

"A short time ago."

I said, "The *Lurline* is booked up months in advance."

"I know, but there are cancellations."

"And the cancellations are distributed among names on a waiting-list."

"Well, I believe that various travel agencies have a certain number of bookings under some sort of an arrangement by which they can keep what amounts to an option on cancellations of their own parties."

"Well?" I asked.

She said, "I managed to get on the ship."

"Why are you going to Honolulu?"

"Could you keep a secret?"

"I don't know."

She said, "I'm going to meet a friend there."

"Man or woman?"

"A woman."

"How long have you known her?"

"For years. She's a good egg and she's in trouble."

"What kind of trouble?"

"I don't want to discuss her troubles. I'm trying to discuss mine."

"Do they have some connection?"

"What makes you ask that, Donald?"

I said, "Let's study the thing from an objective viewpoint. You didn't know very far in advance that you were going to Honolulu."

She nodded. "That's right."

"You had written some letters. Who were they to?"

"I don't want to mention names."

"A married man?"

"Yes."

"And his wife wants the letters?"

"His wife wants to clean him out of every cent he has in the world, and she doesn't care how she does it."

"And Sidney Selma has those letters?"

"He says he has."

"Where?"

"Where he can reach them, where he can make delivery."

"You don't like him?"

"I loathe and detest him."

"When did you find out he had the letters?"

"This morning."

"That's the first time he told you?"

"Yes."

I said, "He has those letters. He knew you were sailing to Honolulu. He evidently came aboard the ship in order to make a contact. Now that doesn't sound reasonable."

"Why?"

"It's costing him money to go to Honolulu. It's costing him time. He had those letters. If you wanted those letters badly enough to pay for them all he had to do was to let you know that he had them and you'd come to him.

"Now you want me to believe that he deliberately got aboard the ship in order to lay the foundation for blackmail; that he's waited for three days before making the first pass? It doesn't sound reasonable."

"But that's the way it happened."

I said, "It sounds reasonable only under one theory."

"What's that?"

"That the blackmail he wants you to pay is to be paid in Honolulu."

"Well, yes."

"And is something other than money?"

"He hasn't fixed his price yet!"

"Perhaps it has something to do with your friend, the one you're going to visit in Honolulu."

She said, "I'd rather not discuss my friend's affairs."

I said, "You can't expect me to advise you unless you're willing to tell me the true facts."

"Well, suppose you're—well, suppose you're right."

"I want to know whether I'm right or not."

"All right," she said suddenly and impulsively. "I'm

afraid you're right."

"What does he want?"

"I think it's going to be something that concerns my friend, Miriam Woodford!"

"What?"

"Donald, I don't know, and I can't afford to guess. That's one thing that—I know it sounds as though I'm not playing fair with you, but after all, well—well, I can't do it."

"Who's Miriam Woodford?" I asked.

"She's a young, attractive widow."

"You're going over to join her?"

"Yes."

"Why?"

"Because she's lonesome and wants company."

"Any other reason?"

Norma shook her head.

I said, "Any time you want to tell me the story I'm listening."

"I can't tell you the story, Donald, and yet I want your advice."

"Advice that isn't predicated on the facts would be completely cockeyed."

She sat in silence for probably as much as two minutes. Abruptly she turned to me. "Donald," she said, "have you noticed a slender man of about fifty who keeps himself pretty well bundled up against the weather at all times? He sits over there in a corner on A deck."

"What about him?"

She said, "His name is Stephenson D. Bicknell. He comes from Denver. He was a partner of Mira Woodford's husband, and under the terms of Woodford's will he was made trustee for Mira's inheritance."

"You know him?"

"I've never met him. I know about him from Mira's letters."

"And he knows about you?"

"I don't know, Donald. I wish I did. I've been trying to

find out whether I mean anything to him. He isn't the kind to circulate around much. He has rheumatism and he keeps very much to himself. There's a woman passenger, a Mrs. Cool, that he talks with once in a while. You know her. I've seen you talking with her."

"Cool," I said, as though trying to recall the name.

"The woman about fifty years old, with the broad shoulders, the—well, broad of beam and small of feet."

"Oh, yes," I said.

"Bicknell is going to Honolulu to protect Miriam," she went on. "Miriam doesn't want him around, she wants him to give her some money to meet an emergency.

"And now this nasty Selma person tells me he expects me to 'play ball' with him. I wish I knew what was going on. It baffles me."

I said, "Perhaps Selma just wants your beautiful brown body."

"Oh, he wants that, all right," she said. "He wants all beautiful brown bodies."

"But he doesn't want to turn over the letters in return."

"Of course not. He wants something else. He expects me to 'play ball'!"

"And what do you want me to do?"

"Give me advice."

I said, "Tell Selma to go to hell."

"He has those letters."

"He won't use them."

"What makes you think he won't? He's utterly ruthless."

"What good would it do him if he used the letters?"

She hesitated for a moment. "He could sell them to the wife."

"Is the husband wealthy?"

"He has quite a few thousand dollars."

"And the wife wants it all?"

"That's right."

"If Selma wanted to sell those letters to her he'd have done it long ago. He wouldn't have gone to all the trouble and expense of getting on this same ship with you.

"On the other hand, if he'd only wanted to blackmail you, he'd have sent you a message to come to him before you ever sailed.

"No, there's something back of all this and the one way to find out what it is is to laugh in Selma's face and tell him to go to hell and do whatever he pleases with the letters."

She thought that one over. "I guess you're right, Donald."

"The letters would hurt you?"

"Not me, the man."

"What's that to you?"

"I want to be a square shooter, that's all. The wife would name me as corespondent, but I can take that. I do want to play square with my friend, that's all."

I said, "The thing doesn't make sense. If Selma knows anything about blackmail he'd offer to sell the letters back to the husband or to the wife. You're the poorest potential prospect of the three."

She nodded. "That's right."

"Therefore, you have something he wants. What is it?"

"Nothing that would be worth a trip to Honolulu—not that I know about now."

"Then tell him to go to hell and we'll force the issue and find out."

"Thanks, Donald, you make me feel better."

"Why did you come to me?" I asked.

"Because I wanted advice."

"Why did you think I could give you advice?"

"Because I think you have brains. Oh, Donald, what must you think of me?"

"What do you mean?"

"About those letters. I suppose you think I'm a bold, bad, wicked woman."

"You're probaby human," I said.

She looked at me warmly. "I am," she said in a low voice. "And I'm *very* grateful."

"I haven't done anything," I told her, "yet."

"Donald, you're a dear," she said impulsively and, suddenly leaning forward, kissed me full on the lips, a warm mouth-throbbing kiss.

At that moment, Bertha Cool, trying to work off the fat she was putting on, rounded the corner on the first lap of her evening mile.

7

IT WAS the last day at sea. An atmosphere of subdued excitement permeated the ship.

The hula dancing class, a group of women of all sorts and shapes, all sizes and ages, now had a pretty good idea of the Hawaiian dance and was ready to take its final examination and receive diplomas. They had a session in the warm sunlight by the swimming-pool.

Suitcases and trunks were being carried up from the baggage room. People were packing, jabbering away excitedly, exchanging mailing addresses, autographing menus and passenger lists.

The spell of the tropics was in the warm, balmy air. The ocean was sluggishly lazy. Flying fish kicked up out of the waves and glided long distances, finally to become engulfed in the top of an oncoming wave.

Behind the ship a black-footed albatross glided and swung at the end of an invisible string. The afternoon trap shooters gathered at the stern.

Sidney Selma passed by, looked at me with a new-found curiosity as though really seeing me for the first time. Norma Radcliff was hardly in evidence. Once when she was on deck Selma had tried to talk with her and she had curtly swung away from him.

Bertha came to stand by the rail where I was looking down at the water.

"You little bastard," she said admiringly.

I turned and raised my eyebrows in silent interrogation.

"Pretending you weren't getting anywhere," she said. "My God, the girl was climbing all over you. I told you she would."

I said, "Bertha, did you ever have the terms of our employment very definitely understood with Stephenson Bicknell?"

"What do you mean?"

"Just what we're supposed to do."

"We're supposed to protect Miriam Woodford."

"From what?"

"From whatever's bothering her."

"And that's all?"

"That's all. Lord, how my feet ache! I wasn't intended to use my ankles and my feet to support a hundred and sixty-five pounds of avoirdupois."

"How're you coming with the fruit and candy?"

Bertha sighed, "I'm getting old. I gave some of that candy away."

"Who did you give it to?"

"The stewardess."

"How about the fruit?"

"I've eaten it—most of it."

"You're doing swell."

"You pull anything like that again and I'll brain you," Bertha warned. "So help me, I'll bat you over the head."

"In the meantime," I told her, "let's not be too friendly. I've already heard it commented that I must have known you before we got aboard the ship."

"I don't believe it!" Bertha said.

I nodded lugubriously.

"Why the question about our duties in the case?"

"Because we're going to land tomorrow and we'll have to start work."

"Donald, what did Norma tell you?"

"Nothing."

I stretched my arms and yawned.

"You smug bastard, you know something," Bertha blazed at me angrily.

"We'd be in a fine fix if I didn't," I told her, and walked off, leaving her standing there gripping the rail.

8

I WAS ON DECK at the first sign of dawn.

Ahead I could see the light on Makapuu Point, and I watched the island of Oahu gradually take shape.

The stewards set up a table and brought fruit juice, coffee, sweet rolls, Danish pastry, and muffins. We passed Koko Head, then Diamond Head, and turned toward the break in the barrier reef. The launch came out from shore. Official greeters swarmed aboard, carrying huge assortments of the colorful Hawaiian leis.

Chosen passengers began to appear decorated with these leis, a riot of colorful flowers, red, yellow, white, crimson, and purple.

Everywhere was the bustle of confusion. To the strains of The Royal Hawaiian Band and a chorus of Hawaiian voices, the *Lurline* eased her way in to the dock.

I managed to be standing near Norma Radcliff when Miriam Woodford came aboard.

Miriam was a radiant blonde, with magnificent legs, plenty of curves, flashing teeth, and laughing eyes.

Looking at her you wouldn't think she had a care in the world.

She flung herself on Norma Radcliff, decorated Norma with flower leis, and was kissing her when Stephenson Bicknell, mincing his way through the crowd, trying to keep from being jostled, but willing to endure the pain for an opportunity to see Miriam, inched his way around a jabbering group and said, "Mira!"

His heart was in his voice.

She turned to him. "Stevie, you old dear!" she said. "You darling. Gosh, but I'm glad to see you. Why in the world didn't you tell me you were coming earlier?"

"I wanted to surprise you," he said, and came toward her, completely oblivious of everyone else on the ship.

She kissed him, and Stephenson Bicknell's cane clattered to the deck as his rheumatic arms circled her and made a pathetic attempt at a robust bear hug.

Mira broke away, picked up the cane, handed it to Bicknell, and said to Norma, "You two should have been getting acquainted all the way across. Norma, this is my trustee—Stevie Bicknell. Stevie, this is Norma, my closest friend."

"You didn't tell me she was coming," Bicknell said.

Miriam Woodford laughed. "Stevie, you've got enough on your mind with all those financial details without worrying about every one of my friends."

Norma turned and caught my eye. She beckoned to me, said to Miriam, "Mira, I want you and Donald Lam to know each other. Donald has been perfectly swell to me."

Miriam Woodford took one good long look at me, smiled, and extended her hand.

"Hello, Donald Lam."

I looked in the laughing blue eyes and something clicked.

"Hello," I said.

"Have you met Mr. Bicknell?" she asked.

"We met on the boat."

Bicknell said, "And here's a friend of mine, Mira, that I want you to know. Mrs. Cool."

After that he introduced Bertha to Mira.

I said, "I already met Mrs. Cool on the boat."

A man from one of the local radio stations came aboard, holding a microphone, dragging a long extension cord after him. I left the group by the rail and tagged along after him.

He had a list of people he wanted to interview and the deck steward was on hand to help him get an identification.

There was some manufacturer who gave an interview interspersed with stuffy comments on the international situation, and then the announcer said, "We have another interesting visitor with us today—Edgar B. Larson of the Denver Police Department. What brings you over to Honolulu, Mr. Larson?"

Larson looked at the radio interviewer in complete, utter surprise, said, "I didn't understand this—I didn't realize this was—I thought it was just an interview with passengers about the trip."

"That's what it is," the announcer said. "What kind of a trip did you have, Mr. Larson?"

"A very good trip," Larson said curtly.

"How long do you expect to remain in the Islands?"

Larson hesitated a moment, then, evidently figuring the cat was out of the bag, squared his shoulders and said into the microphone, "I don't know. When I leave the Hawaiian Islands I expect to have a murderer with me. I'm here on official business. I have information that a murder was committed in Denver and that the murderer is at present in Honolulu."

Passengers who had gathered around in a ring to listen to the interview became completely, absolutely silent.

The flabbergasted interviewer said, "Could you tell us anything more about the circumstances of this murder, Mr. Larson?"

"All I can tell you," Larson said, "is that the murderer thinks the tracks are covered. I can assure the guilty person that such is not the case. We know a lot more than this person suspects."

"Does he know you are coming?" the announcer asked.

"Who said the murderer was a he?" Larson inquired.

"Well, I gathered—you used the term murderer. You mean it could be a murderess?"

"It could be," Larson said.

"You are not at this time giving out any information?"

"Only that I am here to apprehend a person who committed a murder, and that I intend to stay until I do so."

The announcer was back in his stride. "Well," he said, "it's interesting to realize that you feel assured of success, Mr. Larson. Speaking about getting away with murder, that is approximately what our sponsors are doing. They are slashing values to such an extent that some goods are actually being sold below cost."

He went on into another interview.

I approached one of the stewards. "Larson seems to have been rather surprised by the interview," I said.

"I asked him if he would consent to a passenger interview, and he said he'd be glad to. Evidently he didn't know that the announcer was familiar with his connection with the Denver police force."

I took a ten-dollar bill from my pocket. "Do you suppose you could find out how it happened that Larson was chosen for an interview?"

The steward eyed the ten-dollar bill. "I think I could."

I handed him the bill. He folded it and put it in his pocket, grinned, and said, "I'm responsible for it. I was told that Larson was a colorful character who could tell some interesting stories about his occupation, that it would go swell over a radio."

"And who gave *you* the tip?"

"Sidney Selma," the steward said. "And when I see him I'm going to ask him a few questions myself."

I nodded.

"Anything else?" the steward asked.

"That," I told him, "is all I want."

9

BICKNELL CONTROLLED all the reservations for our party on the Islands so he had opportunity to place us where he wanted us.

It appeared that he had assumed that Miriam Woodford was continuing to stay on at the Royal Hawaiian, but as it turned out she had secured an apartment in the Waikiki district within a few hundred yards of the Royal Hawaiian. She had Norma Radcliff move in with her.

Bicknell put Bertha Cool in the Royal Hawaiian, stayed there himself, and gave me a reservation at the Moana Hotel.

Bertha gave me some low-voiced instructions just before we started. "Our client," she said, "is plenty sore."

"What about?"

"He doesn't like Mira's attitude. He thinks she's trying to give him some sort of a run-around. She won't tell him what the trouble is. Told him she'd have to talk with him later."

"Anything else?"

"He doesn't want you to get too prominent. He thinks you should get all your dope about Miriam Woodford from me."

"That suits me fine," I said, "provided the guy is willing to pay our expenses over here while you're getting the stuff, and pay our per diems to boot. By the time he gets done he's going to find he's bitten off quite a financial chunk."

"That's all right," Bertha told me. "He's lousy with money. Now you go on, lover, and go swimming. Just keep out of sight until Bertha gets an opportunity to pump this Woodford widow and see what it's all about."

"How long do you expect it's going to take you?"

"How the hell do I know?" Bertha blazed. "You talk just like a client. We're getting paid. Let's take it easy."

"You'll love Honolulu," I told her.

"I hate the place," Bertha said. "I'm steaming underneath this mountain of flower leis. They smother me."

"Think of it on the mainland," I told her. "Cold winds blowing, cold rain driving down against the windows of the office, the streets all wet, people crowding into streetcars with wet clothes, stinking up the place, and—"

"Can it," Bertha said, and strode off toward a taxicab.

I went over to the Moana Hotel, and found there was nothing cheap about Bicknell when it came to selecting rooms. I was in one that fronted on the beach, with big windows looking out on the white sand of Waikiki Beach, out on the long curling breakers with the outrigger canoes, the surfboards, and the swimmers.

It was okay by me. Somehow I had an idea it was going to be quite a while before Miriam Woodford started confiding in Bertha Cool. In fact I thought it might be quite a while before she confided in anyone, except perhaps Norma Radcliff.

I thought how nice it would be if I had a tape recording of their conversation when they got together, and then found myself wondering if that bright idea hadn't occurred to someone else.

I tried to find out where Sidney Selma was staying, but couldn't get him located.

Edgar Larson, I knew, had gone to the Surfrider Hotel, because that's where his baggage had been taken.

I kept thinking about what Miriam Woodford and Norma were talking about right at this moment and wondering if some smart citizen had managed to install a microphone in Miriam's apartment. I knew I'd do it if I were a blackmailer.

However, it was no skin off my nose, not the way things were at present.

Bicknell wanted to hire us to do a job and then wanted to tell us just how we were to go about doing the job. It was all right with me if he wanted it that way and was willing to pay the price. After all, it was his funeral.

I got my bags placed where I wanted them and started unpacking, wondering if Bertha had thought to put in a bathing-outfit for me.

She had.

It had been hot coming off the pier at Honolulu, and the beach looked cool and inviting. I got into my swimming-trunks and went down on the beach, crossed over to the water, and plunged in.

The water was like velvet, cool enough to be mildly stimulating until the body adjusted itself to the temperature. Then it seemed as natural as being in a bathtub.

I swam out for three or four hundred yards, turned over on my back, floated for half an hour, just soaking up the feel of the salt water, occasionally swimming a few strokes, letting the waves wash me in, until finally I was up on the beach once more.

Then I got out into the dazzling sunlight.

"Well," someone said, "*you* aren't losing any time, are you?"

I looked up. It was Miriam Woodford.

"Hello. Where's everybody?"

"Norma wanted to lie down for a while. I tried to drag her out for a swim. I told her it would make her feel a lot better, but she said she wanted to rest. You going in again?"

"I thought I'd get a little sunlight."

She nodded, sat down on the sand, and indicated a place beside her. She caught the eye of a beach boy, motioned, and in a short time an umbrella was over us. We sprawled out on the sand as though we had known each other for years.

I looked her over and liked what I saw.

She had a body that could have won first prize anywhere. She had the type of skin that browned into a smooth luster. Some women fight to get a tan and their skin loses its sheen. But not Miriam. She was blond and yet she had the type of skin that reacted well to sunlight.

She saw me looking her over and said, "Anything missing?" There was lazy good nature in her voice. She moved her legs a little.

"I was interested in the beautiful tan you have."

"Is *that* all!"

"Not quite."

"I'd have been peeved if it were. You like my tan?"

"It certainly becomes you."

"I went at it gradually. Just a few minutes the first day. A little longer the second day, and, of course, I used preparations that make a tan."

"Looks nice," I said.

She said, "Darn conventions, anyway. If we could go as nature intended us, I'd be nice and brown all over. As it is, the parts the swim suit covers are sickly white. I wish people weren't so narrow-minded, then a girl could get a tan that *is* a tan."

"Make it a constitutional amendment," I told her. "I'll

vote for it."

"I might as well be out here stark naked—as it is now, every time I walk along the beach every man on it is mentally undressing me."

"You wouldn't want to deprive them of that one vicarious pleasure, would you?"

"We-l-l, it's not getting me a uniform sun tan, and, darn it, I want to be tanned all over!"

I grinned at her vehemence.

She suddenly raised her eyes to mine. "Norma tells me that you're a very understanding individual."

"I wish you'd please thank Norma for me."

"I'm not even going to tell her I talked with you."

"No?"

She shook her head. "Norma's worrying too much."

"About what?"

"You know."

I didn't say anything.

She said, "What do you think is the proper thing for Norma to do?"

"That," I said, "is up to Norma."

"What would be your suggestion?"

"I wouldn't have any."

"What do you suppose it is the man wants?"

I said, "Men want various things," and concentrated my attention on a surfboard rider who was gliding in on the crest of a big wave, doing a few fancy turns, guiding the surfboard so that it skimmed along rapidly to the right, then twisted it back to the left, and then came on straight ahead. He was superb, standing gracefully in perfect balance.

"Communicative, aren't you?" Miriam said.

I grinned at her and she grinned back at me.

"I like you that way. I'm going to call you Donald. You call me Mira. Where are you staying?"

"The Moana."

"I come out here for a swim about this time every day," she confided.

57

"I could hardly wait to get out on the beach," I told her. "Isn't this water wonderful?"

She nodded. "Have you ridden in on an outrigger canoe?"

I shook my head.

"Here comes one now," she said. "They paddle way out to where the waves are big, then start coming into shore just in front of a big breaker. They get the canoe going fast enough so it isn't engulfed by the water, and the wave picks them up and lifts them to its crest. Then a few deft paddle strokes, and everybody sits back and enjoys the ride. They come in for almost a mile, roaring along on the crest of the breaker."

"Sounds interesting," I said.

"It's one of the most exciting things I ever did. You've never done it?"

"No."

She said, "I'm going to treat you. This one is on me."

Again she nodded to the beach boy, who in turn raised his hand in a signal. A few moments later an outrigger canoe slid into the water, and Miriam Woodford, taking my hand, said, "Come on, Donald. I want you to sit right up in the bow. That's where it's the most exciting. You're going to have an experience that you'll remember."

I hoped Stephenson Bicknell and Bertha Cool wouldn't come down on the beach, but I saw no reason for telling Miriam Woodford she was off limits.

So we got in the outrigger canoe and paddled and paddled and paddled.

There were three Hawaiians in the back, men who were expert with their paddles. I suppose we didn't help much with our paddles, but at any rate it was exercise. After having been on a ship for five days it was a lot of fun.

We got out to where the breakers were really big.

Miriam explained it to me. "There's an outer reef that runs around this part of the Island," she said. "It's coral and it's just close enough to the surface so that the huge breakers that come sweeping in from the Pacific are turned into smaller breakers that come in at about ten to fifteen miles an hour, running all the way up to the beach. They don't curl over and break. They just reach a crest and then seem to keep breaking and traveling all at the same time. It's the most exciting experience. You're riding in a maelstrom of foam—"

"Paddle, paddle!" the Hawaiians yelled.

We started paddling, toward shore this time, giving it everything we had. The outrigger canoe glided through the water. I looked back over my shoulder. A huge breaker that seemed to be ten feet high was coming in on us. A great big towering mass of water that rose smoothly upward with a hissing crestline of white foam.

The wave picked us up as though we were on an elevator.

"Paddle, paddle!" they shouted, then suddenly: "Pull in your paddles!"

We pulled in our paddles, and one of the Hawaiians, who seemed to be the head man, gave a few deft strokes until he had the canoe right where he wanted it—just on the slope of the wave with the stern right up into the line of foaming water.

The canoe picked up speed. A bow wave sliced up on each side in a delicate curve. Behind, the breaker came on with a roar, seeming to increase its speed as it moved toward shallow water.

I could feel the warm air blowing past me at a speed which tore at my face, could see the sparkling jewels of sunlit water being thrown back, while ahead was a placid sheet of tranquil blue.

I looked back at Miriam.

She had her arms thrown out, the wind whipping her hair, her eyes sparkling with excitement.

She caught my eye and blew me a kiss. I waved at her and turned around to watch the onward sweep of the canoe.

We went out four or five times in the outrigger canoe before deciding we'd had enough.

Miriam said, "Let's sit on the beach for a minute, Donald. I want to talk with you."

I seated myself by her side, relaxed and happy.

"I suppose," Mira said, "you know all about my trouble from talking with Norma, don't you?"

"Norma wasn't communicative about the business of anyone else."

She laughed and said, "You know about it, though, don't you, Donald?"

"Are you having trouble?" I asked.

She said, "Listen. I was a wild harum-scarum babe in New York. I was out for all of the action and excitement there was to be had. Then I went on a cruise. I love cruises. I met Ezra Woodford.

"Ezra was a much older man and he looked it. He had some old-fashioned ways about him, but he was a nice guy and he was loaded with dough.

"Ezra got acquainted with me and finally put up his proposition. He knew that I couldn't love him but he didn't think love would be necessary. He felt that I could give him a certain companionship that he had missed and that he could make me reasonably happy. He promised to leave me half of his property when he died."

"So you married him?"

"Yes."

"And he died?"

"Yes."

"And you got half his property?"

"Yes."

"Was it worth it?"

"Yes."

"Were you happy?"

"No. It's hard to explain just how a girl feels toward an older man who is understanding and broad-minded and companionable. It's a comfortable sort of feeling. It isn't love. It isn't happiness. I suppose it's something similar to the father relationship. I never had a father whom I could look up to and respect, and I suppose there's always been something of that yearning. It's hard to describe, but believe it or not, I really admired Ezra Woodford."

"All right, what's the trouble?"

"Someone is going to claim that I killed him."

"That you killed him?"

"That's right. They think that I wouldn't wait."

"Wouldn't wait for what?"

"Wouldn't wait for him to die, that I had to hurry things along."

"Nice, isn't it?"

"Yes."

She hesitated for a while, then said, "Look, Donald, you're staying at the Moana, aren't you?"

"Yes."

"Go up to your room, get out of your bathing-trunks, put on something light, a sport shirt and slacks, and come on over and let me brew you a cup of tea. I want you to get better acquainted with Norma and—well, I have a feeling that I can confide in you."

I said, "How soon should I be over there?"

"As soon as you can get changed."

"What about you?"

"Don't worry. I'll be ready by the time you are." She laughed.

"It's a date," I told her.

"It's only a few blocks from your hotel."

I got up and started to help her to her feet, but she came bouncing up like a rubber ball, dusting the sand off of her hips, with those blue eyes laughing up into mine as though life were just one big adventure, and she didn't care what came up next just so it wasn't routine.

I went in, took a quick shower, got into slacks and Hawaiian shirt, and walked over to her apartment.

Mira was wearing a housecoat with apparently nothing on under it. She was just out of the shower and had a freshly scrubbed look about her, as fresh as a dew-covered rose petal.

Norma was lying around in silk lounging-pajamas.

They were so relaxed and easygoing, one would have thought I was married to one of them and accepted by the other as a close relative.

Miriam said, "We're having Scotch and soda."

"So am I," I told her.

We sat around and sipped Scotch and soda.

"Go on," Norma said to Miriam. "Unload."

Miriam said, "I'm being blackmailed."

"How come?" I asked.

"It's a long story."

"Condense it," I told her, looking at my watch and thinking of Bertha and Bicknell.

Miriam said, "The first bite is twenty thousand dollars."

"Sidney Selma?" I asked.

She shook her head. "I don't know Sidney Selma."

I raised my eyebrows and looked at Norma.

"Sidney Selma is *my* pet," Norma said.

I said, "Let's put a few cards on the table."

"They're on the table," Miriam said. "At least they're going on right now. I bought some arsenic. Norma knows about it. She has a letter of mine to prove it."

"In your handwriting?"

"Yes."

"That makes it nice," I said.

"Doesn't it," Mira agreed.

"Just what is in that letter?" I asked.

"I mentioned that I'd just returned from an errand, buying enough arsenic to kill a horse—and there were other things in there, kidding things, the way Norma and I joke with each other all the time."

"Where is that letter?"

"We don't know for sure. Norma thinks it's in her things in New York. We didn't think much about it until recently. Then Sidney Selma propositioned her on shipboard. He had some letters Norma wants. He offered to give them to her if she'd give him all of my letters to her."

I turned to Norma, "That was what Selma really wanted?"

"Yes. That was part of it."

"How did you happen to buy arsenic?" I asked Miriam.

She said, "That's the part no one would believe. Ezra asked me to."

"What did he want it for?"

"He was doing taxidermy. It had been a hobby of his. He mixed up some kind of a preparation for preserving bird skins which contained arsenic."

"He was in the habit of mixing it himself?"

"That's right. And he asked me to get him this arsenic."

"Have any trouble?" I asked.

"None whatever. The drug supply house knew my husband and that was all there was to it."

"You signed a poison register?"

She shook her head and said, "That's where I've fooled them—so far."

"How come?"

"My husband dealt with a wholesale supply house. He bought in quantities."

"You can prove that your husband wanted you to get the stuff?"

"No."

"How much did you get?"

"Enough to have poisoned a thousand husbands."

"Where is it now?"

"When I understood there was some sort of an inquiry on, that is, a question as to whether Ezra had died a natural death, I got in a panic and went to the place where I'd put the package. I thought I could show it was unopened and in just the condition I'd purchased it."

"Was it?"

"No."

"What had happened?"

"Someone had cut through the seals on the package and had taken out a quantity."

"How much?"

"I don't know. Some."

"What did you do?"

63

"Dumped the rest of it down the sewer and burned the container."

"That wasn't smart—in case they should ever trace the purchase."

"I know it wasn't. I know it now. I didn't know it then. But when you realize that a quantity had been taken out of the package you can realize what I was up against."

"Who's blackmailing you?"

"A man named Bastion, Jerome C. Bastion."

"Is he here?"

"On the Island somewhere."

"Where?"

"I don't know. He isn't at any of the hotels. The tourist bureau doesn't know where he is."

"And you don't know Selma?"

"Never heard of him."

"How does Bastion get in touch with you?"

"He tells me where to meet him."

"On the phone?"

"Yes."

"How long's he been here?"

"About a month, I believe."

"How long have you been here?"

"A couple of months."

"When did you have your last contact with him?"

"About two weeks ago."

"And what did you tell him?"

"I gave him to understand that I wouldn't be too difficult to deal with, that if he'd let me have all the evidence I might give him not as much as he asked for, but a substantial sum of money."

"He has some evidence?"

"He claims he has."

"And a blackmailer is trying to get the letters you wrote Norma?"

"Yes."

"So you promised Bastion money?"

"I told him I'd try to raise some."

"And he left you alone after that?"

"He knows that I'm taking steps to raise money."

"You intended to pay him off?"

She looked at me defiantly and said, "If I can't get rid of him any other way."

"Did you poison your husband?"

"Would you believe me if I told you the truth?"

"I don't know. Did you poison him?"

"No."

I said, "Promise me one thing."

"What?"

"That you won't pay anyone a thin dime."

"Is that the best way to handle it?"

"Yes."

"All right, I promise."

"And don't tell anyone you've talked with me."

"All right."

I sipped Scotch and soda, looked the place over.

One of the pictures on the wall seemed to be somehow out of keeping with the *décor* of the place. I went over to the picture, moved the picture away from the wall, looked behind it, and then beckoned to Mira and Norma to come on over.

They stood crowded up against me, looking up.

A neat, round hole about the size of a silver dollar had been bored in the wall, and behind it was the unmistakable grid of a microphone.

Mira swayed slightly, grabbed my arm. Her breath was a gasping intake.

I slipped my hand around her waist, quite certain now that there was nothing underneath the housecoat.

Norma pressed the rounded contours of her body against mine, put a hand on my shoulder, and said in a shocked half-whisper, "Donald!"

I let the picture ease back into place so that there would be no perceptible jar on the microphone.

"Well," I said, "*that* does it."

"But—but where could it have possibly come from?"

Mira whispered.

I held my finger to my lips for silence, said in a loud voice, "Where's the little boys' room, Mira?"

She laughed. "Right this way."

I made certain there was the sound of a door slamming, then I drew Mira close to me, whispered in her ear, "Keep up a lot of talk about the kind of a trip Norma had, about all kinds of things. Talk about me. You two girls take me apart, pan the hell out of me. Just keep the conversation a lot of aimless chatter. I've got to find out whether this conversation was monitored or just recorded."

I was kicking myself for being a naïve, gullible amateur. I should have looked the place over for a bug before I let the girls start talking.

The presence of that microphone explained a lot of things. We certainly were in a jam now. If the Hawaiian police, acting in co-operation with the Denver police force, was back of that, we were sunk. They'd be serving a warrant on Miriam Woodford before night. Edgar Larson could be starting back with his prisoner.

If the microphone represented the work of blackmailers we certainly were in their power now, only it meant *they'd* necessarily need a recording.

I went out in the hallway in back of the living-room, pulled up a chair, and started looking for wires.

They had been very cleverly concealed, running up between the walls to the molding, then along the top of the molding.

Once I found a wire I followed it until I located a tape recorder down under the floor of a little service porch in back.

I disconnected the microphone, shut off the tape recorder, and dragged it out where I could get a look at it.

It was a specially designed tape recorder. The reels were the big reels that are used professionally in recording studios.

The average amateur rate of recording is half the speed of the studios, and where complete tone fidelity isn't required that rate is again cut in half, and on some of the smaller machines it is cut in half once more.

This machine was geared to a slow speed, but the big reels, working on a turning unit that had enough power to keep them going on a regular rhythm, were so adjusted that as nearly as I could estimate one reel was good for six hours.

Both girls gathered around me to see what I had.

I figured out the mechanism of the thing, put the machine into high-speed reverse, ran off the tape, and said, "I've got to monitor this stuff and see how bad it is."

"You mean our conversation? All of our conversation is on that?"

"I'm afraid so. All the conversation you had with me and—"

"And all that we had while we were together by ourselves?"

I nodded.

"Good Lord!" Norma Radcliff exclaimed in dismay.

Miriam Woodford laughed. "Well, whoever listens to that is going to hear something that girls talk about in their unchaperoned moments."

I nodded and said, "Right at the moment I'm the one who's going to listen."

I lugged the machine to the bathroom.

"Donald, no. I forbid you. You can't listen. You—"

She suddenly realized what I had in mind and made a dash toward me.

I slammed the door of the bathroom in her face and locked it.

I found a plug for an electric razor, plugged in the machine, turned the tape onto listening, and settled back.

I used the rapid forward feed in order to get over the periods of silence, then put it back to normal speed when I heard the high-pitched squeal which indicated there was conversation.

I came to the place where Norma and Mira Woodford had settled down for their first good heart-to-heart talk after Norma had "got out of her things."

It was some talk.

There was a slight ribbon of light around the bottom of the bathroom door where the door didn't quite meet the floor. From time to time I could see shadows move on this ribbon of light which let me know that the two girls, or at least one of the girls, was outside the bathroom door, listening.

The conversation came in good and clear. It was a swell tape recorder.

When I had finished with the first thirty minutes of that conversation I knew a lot of things I hadn't known before. I knew a lot about the girls' friendship; I'd heard a couple of stories that were new to me; I'd learned a few intimate details about clothes and other personal matters.

I also heard Norma telling Miriam about me, about how nice and helpful I was, and then I heard Miriam ask where she could get in touch with me.

Norma said I was staying at the Moana Hotel.

I heard the sound of a dialing telephone, heard Miriam telephoning, then heard her turn from the telephone and say to Norma, "He's— The clerk says he saw him go out on the beach in a pair of trunks."

Norma said, "Well, get busy. Put on that banana-skin bathing-suit of yours, go down and let him take a look at you."

"Think that'll do it?" Miriam asked.

"Will it?" Norma said admiringly. "Honey, those hips alone would melt the image of a stainless-steel saint."

"You think he can help me, Norma?"

"I'm certain he can."

"Do you think he *will?*"

"Any man who wouldn't would be bats, walleyed, and a hundred and two," Norma said. "You've proved it often enough. It makes me envious just to think about it."

"You should worry," Miriam said. "Look at yourself."

"I'm all right in the flesh," Norma admitted, "but I don't always want to go that far."

There followed more of the same. Evidently Miriam had been getting into her bathing-suit, and the almost clinical anatomical comparisons which followed made my cheeks burn.

"Donald Lam, you shut that dreadful thing off or I'll club you to death," Miriam said in a voice that sounded oddly strangled.

I kept the tape recorder running until I heard the sound of a door slamming when Miriam Woodford had started out for the beach to meet me.

I shut the tape recorder off and opened the bathroom door.

Miriam was sitting on the bed, a picture of mingled embarrassment and amusement.

Norma was already beginning to laugh.

"Now you know!" she said.

"Now I know," I told her.

"You not only know what women say to one another in privacy," Norma said, "but as much about me as if I had been married to you for the last five years."

Then they both started to laugh.

I said, "This is no laughing-matter. Whoever put that tape recorder there now has—"

"I know, I know," Miriam shrieked. "It's a time for tears, but it's just so funny, just so terrifically funny that you would sit in there and listen to all that stuff about yourself and how I was going to hypnotize you."

"And it worked," I said.

"Sure it worked," Norma told me. "We planned it that way."

They both went into another gale of laughter.

"Who does the work around here?"

"Mitsui, a little Japanese-Hawaiian girl."

"Do you suppose she could have—"

Miriam shook her head. "She's a most unobtrusive little thing. Just moves around doing the work, putting out clean towels and all of that."

"Where is she now?"

"I sent her uptown for some things."

"Does she have a room here?"

"She doesn't sleep here. She comes in about eight o'clock in the morning and leaves around eight o'clock at night."

"Carry anything with her?" I asked.

"A bag," Miriam said. "She has her uniform in that and she changes in the maid's bathroom."

"Let's take a look."

We went into the maid's bathroom. The little bag was over behind the tub. I pulled it out. Sure enough there were two more of the big spools of tape in it.

"What do we do?" Miriam asked.

"We replace this machine right where it was."

"What do we do with all the tape?"

"We erase it."

"How can you erase it?"

I showed them how to put the tape on, feed it through, then depress the button which released the magnet and put the machine into high speed.

I had the tape all arranged, the spool put back in its proper position, and the tape recorder back under the porch with the microphone all connected before the maid got back from shopping.

I left the button in such a position that whoever had set up the recording-machine would think he had forgotten to push the button down so that the sounds would be recorded and this would account for the blank tape—at least I hoped that would be the result.

"Now what?" Miriam asked.

"Now I have to follow your sweet little maid when she quits work," I said, "and find out what she does with those spools of tape."

Miriam said, "Do you think you can do that, Donald?"

"I think so. I'll rent a car. You say she gets off at eight?"

"Yes. I can delay her for a few minutes if you want."

"No. Eight will be fine."

"When she comes in you'll have tea with us? That will give you a chance to size her up."

"I have her sized up right now," I said. "Now you girls remember that everything you say is going to be monitored. As nearly as I can figure out that reel that was on there was scheduled to run until about four o'clock this afternoon. She'll put another reel on there before she leaves. All of your conversation will be monitored and recorded. If you make it too stilted they'll know you've found the microphone. But you—"

"Don't worry," Miriam said, "it won't be stilted."

They looked at each other and giggled.

"Under the circumstances," I told them, "I don't think I'd better stick around. I'll be out here where I can pick Mitsui up when she leaves. I don't want her to see me here. I'd prefer that I remain a perfect stranger to her. I can tail her better that way."

Miriam nodded. "When do we see you?"

"I'll be in touch with you, but remember to be very careful. Everything you say is going to be recorded on tape. If I call up you'll have to disguise the conversation at this end. In fact your phone may be tapped so I'll talk in circles."

"Okay," Miriam said. "And after this, Donald, when you see me in that bathing-suit you'll know that it's a come-hither sign."

"*Now* I know," I told her.

Each of them kissed me good-by.

They weren't Platonic kisses. They weren't meant to be. They were putting on a show.

"Blood pressure, 180," Mira reported.

"Pulse, 125," Norma said.

They grabbed each other in an ecstasy of mirth. I knew it would be the same way with them even if they had known they'd both be arrested as soon as I stepped out of the door. If there was a funny side to anything they saw it.

When I got out I was tingling all over and wondering if any of the gold fillings in my mouth had melted.

They certainly were a couple of babes.

I wondered what Bicknell was doing.

10

THE ROYAL HAWAIIAN HOTEL was saturated with an atmosphere of deep, quiet luxury. The royal palms furnished dappled shade; the air was a combination of ocean tang and the scent of flowers.

I wandered through the lobby and a couple of shops before I found Bertha Cool seated at a table out on a lanai overlooking the ocean.

There was a planter's punch in front of her, and Bertha was just a little flushed, her eyes just a little watery, her lips pressed in a tight line.

I took a good look and decided that Bertha was just a little bit high and very, very mad.

I drew up a chair and sat down across the table from her.

Bertha glared at me with eyes slightly reddened from the effects of the drinks and glittering with rage.

"And what do you think *you've* been doing?" she asked.

"Looking for you."

"A fine detective you are!"

"Of course," I said, "I unpacked and went for a dip."

"Oh, of course," Bertha said. "My God, our client didn't pay seven hundred and fifty bucks for a round-trip ticket for you because he expected you to do anything else, did he?"

"What *did* he expect me to do?"

"To protect Miriam Woodford."

"From what?"

"That's what we're here to find out."

"I thought I was to be your leg man."

"With legs like that," Bertha said, "I'd fall flat on my face."

"What's wrong?"

"Everything."

"How come?"

"Bicknell's sore."

"At whom?"

"You, me, himself."

"A nice combination."

"Isn't it?"

Bertha sipped the drink, said, "I knew I'd hate this place!"

"What do you hate about it?"

"The whole thing. Seeing these slick chicks in their two-piece swim suits makes me conscious of my figure and my age. Look at that one going around with a postage-stamp bathing-suit plastered so tight it looks like the skin on a sausage."

I looked.

"Look at that wiggle," Bertha said. "They didn't wiggle like that when I was a girl, and they weren't that good-looking."

She took another sip of the drink.

"Well, why don't you relax and watch them?"

"I get mad," Bertha said. "Here I am all cinched up in a girdle to keep my fanny from spreading out farther than the seat of the chair. Just look at that blonde over there in that white suit. See the one I mean—".

"I saw her long before you saw her," I told Bertha.

"You would!" she snapped, and took two big swallows of the drink.

"After all," I told her, "your forte is not two-piece bathing-suits, it's making a bank account build up."

Bertha glared at me. I gathered she didn't like what I'd said.

A graceful Hawaiian woman in some kind of a near Mother Hubbard wrapper, all printed with vivid Hawaiian designs, walked across the lanai.

"Look at her," I said to Bertha. "*She* doesn't have a girdle."

"She doesn't need one," Bertha said.

"She weighs twenty pounds more than you do," I said, "and she isn't any taller."

Bertha looked at her with interest. "It's something in

the way she stands," she said thoughtfully. "Her back is straight, her shoulders are right in line with her hips, and her head is erect."

"I wonder if they carry things on their heads," I said.

"Damned if I know," Bertha said, looking at the woman enviously. "She could—and she's older than I am, Donald."

I said, "Finish your drink, Bertha. We're going in that shop and get one of those Hawaiian dresses for you."

"For me?" Bertha snorted.

"For you."

"Why I couldn't wear one of those things—why, Donald Lam, are you nuts?"

"That," I said, "is the way you're going to break the ice with Miriam Woodford. You come over here looking like a conventional businesswoman, laced up in a steel armored girdle and hating the place. No one's going to give you a tumble on that basis, but you go native and everyone will be talking about it. From all I hear Miriam Woodford is an impulsive girl. She adores the unconventional—why don't you obey the impulse, Bertha? Come on, finish your drink."

I got Bertha to finish her drink, got her arm, and piloted her across to one of the Hawaiian shops.

Bertha glared at the girl clerk defiantly as though challenging her to smile.

"I want one of those Hawaiian things," she said.

"Certainly," the girl observed as casually as though Bertha was ordering a package of cigarettes. "I think we have something in exactly your size. Would you care to look at patterns? Perhaps you'd like to step in the fitting-room and try one on for size."

Bertha pawed through four or five different designs, selected one, went into the fitting-room, and came out with a devil-may-care look in her eyes composed half of impulse and half of alcoholic stimulation.

"How do I look, Donald?"

"Stand a little straighter," I said, "and don't be so stiff."

"Good Lord," Bertha said, "without my girdle I can't."

"But that's the trouble," the girl said. "You've girdled your muscles until you've made them flabby. They've been receiving support from a girdle. Just notice these Hawaiian women. They walk straight and true, and their figures are firm even when they're large. That's because their muscles are built up."

"How do they build them up?" Bertha asked.

"Doing the hula."

Bertha said, "I'll take this. Send it to Mrs. Cool, room 817."

"I think you should have two of them."

"All right, I'll take this one and that one over there with the palm-frond pattern."

"Will you wear it and have the other delivered?"

"Wear it?" Bertha said. "Me walk out in public with this thing?"

"Why, certainly, Mrs. Cool. We'll send your clothes up to your room. This is regular garb in Honolulu."

Bertha said, "I feel naked."

"You look fine," the girl told her.

"Come on," I told Bertha. "You'd better get used to the thing and you've got to get used to going without that girdle."

Bertha put her hands on her hips, pressed a couple of times, said, "I'm soft as melted butter."

"You should try swimming and the hula," the girl said seriously.

"Me dance a hula?" Bertha said. "Are you trying to spoof me?"

"Certainly not. It will firm up those muscles in no time. It's the best exercise you can get, and it teaches you rhythm and grace."

"At my age—with my figure?"

"Just look at these Hawaiian women. Look at that woman walking past there."

Bertha looked.

"All right," she said. "Do up the girdle and the skirt and blouse and send them up to room 817. Donald, if you take a picture of me and send it back to the office I'll kick you overboard some dark night going back even if they hang me for it. I don't know what's got into me but—come on, Donald."

We marched back across the lobby of the hotel.

"I feel as conspicuous as though I didn't have a stitch on," Bertha said.

One or two of the tourists who had been on the boat and who were in the lanai looked at Bertha in astonishment, then broke into smiles of amusement.

That did it.

"Go on and rubber," Bertha said venomously under her breath. "I'll wear anything I damn please. You can stare at me until your eyes pop out. After all, it's my figure and I'm going to build up those muscles."

"That's the spirit," I said. "Now what you need is a bathing-suit."

"A bathing-suit!"

"It's better to bathe with them on. There are certain ordinances—"

"I wouldn't go out on that beach in a bathing-suit for—"

"Come on," I said. "Take a walk. Look at some of the people out there on the beach. Now, then, your figure isn't half as bad as that woman's."

Bertha stared at the woman I indicated.

"My God!" she said under her breath.

"Well," I told her, "that's it. Nobody knows you here. You came out here to have a good time. Go back there and get a bathing-suit and get out on the beach."

"I burn," Bertha said.

"Sure you burn. You haven't had any sun on your skin for thirty years. Go ahead and get out on the beach. The afternoon sunlight won't bother you. The water is fine. Take a quick dip, get out and swim, then take about ten or fifteen minutes of late-afternoon sunlight, then go put on a good skin lotion."

Bertha said, "Donald, I believe I'm drunk."

"Well," I told her, "what did we come over here for?"

"We came over because a creaking Don Juan paid our expenses and is crabbing because I haven't made a contact."

"Well," I said, "you won't make a contact sitting on the lanai and drinking planter's punches. Go on out and dunk in the surf."

Bertha said, "I'm just in the don't-give-a-damn-if-I-do mood that is going to start me doing it."

"Where's Bicknell?" I asked.

"Up in his room. Sore as a bear. He couldn't find you. He telephoned and left word for Mira to call back, and she hasn't done it. And he's gritting his teeth and creaking like a rusty door hinge."

"Get in your bathing-suit," I said. "I'm going up and see him."

"He'll throw you out on your ear. He's sorry now that you came over here."

I said, "That's fine. I'll go up and make a report."

Bertha looked at me suspiciously. "What do you have to report?"

"That we're here and at his service," I said, "and that you're preparing to make a contact on the beach."

Bertha said with a sudden giggle, "Pick me for a sprig of mint and stick me in the top of a julep, Donald, but I feel fine. And I *was* sore at the place."

"Go ahead," I told her. "Go back in that store and get yourself a bathing-suit and—Bertha, did you ask what these things cost?"

Bertha looked at me in sudden dismay. "Good God, no," she said.

"Well," I told her, "you've worn this one so it's too late to do anything about it. Figure some way of putting it on the expense account."

Bertha said, "It isn't that. It's the fact I bought something without finding out how much it was. Heaven help me, Donald, I'm not *that* old! And I know damn well I couldn't get *that* drunk!"

"Sure not," I said. "You're beginning to relax and enjoy

the place. Go get a bathing-suit. I'm going up and see Bicknell."

Bertha stood there looking at me in grim-faced dismay. Her lips were quivering as though she was going to cry.

"I didn't ask what the goddam things cost," she wailed, her voice bitter with self-reproach.

I walked away hoping she'd get in the surf before she realized that the planter's punches they make at the Royal Hawaiian Hotel have a wallop that can jar a babe as hard-boiled as Bertha Cool. Add the Hawaiian air, the lazy, luxurious environment, and women who have put sex in moth balls years ago suddenly start studying the hula and shopping for two-piece bathing-suits.

I stopped at a snack bar, had a sandwich and a glass of papaya nectar, then went to hunt up old grouch-face Bicknell.

11

BICKNELL WASN'T in his room. A bellboy told me he thought he was on the beach.

I went down to the beach, walked up and down looking for Bicknell, and couldn't see him. I was on the point of starting back when a figure in swimming-trunks caught my eye.

I hadn't been looking for Bicknell in trunks so it came as a shock when I recognized him seated there under an umbrella, reading a book.

He hadn't seen me.

I walked up and sat down beside him.

"Hello, Bicknell. How goes it?"

He turned his eyes on me and his face set in lines of dislike.

"Where have *you* been?"

"Looking for you."

"Don't look for me. You keep in touch with Bertha Cool. I'll keep in touch with her."

"Okay. Do you know anything new?"

"I know that Mira is avoiding me."

"Why?"

"Presumably because she doesn't want to tell me some-thing."

I said casually, "I saw her walking along the beach half an hour or so ago in a swim suit, and she seemed to be looking for someone. I gathered she was looking for you."

His face lit up as though someone had turned on an electric light inside his brain.

"You saw her? Where, where?" he asked. "Where was she? What did she say?"

"Right along here," I said. "She was looking for some-one."

"When? How long ago?"

"Must have been half an hour or so, I guess. She asked if I'd seen you anywhere."

Bicknell said, "Well, I've missed her, then. They told me that she went down on the beach every afternoon."

"Have you tried calling her?"

"I called her and she said she didn't want to see me today."

"Well," I said, "that's understandable."

"What do you mean?" he asked, turning toward me savagely.

I said, "If she's smart she certainly has an idea that her telephone is tapped and there's probably a microphone somewhere in her apartment. Naturally she wants to see you where the conversation won't be monitored, and what would be better than running into you on the beach and sitting down for a little confidential chat?"

"By George, Lam," he said, "I believe you're right. I believe you've got the thing! That's why she was so short to me over the telephone. She thinks her line's tapped. Who could be doing that?"

"Some blackmailer who wanted to get the goods on her."

"He wouldn't be blackmailing her unless he had the goods on her."

"He might be blackmailing her on bluff. If she babbled

out a lot of stuff over the phone to you he'd be able to back it up with proof, provided he had the line tapped. And the same is true about a conversation in the apartment. If I were you I'd steer clear of that apartment and try to talk things over when I met her casually."

Bicknell grabbed at that explanation. "That's it! That's the reason she was so curt over the telephone. Lam, Bertha's right. You're smart. By golly, you *are* smart."

I said, "That's just experience, Mr. Bicknell. We've had lots of these cases, and many, many times we find that the telephone lines have been tapped and someone has installed a bug in a room where conversation would logically take place."

"You say she's been down here on the beach and gone back?"

"I don't know whether she's gone back or not. I saw her."

"Poor kid," he said. "I guess I let her down. She probably thought I'd have sense enough to come down here and wait where we could have what would appear to be a casual conversation, and I muffed it. Well, I guess there's no use waiting now. Lam, would you mind helping me up?"

I helped him to his feet.

He dusted the sand off his dry bathing-trunks.

"You want to watch this sun," I told him. "If you've been out in it for a while you'll burn pretty badly."

"Oh, that's all right. I am not the type that burns. I— Lam, if you see Mira anywhere on the beach or around where I can talk with her, you let me know, will you?"

"Where will you be?"

"I'll be in my room all afternoon, and then I'll be down at the cocktail lounge, and then I'll be having dinner. She can find me, all right. I'll leave word with the bell captain where I can be located at any time."

"Okay," I told him. "I'll do that, but she *may* not have another chance until tomorrow—she'll probably call you from somewhere, but your calls may be monitored. You'll have to keep that in mind. And she's probably being shadowed."

"You think it's like that? I mean, do you think they'd go to all these lengths—whoever they are?"

"How do I know? In my business you are supposed to figure everything, hope for the best, and prepare for the worst."

"Yes, that's so."

He put his hand on my shoulder. "Donald," he said, "you're all right. You're doing fine. I'm certainly glad that Bertha insisted on you coming. I think we're going to get this thing licked. But let Bertha handle all the contacts. Well, we're doing all right, Donald, all right!"

"Sure we are," I told him.

He hobbled away toward the Royal Hawaiian, and I went back to the Moana, rang up one of the car agencies that makes a specialty of renting cars, and arranged for a car.

At eight o'clock I was waiting where I could keep an eye on Mira's apartment.

The Japanese-Hawaiian girl came out carrying her bag, looking completely innocuous.

She waited at the bus stop and took a bus just like any other servant.

I tagged along behind the bus.

The bus went on down on Kalakaua Street and then turned left on King Street. After it had gone half a mile or so on King Street it stopped, and who should get off but my little Japanese-Hawaiian girl.

She walked along the curb for thirty or forty feet, slid in behind the steering-wheel of a sleek-looking car, eased it away from the curb, and almost immediately gunned the motor into speed.

They have a technique of driving in Honolulu that scares a newcomer to death, a relaxed, casual way of hurtling around corners, whizzing through the narrow streets, threading their way in and out of traffic. They have intersections where four and five through roads all run in together, and by some occult method of telepathy each driver seems to know what the approaching driver is going to do. They twist and turn and weave, and somehow or other they always seem to get there, but it seems a miracle when they do.

This girl was a typical Honolulu driver. I had the devil of a time trying to keep her in sight. I didn't dare get too close but I knew I'd lose her if I dropped too far behind.

She swung around corners until she was headed out toward Koko Head, and then she really settled down to travel.

I followed along behind, sometimes fairly close, sometimes quite a way behind. Once or twice when I felt sure she wasn't going to turn I got ahead of her.

That did it. She didn't want people to pass her. She slammed down the throttle and burned up the road until she passed me.

At length she slowed, and then abruptly turned down a steep hill toward the beach.

It was rather tricky following her here, but I turned off the lights and eased down the road to where she swung in on a driveway.

I was able to keep on going for a hundred yards, until the road ended, then I made a U-turn, came back to the side road, and found her car parked in front of a cute little house perched on rocks above a nice swimming-cove—a house shaded by banana trees, palms, and the lush Hawaiian tropical growth.

I drove back down the road, parked, switched off the motor and the headlights, and sat there waiting.

She came out in about ten minutes and headed back toward Honolulu. I tagged along behind for a few minutes until I was satisfied she was on her way back, then I hightailed past her and drove rapidly.

I kept watching her lights in my rearview mirror. She wasn't in such a hurry now, not nearly so impatient or angry when cars passed her.

When we got back to where there was more traffic and

more intersecting roads, I slowed down and she passed me, driving at a steady pace.

She wasn't at all suspicious, but was driving wide open. Evidently she'd paused somewhere along the road and made a check to make certain she wasn't being followed.

It was a cinch to tag her now. She turned down into a cheaper quarter, made three or four sharp turns, parked the car, and went into a small house. I saw lights come on in the house, and saw her pull the shades.

I got out and took a look at her car. The doors were locked and, of course, the ignition was locked.

By using my small flashlight I was to able to read the mileage figures on the speedometer. I jotted them down, then drove back to the Moana Hotel, keeping track of the mileage on my own car.

I hunted up Bertha at the Royal Hawaiian.

"How's Bicknell?" I asked.

"He was all perked up at dinner," Bertha said. "The old goat seemed to be really feeling his oats. We had a couple of drinks and he ate a good dinner. Afterward, he began to get moody. He kept looking at his watch."

"I'll fix that," I told her.

I went back to the Moana, rang up the hotel, and asked for Bicknell.

They rang his room and Bicknell answered immediately, a note of eagerness in his voice.

"Gosh, Mr. Bicknell," I said, "I had the deuce of a time getting to a telephone that wasn't busy. I'm over at Lau Yee Chai's now. Mira was over at the Moana Hotel when I left, walking around the lobby as though looking for somebody. Did you say something about being over at the Moana Hotel later?"

"Me? No."

"I think you did," I said. "I think you made some statement when she met us at the boat about the way you liked the Moana or something."

"I said I'd stayed there when I was here before," Bicknell said.

"Perhaps that's what you intended to say," I told him, "but I had the idea that you liked to go over to the Moana and—"

"Well, thanks a lot, Donald," he interrupted. "I'd like to chat with you, but right now I'm very busy. I have to see a man on a business matter. Good-by."

He hung up.

I went to one of the near-by food mills and slipped one of the waitresses five dollars.

"What's that for?" she asked.

I said, "Come with me and make a telephone call."

"That's all?" she asked.

"That's all."

I took her to the telephone booth, rang the Royal Hawaiian.

"What do I do now?" she said.

"Ask for Stephenson D. Bicknell," I said. "He won't be in. Ask if you can leave a message for him. Make your voice sweetly seductive. Tell the operator to please tell him that a young woman called who wouldn't leave her name, but that she'll try and see him sometime tomorrow."

The waitress did what I told her and I gave her a wink after she'd hung up.

"This man has been making passes at a girl, and I want him to think he's getting somewhere," I said.

"Oh." She laughed at me and said, "Don't encourage him *too* much. There are plenty of wolves around here."

"It's competition that counts," I told her.

"How would you know?"

"Powers of observation. Why?"

"Nothing," she said archly. "I just didn't think that *you* encountered much opposition."

"You'd be surprised," I told her.

"I'd be willing to," she said, then laughed. "Any time you want any more calls put through, just let me know. That's the easiest money I've made in a long time."

"I may take you up on that," I told her. "Thanks a lot."

"You're welcome," she said. "Good night."

She stood looking at me.

I went back to the Moana, took my clothes off, and lay in bed reading. Before I went to sleep I called Mira.

"This is your swimming partner."

"Oh, yes, hello—"

"Don't mention names," I warned.

"Oh, yes, when will I see you?"

"Tomorrow maybe."

"Not tonight?"

"No."

"I'm sorry. I was hoping—did you do what you said you were going to?"

"Yes."

"Find out anything?"

"Yes."

"Can you tell me?"

"Not now."

"I think you're mean. You could drop in and—"

"Not tonight. We haven't got a certain problem solved yet.

"Now here's something important for you to remember. You've been all over Waikiki hoping to run into Steve Bicknell."

"The hell I have!"

"Yes, you have. You've missed him everywhere. You wanted to run into him so it would seem like a casual meeting. You think you're being watched. You're nervous. You called up once and he'd gone out."

"Do I *have* to pull that line?"

"If you want me to work with you," I said and hung up.

Then I read for a while and went to sleep.

12

AT FIVE MINUTES TO EIGHT O'CLOCK in the morning, Mitsui, the Japanese-Hawaiian maid, got off the bus and, carrying her bag, walked into Miriam's apartment, a demure, self-effacing, efficient servant.

I got in my car and cruised up along Kalakaua Street. I had a feeling someone was following me, but I couldn't verify it. It was just a feeling. I made twists and turns until I knew no car could have stayed behind me without becoming conspicuous, and then I violated a few speed laws. When I was sure I'd shaken any possible shadow, I turned left on King Street and drove along slowly, looking at the license numbers on the parked automobiles.

Her automobile was in just about the same place it had been the day before.

I got out and looked at the figures on the speedometer. They checked. She had driven directly from her place to the place where she'd left the car and hadn't made any side excursions.

I drove back over to the neighborhood where she had gone calling the night before.

By that time it was around nine o'clock.

A rather friendly looking guy was emerging from his house with a briefcase, getting in his automobile.

I drew up alongside and said, "I'm sorry to bother you, but do you know where the Smith house is?"

"The Smith house?"

"That's right. It's around here somewhere. I understand it's for rent."

"I don't know of any houses for rent around here," he said. "Are you sure of the address? Do you have the right place?"

"Not sure," I said, "but this is the description of how they told me to get here."

"There was only one house for rent," he said, "and that's the one down at the end of the driveway there, to the left. It's been rented for over a month now."

"A man by the name of Smith?" I asked hopefully.

"No," he said. "It's—it's an odd name. Wait a minute. I'll think of it. I met the guy—oh, yes, a man by the name of Bastion. He keeps pretty much to himself."

I sighed wearily. "Well, I guess I'll have to go back and get another chart of sailing-directions. I must have made a wrong turn somewhere."

He said, "There aren't many houses for rent. They're snapped up pretty fast. With whom are you dealing?"

"A regular real estate operator," I told him. "I should have let him drive over with me, but I thought I could find my way. Well, thanks a lot."

I drove back to Waikiki and found Bertha Cool at breakfast at the Royal Hawaiian. She was eating papaya.

"Hello, Donald," she said. "Sit down. Say, do you know something?"

"What?"

"This stuff is good," Bertha said, indicating the papaya with a spoon.

"Sure it's good. Moreover it's good for you. It has pepsin in it and helps digest food. That's why they use it to tenderize meat."

Bertha glared at me. "I wish you could talk without listing statistics. I don't need help to digest my food. I, me, personally digest my own food, gobs of it. I squeeze all the nourishment out of it right in my own stomach, all by myself, every damn bit of it. What the hell are we doing here, anyway?"

"Waiting for you to make the contacts," I said, grinning.

Bertha said, "There's something fishy about this whole business. I can't seem to get to first base. I've called that God's gift to man half a dozen times. They say she's out every time. Some snippy maid that says she's down on the beach swimming. You know what I think? I think it's a run-around. I don't think she wants help from anybody. This is a fine way to run a detective agency. Why don't *you* get busy and do something?"

"Such as what?"

"Find out what the hell it's all about."

"I thought that you were going to do that. I thought I was supposed to be just a leg man."

"You're talking like Bicknell!"

"Well, what do you want me to do?"

"Find out what's going on. I wish I'd never left the office. Business is different from what it used to be, Donald. You're the one to go out and plan all this stuff. Bertha is the one to sit in the office and make the clients get the long green lettuce into the bank account.

"Out here I'm a total loss and that numskull client of ours is going to fire us. He's got things all fouled up insisting that we play it his way, and now he's going to blame it on us."

"All right," I told her. "For your information here's the low-down. Sidney Selma, who came over on the ship with us, is a blackmailer. He tried to blackmail Norma Radcliff, and I think made some headway. I think some things happened that Norma hasn't told us about."

"So what?" Bertha said.

I said, "There's another blackmailer who's after Miriam. He's a man by the name of Jerome C. Bastion, who lives in a rented house in a little subdivision. The address is 922 Nipanuala."

Bertha stared at me. "What the hell are you talking about?"

"Telling you what it's all about."

Abruptly Bertha opened her purse, pulled out a pencil and a notebook. "What's that name?"

"Jerome C. Bastion."

"And the address?"

"922 Nipanuala."

"Spell it," Bertha said.

I spelled it for her.

"These Hawaiian names," Bertha said. "They give you the willies. The crazy language is all cockeyed."

"*Kapakahi*," I said.

"What's that?" Bertha asked.

"Cockeyed," I said.

"That's what I'm telling you," Bertha said. "But what does *kapakahi* mean?"

"Cockeyed."

Bertha got red in the face. "I'm telling you the language is cockeyed and you come back with some idiot Hawaiian stuff. Now what the hell are you talking about?"

"*Kapakahi*," I said, "is Hawaiian for cockeyed."

Bertha puffed up like an adder, gradually subsided. "Sometimes," she said, "I could strangle you with my bare hands. How did you find out about all this?"

"Doing detective work, renting a car, trailing spies."

"You're keeping an expense account?"

"Of course."

"Now *that's* more like it," Bertha said, relaxing. "Tell me about this sonofabitch, Bastion."

"He wants twenty thousand dollars from Miriam Woodford."

"What does he want it for?"

"To suppress evidence that would indicate she murdered her husband."

Bertha thought that over. "Fry me for any oyster! And this guy from Denver—what about him? This Edgar Larson. I am beginning to get a little afraid of him, Donald. He's dangerously unobtrusive and so smug. If he wasn't getting somewhere he'd be running around in circles. We'd be cutting his back trail. We don't do it. He's crawled into a hole and pulled the hole in after him. He wouldn't be so hard to find if he wasn't getting somewhere."

"That," I said, "is why I'm telling you about Bastion."

"Why?"

"Because I think Larson is smart and I think we've got to beat him to the punch."

"What would Larson do?"

"He might go out and make a dicker with Bastion."

"For what?"

"For whatever Bastion knows."

"What does Bastion know?"

"I'm not too certain he knows too much at the present time, Bertha. He knows enough to make him suspicious and he's trying his best to get more information. I think he may be bluffing."

"So what?"

"So," I said, "you stroll down on the beach and—"

"Me on the beach?" Bertha Cool said. "Go down and get sand in my shoes, get my stockings snagged?"

"In your new bathing-suit," I told her.

Bertha glared at me.

"Your feet will be bare," I told her. "You won't have any shoes. You won't have any stockings. Or you can put on some of these beach sandals if you want. You go down there and you'll find Bicknell sitting under an umbrella. He's going to be a little bit impatient by the time you get there. He'll be just a little bit sore. And he'll probably start jumping on you, asking what you've done, pointing out that you've been here long enough to have accomplished *something*."

Bertha grunted and said, "Are you telling me? That's what comes of having a detective job and running it the client's way. The client wanted me to establish a contact with Mira. Why, Mira hasn't any more intention of talking with me than I have of ringing up the Bureau of Internal Revenue and asking them to look over the books and see if they can find some way of getting a little more money on my last income tax return."

"Bertha," I said, "you'll have some news to tell Bicknell. You can show him that we're on the job. You can also tell him that the maid who is working at Mira's place is a spy in the employ of the blackmailers, and that he mustn't go near the place but will have to contact Mira out here on the beach."

Bertha's greedy little eyes glittered at me as she blinked the information back into her brain.

"Is all this on the up and up?"

"It's on the up and up."

"How did you find out about the maid?"

"I shadowed her last night."

Bertha said, "Dammit, Donald, there are times when I'm really proud of you. Go ahead, give me some more low-down."

I said, "Mira's place is bugged up. There's a tape recorder that's serviced by the maid. All conversation from the living-room is recorded on plastic tape."

"Pickle me for a peach!" Bertha exclaimed, "and throw in a black clove for seasoning. How did you find all that out?"

"Just looking around. That's all the low-down I have at the moment."

"Well, go get some more."

I said, "You put on your bathing-suit, go on down, and find Bicknell. He'll be sitting under an umbrella."

Bertha said, "I was half-plastered when you sold me on the idea of buying a bathing-suit. I tried it on this morning. I stick out in places."

"Go ahead and stick out. What did you come over here for? To make money or to win a beauty contest?"

Bertha glared.

I said, "You've got to work fast because Bicknell is beginning to wonder just what we're doing. I think he's going to be peeved."

Bertha grabbed her knife as though she intended to stab right through the plate of ham and eggs that the waiter had just brought.

"Well," I told her, "go ahead and enjoy your breakfast."

"Donald," she said sharply, "where do you think you are going?"

"Out," I told her, and waved good-by as I walked across the dining-room, leaving Bertha sitting there glowering.

I knew she wouldn't try to follow. The ham and eggs were already paid for, and Bertha was going to sit there and eat them regardless of flood, famine, and pestilence.

I went into a phone booth and called Miriam Woodford on the telephone.

The maid answered. "Mrs. Woodford not up," she said.

"How about Miss Radcliff?"

"Not up."

I said, "You take a message for them."

"I can't take a message," she said in a somewhat stilted manner, pronouncing each word distinctly and separately. "They are asleep."

"Wake them up," I said. "Take them a message. Tell them that this is Donald Lam and I am coming over."

"They are not up," she said.

"Take that message to them," I told her and hung up.

I gave them about ten minutes and then walked over to Miriam's studio apartment.

Miriam herself let me in. She had on an opaque silk negligee with nothing under it. For a moment as she stood in the doorway I saw the silhouette of a beautiful figure outlined against the silk by the illumination of a sunlit window in the dining-room behind her.

"Well," she said, "you're an early bird. What's the idea, waking us up this way?"

"There's work to be done."

"Come on in, Donald. We're just getting in circulation. Norma's in the shower."

I walked into the living-room, motioned toward the picture with the concealed microphone back of it, then toward the bedroom.

"Come on in here for a minute," Miriam said. "Norma said she had something to tell you. Norm, are you decent?"

Norma called out, "Who is it?"

"Donald."

"I'm in the shower."

"Stay in there for a minute," Miriam said.

She took me into the bedroom, said, "Sit down, Donald."

I closed the door, went around and looked behind all the pictures, looked around the walls. Miriam watched me with thoughtful eyes.

When I had finished she raised her eyebrows in a silent question, and I shook my head and said, "Probably they just had room for one bug and they put that in the living-room."

"Give," she said.

I said, "I followed your maid. She took a bus just like any other maid would do, but she got off the bus as soon as it turned on King Street. She had a good-looking Chevrolet parked there. She got in it and went out Koko Head way to a little house above a cove with a little swimming-beach down below it. There are half a dozen houses cling-ing to a steep side hill there."

"Where, Donald?"

"A place called Nipanuala Drive, 922. That's where Jerome Bastion lives."

"What did Mitsui do?"

"Stayed there long enough to deliver a couple of re-corded spools of tape, pick up some fresh tape, then came on back, got in her car, went to her own house, stayed there until this morning, got up, drove the car down to King Street, parked it, got on the bus, and came to work."

"The double-crossing cat," Miriam said. "I could gouge her eyes out—"

"That wouldn't do any good," I said. "What we have to do is to play it close to our chests."

"Such as what?"

I said, "I want both you and Norma to put on the most seductive bathing-suits you have. I want you to go down to the beach as soon as you've had breakfast. You'll find Stephenson D. Bicknell sitting on the sand under a beach umbrella."

For a moment Miriam's face twisted with a grimace of dislike.

I raised my eyebrows in silent interrogation.

She said, "I don't know. He was Ezra's partner and I liked him all right in that capacity, but now he's in charge of all my money. I don't like him in that capacity."

"Why not?"

"I don't like guardians. I don't like chaperons. I don't like spies. I don't like snoops. I don't like discipline. I don't like conventions. I never did."

Norma stuck her head out of the bathroom door. "The coast all clear?" she asked.

"Donald's here."

She turned to look at me. "Hello, Donald. How's for a girl getting some clothes?"

"Oh, don't be so shy," Miriam said carelessly. "Donald

knows all about you."

"Not like this," Norma said.

"I'll bet he will."

"How much?"

Miriam thought that over. "Two hundred."

"You've made a bet. No, you haven't, either. You're just trying to spoil my chances." She laughed. "Donald, if Mira won't do it, will you hand me that robe?"

I laughed. "Why should I? Give me two good reasons."

She thought that over. "You're putting me in a spot. Good grief, who's that?"

She pointed a bare arm at the door. Miriam and I turned our heads.

I heard the thud of bare feet and whirled just in time to see Norma clutching the robe in front of her.

Miriam burst out laughing as Norma's naked back turned toward the bathroom. Then, a moment later, Norma, a grin wrapped all over her face, came out, the robe belted at the waist.

"Smarties," she taunted.

"Good work," Miriam said, "you had us fooled."

I said, "Now I want some information. What would you have said, or how would you have felt, Norma, if I'd meekly handed you that robe when you asked me to?"

"Why, I'd have thought you were a perfect gentleman," Norma said. Then she added, "And I'd have hated your guts for being uncomplimentary."

"I'd have thrown him out on his ear," Miriam said.

"The heck you would," Norma taunted. "Any old time."

"Well, let's get back to business," I said. "Go down to the beach. Separate if you want to, but when Mira finds Bicknell I want Norma to come along almost immediately."

"And do what?" Norma asked.

"Just be there, stick around, be nice. Show him anatomy, be alluring."

Miriam said, "I think he has matrimonial designs, Donald. He saw how happy Ezra was and he's started getting romantic. When he kissed me yesterday he was being a regular Romeo."

"Could be," I said.

"I married an older man for money once," Miriam said, "and now I have money."

"Want more?"

"Not by marrying Steve Bicknell and waiting for him to kick the bucket."

"Speak for yourself," Norma said, laughing. "Don't forget me."

"*You* wouldn't wait," Miriam said.

She turned to me. "We hunt up Bicknell. Then what do we do?"

"Then," I said, "you are inseparable. You keep giving hints to Norma, but she just doesn't get them. You tell her that she really should go in the beach shops and pick out some clothes, that you'll hold the fort while she's gone."

"And what will I do?" Norma asked.

"Tell Miriam that you want her along when you make your purchases, and just don't take any hints."

"Do I have to be that dumb?"

I nodded.

"Oh, well," she said, "I can probably make the act sound convincing at that."

I said, "The idea is that Miriam is very anxious for an opportunity to talk with Bicknell alone, but you are her guest. You are inseparable friends and it just doesn't occur to you that there could possibly be any reason why Miriam should want to get rid of *you*. You're intimate friends and haven't any secrets."

Norma nodded. "When do we do this?"

"Right after you've had breakfast."

"What about the servant, Mitsui?"

I said, "The servant is naturally wondering about me. I've got to have a part in this thing and be in character."

"How do we account for you?"

I said, "I knew you girls in New York. I knew both of

95

you well. I'm making passes at Norma."

"Getting anywhere?" Norma asked.

I grinned and said, "It would look better if it appeared I had in the past."

"Okay," Norma said. "Give me a ready-made purple past and I'll live up to it."

"Now don't try to leave me out of this," Miriam said.

"You won't be left out," I told her, "not by the time Mitsui gets done reporting to Bastion."

"Then what'll happen?"

"You can't tell. He may be looking for a new angle of blackmail. Now remember that tape recorder is operating, and as soon as you get out in the other room you'll have to start talking about things that sound intimate. You can make little hints, talk about me, and then get together and whisper. Be damned certain that the whispers won't register. They can be just a lot of hissing s sounds, but it will sound like genuine whispering."

"Why should we whisper if we aren't supposed to know there's a microphone?" Norma asked.

"Because of the servant," I said. "You're protecting Norma's good name."

"Protecting my good name after receiving my former lover in a bedroom before breakfast, while we're dressing?"

"You forget that Miriam's here. There's safety in numbers."

Norma suddenly threw back her head and laughed.

"What's the joke?" I asked.

"The idea of Miriam being a chaperon or that she'd make for safety."

Miriam said thoughtfully, "Donald, why couldn't you—"

"Go on," I said as she stopped.

She hesitated a moment, glanced at Norma, and then said, "Why couldn't you go over to that house of Bastion's? When he's out swimming, get in there, go through the house, and see if you can't find the incriminating evidence that he has and—well, he could hardly go to the police and make a complaint because he wouldn't dare to state that he was holding evidence for purposes of blackmail."

"Are you telling me my business?" I asked.

She looked at me and said, "Yes."

"Don't," I told her. "I've handled so many blackmail cases they're commonplace to me. There are complicating factors in this case you don't know anything about. Try doing exactly as I say."

Gentle knuckles sounded on the door.

Miriam hesitated, looked at Norma.

The door opened. Mitsui's inscrutable eyes, looking like lacquered ripe olives, slithered around the room. "I go shopping now," she said. "Breakfast is on the table."

She closed the door.

"Can you beat that?" Miriam asked. "The independence of the little devil. Just because we're a little late coming out for breakfast. You'd think she was catching a train or something."

"She goes shopping every morning?" Norma asked.

"That's right, and she has to go at a certain fixed time."

Norma laughed. "Trouble with independent help, even in the Paradise of the Pacific!"

I said, "Well, I'm getting out of here. You girls hurry through breakfast and get down to the beach."

"It won't take any time," Miriam said. "We'll just step into our bathing-suits and be all fixed."

"Okay," I told her. "I'm on my way."

"Where are you going, Donald?"

"Places."

"Want to go swimming with us?"

"No. You two play it the way I said."

Miriam said, "I've got to see him *sometime*. No use dragging Norma in and spoiling her morning. She might see someone—"

"No, you do it the way I told you," I said, and walked out.

I hurried back to my hotel, changed back into my swimming-trunks, rented a surfboard, and paddled down the edge of the beach to where Bicknell was sitting in the space reserved for the Royal Hawaiian guests.

I dragged the surfboard out of the water and walked up the sand to drop down by Bicknell.

"Hello," I said. "How are you feeling?"

"I'm feeling a lot better. I think the sunlight and the fresh air is doing my arthritis a lot of good. Look, I'm beginning to tan."

"Be careful you don't burn."

"I won't burn, but I can feel a little tingling sensation in my skin. I think I'm going to develop a nice tan. Donald, what are you and your partner finding out?"

"We're laying the foundations," I said airily, "and—"

"Don't hand me a line like that."

I turned and raised my eyebrows.

He said, "You're either utterly incompetent as investigators or else you're getting some place and holding out on me."

"How could we be getting any place," I asked, "when you insist that we make our contacts through Miriam Woodford and Bertha can't get in touch with her? You wanted Bertha to make a contact on a woman-to-woman basis."

"Well, what's wrong with that?"

"Nothing, except that it hasn't worked and I don't think it's going to work."

"Why can't Bertha do it?"

"Because Bertha can't go to Miriam's place, ring the doorbell, and say, 'Hello, you're a woman, and I'm a woman, so why don't you confide in me?"

"You're trying to make my plan sound ridiculous. I don't want Mrs. Cool to go to the door. I want her to be around here on the beach where she can see Miriam casually, speak to her, perhaps, if she has to, tell her that she's a detective from California. Then Miriam will think things over, ask her advice, and you'll be all set.

"I confess I'm a little disappointed in your partner, Donald. She seems to lack imagination."

"Well, she'll be down here any minute now, and you

can tell her so."

"I will."

I went back to my surfboarding, made a great show of paddling out to the surf, then worked my way unostentatiously through some other surfboarders back to the Moana Hotel, turned in the surfboard, went into my room, showered, rinsed out my bathing-suit, hung it out to dry, and went out to stand at the window of my room looking over the beach trying to see Mira and Norma.

The distance was too great for recognition. I didn't have any binoculars and there were too many beautiful girls on the beach.

I went back and sat down and waited. The hardest thing of all.

Nothing happened.

An hour passed, two hours. The telephone rang.

I was as jittery as a girl waiting for a bid to the senior prom. I fairly grabbed at the telephone.

Bertha's voice, all choked up with emotion, said, "Donald, for God's sake, get down here quick."

"Where?"

"Police headquarters."

"What's happened?"

"Plenty. Get down here."

"Where do I find you?"

"Office of Sergeant Hulamoki. He's in charge of Homicide."

I hung up and rang Miriam's telephone.

Miriam herself answered.

"Donald talking, Miriam," I said.

"Hello, Donald. What's new?"

"Did you see Bicknell?"

"Now aren't *you* funny?"

"Did you?"

She said, "Norma and I put on bathing-suits that made even me feel indecent. We went down to the beach. No Bicknell."

"Sure. He was there—under an umbrella."

99

"No Bicknell."

"You're sure?"

"Of course I'm sure."

"Bertha Cool?"

"You mean the woman who came over on the boat with you?"

"Yes."

"We didn't see her. Would she have been in a bathing-suit?"

"Probably."

Miriam tittered, then said, "No, we didn't see her."

I said, "Okay, sit tight. Something's happened. I don't know what," and hung up.

I went up to police headquarters, asked for Sergeant Hulamoki, and was shown right in.

Bertha and Stephenson Bicknell sat rigidly erect, looking frightened. Sergeant Hulamoki sat on the other side of the desk.

The sergeant and I shook hands.

"Just trying to clear up a certain little matter," the sergeant said. "Mrs. Cool thought you might help."

"Something serious?" I asked.

"Mr. Bicknell," Sergeant Hulamoki said, "is an unwilling witness."

Bicknell looked at me, clutched the head of his cane a little tighter, fidgeted.

Sergeant Hulamoki looked at me and said, "There is, of course, no need to maintain the guise of being strangers. The Island police has a passenger list of the *Lurline* several days before it docks here. We look over the list in order to find out just who is favoring our Islands with a visit."

I nodded, saying nothing, because saying nothing was the safest thing to do.

"So we know all about Cool and Lam, Investigators. We are familiar with the background and history of Stephenson Bicknell. And we have *surmised* that there was a rather urgent reason for his visit."

"Urgent?"

"Mr. Bicknell started pulling wires to get reservations on the *Lurline*. He went to considerable trouble and some expense. He didn't know exactly who was going to occupy the reservations until the day before sailing."

I nodded again, looking wise.

"We would like very much to receive a frank statement," Sergeant Hulamoki said. "You people came over here because you were hired to come over here. You occupied staterooms that had been reserved by Mr. Bicknell. It is quite obvious that you are traveling on his business.

"Mr. Bicknell is, of course, interested in financial matters in which Mrs. Ezra P. Woodford is also interested."

"I think she prefers to be called Mrs. Miriam Woodford," Bicknell interpolated, "and don't try to put two and two together so as to make twenty-two."

"All right, Mrs. Miriam Woodford," Sergeant Hulamoki agreed affably. "It is to be assumed that Mr. Bicknell came over here because of certain important business matters having to do with Miriam Woodford?"

"What makes you think so?" Bicknell asked.

"You have no other business in the Islands. You have no friends in the Islands. Yet you told the Matson Navigation Company that your trip was an extremely urgent business trip."

"I just wanted to get over here," Bicknell said.

"And you employed the firm of Cool and Lam to help you with your enjoyment?"

Bicknell was silent.

Sergeant Hulamoki shook his head. He said, "How do you account for the fact that Donald Lam has visited Mrs. Woodford in her apartment?"

Bicknell stiffened and glared at me.

"The last time," Sergeant Hulamoki said, "was before breakfast this morning, while both girls were dressing. Donald Lam is evidently a friend of long standing."

"Why the double-crossing sonafabitch!" Bicknell said, walking right into the trap.

"They entertained him in their bedroom while they

were dressing."

"*Both* girls?" Bicknell asked.

"Both girls," Sergeant Hulamoki said.

"Do you," I asked, "make detailed checks on all of your visitors like this, sergeant?"

He looked at me, smiled, and said, "No."

"Thank you," I told him. "I'm honored."

"You should be."

Bicknell was gazing at me with cold, angry eyes.

Sergeant Hulamoki said to me, "We have reason to believe that Mr. Bicknell saw a murder committed, and Mr. Bicknell is exceedingly vague in the information he is able to give us."

Bicknell said, "I've told you everything I know."

"We think you could be of greater assistance."

"Would you," I asked, "mind telling me just who was murdered?"

Sergeant Hulamoki said, "The murder was committed at 922 Nipanuala Drive. The victim was Jerome C. Bastion, who has been a visitor here for some four weeks."

Bicknell said to me, "Bertha Cool and I drove out to this place. I wanted to talk with this guy."

"Why?" I asked, keeping my face a mask of innocence.

"Because I had a business matter I wanted to discuss with him."

"What was it?"

"It was purely private."

"Go on," Sergeant Hulamoki invited.

"I've told you the story a dozen times."

"You haven't told it to Mr. Lam, and I can see Lam is all agog with curiosity."

Bicknell said, "It's a narrow driveway. There was no place to park the car where it wouldn't block the road unless we turned it around. I got out of the car. I rang the chimes. There was no answer. I rang again. There was no answer. I thought the occupant of the house might be down in the cove, swimming. I could hear someone splashing around down at the cove and the sound of voices."

"Go on," I said.

"I stepped up to look through one of the windows where the Venetian blind was open."

"Then what?"

He said, with a little shudder of nervousness, "I don't like to think about it."

"Go right ahead," Sergeant Hulamoki said. "You're going to have to think of it a lot. You'll get over the shudders after so many repetitions."

"Well, I saw a man sprawled on a bed. He evidently had been shot between the eyes."

"What else did you see?" Sergeant Hulamoki asked.

"I saw someone running."

"Man or woman?"

"It was a woman. I've told you that."

"What did she look like?"

"That I can't tell you. I saw only her back. A flash of leg and her hips. She was either in a bathing-suit or completely in the nude—I don't know which."

"And what was she doing?"

"I had just a fleeting glimpse of her as she ran through the doorway."

"Could you describe the bathing-suit?"

"It was so tight-fitting that I can't be absolutely positive that it *was* a bathing-suit. It may have been a nude woman."

"And what did you do?"

Bertha interposed and said, "He came back to the car. I was waiting to see if anyone was home before parking the car. Bicknell rang the doorbell. I sat there watching him at the door and decided there was no one home. Then I saw him look through the window. Then he came hurrying back toward the car, waving his hands and moving as fast as he could. He has arthritis and he can't run, but he was shuffling along as fast as he could."

"Then what happened?" Sergeant Hulamoki asked, studying Bertha thoughtfully.

Bertha said, "He told me what he'd seen, and told me

to rush to a telephone and notify the police."

"So what did you do?"

"I left the car where it was, went, and phoned the police."

"Then what?"

"Then I went back, looked in the window, saw the body, and got Bicknell to come and sit in the car with me while we waited for the police. It was only a few minutes."

"Where did you go to phone?"

"Right where I told you the first, second, third, fourth, and fifth times," Bertha snapped angrily. "I climbed a million and five stairs to a house up on the hill and asked if I could use the phone."

"You didn't go into the house, the one where the body was?"

"Certainly not! I have *some* sense."

"Did Bicknell?"

"Of course not."

"You could see him from the place where you were telephoning?"

"As it happens, I could. After I got in and explained what I wanted and the woman showed me the phone, I could look out of a picture window and I saw Bicknell standing there looking like a lost sheep."

Bicknell said, "I didn't even try the door. I'm not foolish enough to go in."

"No, I dare say you're not," Sergeant Hulamoki said, "but I do think you saw more of the girl than you're admitting."

"Well, I didn't."

Sergeant Hulamoki turned to Bertha. "Now, when you got back, after you'd phoned the police, did you make any attempt to go to the back door?"

"No, why should we?"

"Because there was a killer in the house."

"Because a killer *had been* in the house," Bertha corrected. "You wouldn't expect her to stay there. Bicknell saw her running from the room. She heard the chimes of the front door, and she got out of there fast."

"How did she get out?"

"Through the back door, probably, then down the steps to the cove, in for a swim, out on the other side, and up to her car, or the house where she was staying. Dammit, *I* don't know how she got out, but she must have got out."

"And wouldn't it have been easy for you to have climbed up to where you could command a view of the swimming-cove and the stairs so as to have seen this figure—in case Mr. Bicknell hadn't already recognized her and didn't want you to know who she was?"

Bertha said, "I'm not a gazelle. My activities as a mountain goat have been greatly curtailed of late. Springing up to the crest, jumping from rock to rock are activities tha: just don't appeal to me."

"There was Mr. Bicknell. He had all the time you were over in the neighboring house telephoning. Apparently he just stood there on the front porch. The point I'm trying to make is that there seems to have been a singular lack of curiosity as to the identity of this young nude woman who ran out of the house."

"Bicknell is all crippled up with arthritis," Bertha said. "He has a hard time moving around."

Sergeant Hulamoki shook his head. "I think that Mr. Bicknell should be able to give us a more accurate description of the young woman who was in the house."

Bicknell made a little shrugging gesture with his shoulders.

"Is there someone you are trying to protect?" Sergeant Hulamoki asked.

"Of course not," Bicknell said indignantly.

The sergeant said, "It is strange, Mr. Bicknell, because, as it happens, we know a great deal about Jerome C. Bastion."

Bicknell sat up in his chair, but his face remained without expression.

I glanced at Bertha. Her face was like granite.

"This gentleman," Sergeant Hulamoki went on, "was

a very expert, adroit, professional blackmailer. He made a living, and a very good living, from blackmail.

"Now, then, as it happens, Detective Edgar B. Larson of the Denver police force came over on the ship with you. Sergeant Larson's trip was professional. He had learned that Jerome C. Bastion was over here and that Bastion was here for purposes of blackmail. Sergeant Larson had reason to believe that the victim of Bastion's blackmail was none other than your ward, Miriam Woodford."

"I'm not her guardian."

"Well, you're her financial guardian."

"That doesn't make her my ward. I wish it did."

"Why?"

"Because I can't control the woman. I can't get her to realize the seriousness of the situation."

"What situation?"

"Her financial situation, her social situation, the fact that there should be more of a semblance of mourning regardless of how she felt toward Ezra. Now that's not right, either. That's not exactly the way I want to express it. What I mean is that I tried to impress upon her that her naturally spontaneous character should be—well, there shouldn't be any levity."

Sergeant Hulamoki looked at Bicknell thoughtfully. He said, "Here in the Islands, Mr. Bicknell, we are not greatly impressed by wealth or influence. When we investigate a case we try to do the very best job of which we are capable."

"I'm glad," Bicknell said.

"And if we find there have been any misrepresentations by anyone, we are very harsh."

"That's a good attitude to take," Bicknell said.

"Do you have anything to add to your statement?"

"Not a thing."

"You think this girl you saw was in a bathing-suit?"

"I think so."

"You think she was young."

"She was very lithe, very graceful, very quick in her

motions."

"About how tall?"

"Rather a tall girl."

"Slender?"

"No, she had a good-looking leg and—and back."

"Well-formed?"

"Well-formed," Bicknell said.

Sergeant Hulamoki got up from behind the desk. He said, "If you people will excuse me for a moment I have an appointment with Sergeant Larson. I want to confer with him."

Sergeant Hulamoki walked out of the room, and the door slammed shut behind him.

I got up out of my chair, pointed to a desk lamp with a peculiar base, and made warning motions by putting my finger to my lips. Then I said, "All right, quick, folks, give me the low-down on this thing. What is it?"

Bicknell said, "Well, as a matter of fact, we—"

Bertha kicked him on the shin, and he went into a convulsion of agony.

Bertha said, "We told the whole truth, Donald. The thing happened exactly as Bicknell has outlined."

"Did he recognize the girl?" I asked.

"Ask him," Bertha said.

I made a warning sign with my hand, said, "Bicknell, give it to me straight and give it to me fast. Now we're working for you and you've got to tell us the truth. Did you recognize the girl?"

"Definitely not," Bicknell said, finally getting the idea. "I told it to the police exactly as it happened."

"Exactly?"

"Exactly."

"You haven't held out a thing?"

"Not a single thing."

I said, "We've had a lot of experience in this stuff and you haven't. Now give it to me straight, Bicknell. Are you telling us the whole truth?"

"The whole truth, every bit of it."

"Well," I said, "that's that, then. It seems funny you'd have seen the girl go through the door and not have been able to tell more about her. Where was she when you first looked in the window?"

"I don't know," Bicknell said. "She may have been standing in the shadows somewhere. You know how it is. A flash of motion will arrest your attention. The first thing I saw was something white moving and then I saw this girl's leg—it wasn't too light in there, you know, Donald. There were shadows in the room and it was hard to see looking through the window. I think there were reflections from the outside that bothered me. Anyway, all I know is that the first good look I got at this girl was when she was running through the doorway."

I turned to Bertha. "Give me the low-down, Bertha. Don't try to hold out."

"Dammit," Bertha said, "I wouldn't hold out on anybody. This is a murder rap. I'm not going to take a murder rap for any client. I'm giving you the low-down. Personally I don't think he recognized her."

"But you think it was a woman?" I said to Bicknell.

"It was a woman's leg and—and rump."

"What kind of a bathing-suit?"

"If there was any bathing-suit it was—I'm not prepared to say there was a bathing-suit. I think she may have been completely naked."

"And what happened to her?"

"She evidently went out the back door."

"How do you know?"

"I think I heard the back door slam while I was standing there."

"And you did nothing about it?"

"What could I do? Did you think I was going to go hobbling around the cement walk and confront some woman who had just killed a man? Don't be silly! That's a job for the police. I'm no longer a young man. I'm not a physically robust man and what chance would I stand of grappling with someone who had just committed a murder?"

"She didn't come around in front of the house?"

"No. The way I've figured it out," he said, "although I haven't told the police, is that she'd gone to the cove for a swim, wearing a robe and nothing else. I think she opened the back door, dropped the robe, and went in there naked. In that way no one would stand any chance of finding any blood spatters even on a bathing-suit. After the murder she ran out the back door, slipped on the robe, and went down the stairs toward the beach.

"At the first landing she turned up one of the other flights of stairs, apparently a young woman returning from a morning swim. No one would have paid any attention to her, and if there was no swimming-suit under the robe, who was to know anything about it?"

"Then where did she go?" I asked.

"That place is terraced with half a dozen houses clinging to the hill above the cove. There are roads on three levels. She simply climbed to one of the upper roads. She had a car parked there. That's all there was to it. She had gone before Mrs. Cool had the police on the line."

"Well," I said, "there's nothing much we can do until the police find out more about it. Did you ever know Bastion?"

"No."

"You'd never met him?"

"Never."

"Did you know him, Bertha?"

Bertha shook her head. "I didn't recognize the body, and the name means nothing to me."

"All right, now why did you go out there?"

"We went out there," Bertha said, "because I had a tip that the man who lived there was trying to blackmail Miriam Woodford."

"Where did you get the tip?" I asked, looking her straight in the eyes.

"That's one thing," Bertha said, "I'm not going to tell even you—not yet."

"Why not?"

"It's a confidential communication. I'm not going to divulge my sources of information to anyone. I promised I wouldn't and I'm going to keep that promise."

"Just what did you intend to do when you got out there?" I asked.

She said, "I intended to put the fear of God into him. I hate a slimy blackmailer, and I intended to call for a showdown."

"Suppose he didn't scare?"

"Then," Bicknell said, "I was along with a checkbook, Mr. Lam, if you really want to know the low-down on the thing."

"Well, I wanted to know the low-down," I said. "Thanks a lot. Anything else?"

"That's all," Bicknell said.

"Nothing else," Bertha told me.

We lit cigarettes and sat waiting.

In about two minutes the door opened and Sergeant Hulamoki came in with Detective Edgar Larson of the Denver police force.

"Hello, Mr. Larson," I said.

He nodded to me, said tersely, "We may as well get some cards on the table. I came over here ostensibly as a tourist. Actually I am on the Denver police force and am assigned to cases of homicide."

I nodded.

"I won't go into details," he said, "but we had reason to believe that Miriam Woodford may have murdered her husband, Ezra P. Woodford."

Bicknell straightened in his chair, tried to pull himself up, but he couldn't make it. His weak wrists wouldn't furnish the power. He reached for his cane.

"You're not going to make statements like that with impunity," he said, "you—"

"Shut up," Larson told him, "and listen. We have reason to believe that Jerome C. Bastion, who was occupying that rented cottage, had some evidence that would tie

Miriam Woodford in with the murder of her husband."

"In the first place, Ezra Woodford wasn't murdered," Bicknell said. "In the second—"

Larson interrupted. "How much do you know about Miriam Woodford?"

"I know she's a square shooter. She probably wasn't madly in love with Ezra, but she made a business deal with him and she upheld her end of that business deal."

"How much do you know about her past?"

"Nothing," Bicknell said, "and what's more I don't want to know anything about it."

"Her past," Larson said, "is a little checkered so far as the conventions are concerned. There are a few splotches of purple in the picture."

"In other words," Bicknell said sarcastically, "the moment a girl ceases to be a virgin she can be convicted of murder, is that it?"

"That's not it," Larson said calmly, with no outward indication that he resented the sarcasm. "We are simply trying to get a clear picture of the characters involved."

Bicknell sat in tight-lipped, indignant silence.

"Miriam was a playgirl who went on cruises," Larson said. "It was on one of those that she met Ezra Woodford. Her name was Miriam Vernon then. Woodford was a lonely, rich man. Miriam was a package of human dynamite. She had Norma to back her play. They played their cards very, very well. Ezra Woodford married Miriam."

Bicknell said, "Now look here, I was Ezra Woodford's partner. I know a lot about how he felt and a lot about what he thought. Since you've brought the matter up I'm going to tell you he wasn't under any illusions about Miriam. He knew that she was a party girl who had been playing around, but he liked her. She had the knack of making him laugh. She kept him on his toes. He was lonely and he wanted to have youth around him. He was willing to pay for it. He made a deal with Miriam. She was going to marry him and be taken care of for life. She kept her end of the bargain—he kept his."

"The trouble," Sergeant Larson went on, "is that Ezra Woodford was rather durable. He turned out to be a man with a strong constitution and definite notions of his own. Miriam was willing to play the game for a while, but the trouble was she wouldn't wait."

"What do you mean, she wouldn't wait?"

"Just that," Sergeant Larson said. "Miriam isn't a good waiter. She's long on impulse and short on patience. She decided to help matters along a little bit with a dose of arsenic."

"Arsenic?" Bicknell said. "You're nuts."

Larson said, "I have some proof. I think I'm going to get more proof. When I get it I'm going to have an airtight case."

Bicknell said, "Ezra died of natural causes. The doctors said so."

"The symptoms were those of arsenic poisoning."

"The death certificate shows it was acute food poisoning," Bicknell snapped.

Larson said nothing.

Sergeant Hulamoki looked at him.

Larson nodded.

Sergeant Hulamoki said, "Well, I guess that's all for the moment. You folks can go now. We may call on you again."

We got up and filed out.

Bertha said, "I'll ride back with you, Donald. Bicknell has a rented sedan. He can drive it back and we'll meet at the Royal Hawaiian."

We got in my car. I looked the thing over to see that there were no wire recorders, no microphones, then said, "All right, tell me what happened."

Bertha said, "My God, Donald, I'm in a mess. I'm scared stiff!"

"What did you do?" I asked. "Did you go in the place?"

Bertha nodded. "Bertha went in."

"Tell me about it."

She said, "Bicknell talked me into it. I realized it was

taking a terrible risk, but Bicknell was there dangling that checkbook, and—well, you know how it is with Bertha. She can't resist picking up a little something extra."

"Go on," I said. "Tell me about it. When was this? Before you telephoned the police or afterward?"

"No, it was afterward. I phoned the police just as I said I did and went back and joined Bicknell there on the porch, waiting for the police to come."

"Then what?"

"Then," she said, "was when Bicknell got the idea. He told me that Bastion was a blackmailer, that Bastion was blackmailing Miriam; that his murder was the worst thing that could possibly have happened because he must have some incriminating stuff of some sort there in the house. He said the police would find it and then the fat would be in the fire."

"Did he have any idea what it was that Bastion was using as a blackmail lever?"

"Something about Miriam's past. I guess she was a playgirl, all right. Apparently Bicknell knows all about it, but isn't concerned about that. I don't know, Donald, it may be something more serious. Perhaps she did decide to hurry things up with her husband. You can't tell about these wild babes. They get ideas. This Miriam has me stopped. She and Norma are modern girls and they're a different breed of—"

"Never mind that," I interrupted. "How did Bicknell know about Bastion in the first place?"

"I told him."

"When, where, and why?"

"Right on the beach, just a few minutes after you left, and because the sonofabitch was riding me, claiming we weren't getting anywhere, that he'd wasted his money getting us over here, and that he was dissatisfied."

"Did you tell him how you knew?"

"Not me, lover. You can trust Bertha for that. I told him I had to protect my sources of information just like I told the police."

"Keep playing it that way," I told her, "because I drove out there early this morning to scout around. It might be better if the police didn't know that."

"Well, they can't pin anything on you because the murder was committed just before we arrived," Bertha said. "The doctor confirms that."

"All right," I told her, "give me the low-down. Was it Miriam that Bicknell saw out there?"

"I think it was."

"You don't know?"

"No. He won't admit a thing."

"Then why do you think it was Miriam?"

"Because he's so damned evasive in his description. I think he had a better look than he said he did."

"All right, here's the next question. Did Bicknell do it?"

"No, he couldn't have."

"How do you know? Was he on the beach?"

"He was with me. I picked him up on the beach right after you'd left. He was out of my sight while we were changing clothes in the Royal Hawaiian, that was the only time, except when I was climbing the stairs up to that house to phone the police, but that was *after* the murder was—"

"When he got out of the car and went to the door?"

"I was watching him all the time. He rang the bell, looked in the window, and came running over to me. I think it was Miriam Woodford, Donald. And if it was we can't protect her."

I thought that over, said, "It depends on what the police find. What happened out there? Give me the whole story."

"Well, after I'd phoned, Bicknell pointed out that the evidence showed Bastion had been shot while he was in bed. Apparently he'd been reading the paper. The paper was lying there on the floor beside the bed. Bicknell said probably Bastion had opened the door, got the paper, and was lying in bed reading. That would mean the front door might be unlocked."

"Go ahead," I said to Bertha. It was like pulling teeth.

"Well," Bertha said, "I was willing to let him satisfy his curiosity on that point, so I didn't protest when he tried the knob on the door."

"And then what happened?"

"It was just like he deduced the damn thing from sizing up the way the body was lying. The door was unlocked. He opened the door and there we were, able to walk right in. It seemed a simple matter to step through the door. I held back, but Bicknell got busy with the siren song of his checkbook. Bertha couldn't resist."

"You fools," I said. "You couldn't have gone in there without leaving fingerprints and—"

"Now wait a minute," Bertha said. "Bicknell isn't that dumb, and even if he were I'm not a babe in the woods. I had my handkerchief out polishing the doorknob before we even took a step inside the place, and I warned Bicknell about fingerprints.

"Bicknell had a pair of light gloves in his pocket, and he put those on and told me that he'd look around and that I wasn't to touch a thing."

"Go ahead," I said. "What happened?"

"We went in the murder room and looked around. Bicknell opened a few drawers and looked through Bastion's clothes until he found his wallet."

"What was in his wallet?"

"Oh, a whole gob of money," Bertha said, "and some papers."

"What were the papers?"

She said, "That I don't know. Bicknell gave them a quick look, then put them in his pocket."

"The crazy fool," I said. "The police will search him and—"

"Now wait a minute," Bertha said, "don't go jumping at conclusions. Bicknell's smart. He wasn't in there over five or ten minutes. I wasn't in there two minutes.

"Bicknell was afraid the police might take him to headquarters and search him, so he wanted to ditch those papers some place where they wouldn't be found by the

115

police, but we could pick them up later."

"So what did you do?"

"There's a stone wall out in front of the place. When he went out he slipped the papers into one of the gloves, balled up both of the gloves, and stuck them in a little hole in the wall and plugged it up by inserting a loose rock that was lying at the bottom of the wall."

"You don't know what was in those papers?"

"No. I doubt if Bicknell does. He just gave them a hasty glance, but apparently it was pay dirt, something he wanted."

"Anything else?" I asked.

"In a closet," Bertha said, "there were a lot of spools of tape, and there was a machine on which they could be played. I think some of the spools were blank and some of them were spools that had something on them. I suppose these are the conversations between Miriam and Norma, but we didn't dare touch them. We couldn't have got them out of the place."

"The police will find them, listen to them, and be coming down on Miriam Woodford like a thousand ton of brick before the day's done. Go on, what else?"

Bertha said, "Now I'm coming to the part that bothers me. Donald, I must have been completely nuts."

"Go on," I said impatiently. "We haven't got all day. Let's have it straight. You're not helping things any being so coy."

Bertha said, "Up to this point I was pretty much in the clear. It was Bicknell who was doing all the illegal stuff."

"You'd gone into the place."

"That's right, I'd gone into it, but I hadn't touched anything."

"Go on."

Bertha said, "I began to get cold feet, awful cold feet."

"It was about time," I told her.

She said, "I told Bicknell that I was going outside and keep an eye on things and that I'd whistle in case the police came."

"So what did you do?"

She said, "I walked out."

"Leaving Bicknell in there?"

"Yes."

"Go on," I told her. "You've got something on your mind. For heaven's sake, get it out in the open."

She said, "It was as I was walking out of the door, Donald. I was just standing there in the little entrance hallway for a second. There was a bookcase with some books in it, and one of the books was a little bit out of line. I suppose I should have claimed it was the detective in me that noticed it, but it wasn't. It was the natural feminine instinct, the housekeeper. And, dammit, don't you laugh at me having feminine instincts!"

"I'm not laughing."

"The book was just a dummy. As soon as I touched it I could tell there was something wrong with it. I pulled it out. It was just half a book. The inside pages had been cut out, leaving just the cover."

"Go on," I said, "we haven't got all day. Get it out of your system. Let's find out what we're up against."

Bertha said, "Bicknell was in the other room, rummaging around. As soon as I touched the book I knew the balance of it wasn't right. I tried to push it back in and it didn't feel right, so I pulled it out and saw it was just a half a book like I said. In the cut-out part of the book was just a common, ordinary, motion-picture camera."

"That's all?"

"That's all," she said.

"What did you do?"

Bertha said, "Before I thought, I had the motion-picture camera out and was looking at it, and then I suddenly realized that I was leaving fingerprints all over everything.

"Well, I grabbed my handkerchief and scrubbed off the book as best I could, and then I started to do something with the motion-picture camera and realized that I'd got fingerprints all over it and it might be awfully hard to get them off."

"So what did you do?"

"I stole the motion-picture camera and put the fake book back on the shelf."

"And what did you do with the camera?"

She said, "Well, I was afraid the police might search me. I was pretty certain they'd make some excuse to go through the automobile.

"I walked out and stood on the porch holding the thing, and then I got a bright idea. I walked down the road to the junction of the driveway. There were half a dozen mailboxes there. One of the mailboxes was in the name of Abney. I don't know what time mail gets distributed around there but I have an idea it's late in the afternoon. Anyway, I was taking a chance on it. I opened the mailbox and stuck that motion-picture camera in there."

"Leaving fingerprints on it?"

"No. I wiped it off as best I could, but I'm still worried about it. I may not have got 'em all off. I didn't have any gloves."

"Then what?"

"Then I walked back to the porch and about that time I heard a siren coming. I gave Bicknell a signal and he came out. I asked him if he'd found anything more and he said he hadn't, just the papers."

"And he'd hidden those?"

"No. He was still holding them. It was at that time that he put them inside one of the gloves, balled the gloves up, put them in his little chink in the stone wall, and then plugged that up with the loose stone that was lying on the ground by the wall. I think probably the stone had fallen from the wall in the first place."

"And you didn't tell Bicknell anything about the camera?"

"Donald," she said, "I haven't told *anybody* about that camera, and I'm not going to tell anybody. I'm going to lie like hell if they try to pin it on me. It was a fool thing to do. But I have an idea there may be some films in that camera that are significant, stuff that perhaps he was using in his blackmail."

She paused to look pleadingly at me. "Now you are daring and resourceful, suppose you get the films out of the camera and send them in and have them developed. The police will be watching Steve Bicknell and they'll be watching me, but there should be an opportunity for *you* to get out there and strut your stuff."

"Why didn't you tell Bicknell about the camera?" I asked.

"And put myself in the power of a creaking client?" Bertha retorted. "Hell, that puts my neck in a noose. You know it, I know it, and what's more, Steve Bicknell would know it. When it comes time to make a financial adjustment do you think Bicknell will say, 'Well now, Mrs. Cool, you've risked your license by doing something illegal trying to help me and I want to give you a little bonus.' Fat chance. He'll know that he knows something that would put me out of business and he's just ornery enough and tight enough to try to make something of it. Just as I'm ornery enough and tight enough to look at him in an accusing way and remind him of the fact that *I* know *he* violated the law in going in there and searching."

"You didn't search?"

"I was careful not to search. I just stood there in the doorway and watched."

"And while you were out putting the motion-picture camera in the mailbox you don't know what Bicknell was doing?"

"He was searching."

"I mean you don't know what he found."

"He said he didn't find anything."

"That's what he told you. You have no way of knowing."

"That's right."

"Now can you tell me just about where those gloves were put in the wall?"

"About ten feet to the right of the walk, and about two-thirds of the way up the hall. There's a stone with a splash of white on it, and it's directly underneath that stone."

"All right," I said, "I'll see what I can do. Keep your mouth shut."

"That I will," Bertha said. "Don't think I'm going to go blabbing this stuff to anybody."

I said, "Now here's one other thing, Bertha. How much blood was there in that room?"

"Quite a bit. It was a messy job."

"The police probably aren't quite ready to start looking you over with a microscope for blood spots and—"

"I never got near any blood," Bertha said.

"How about Bicknell?"

"He tried to be careful."

"He tried to be," I said. "You can't tell just what happened. Now, remember this, Bertha, the police here are pretty competent. They looked your shoes over. They saw exactly what you were wearing. They looked Bicknell's clothes over."

"Well?" Bertha asked.

I said, "Later on today they'll make it a point to go through your rooms. If they find that the clothes you are wearing now, and particularly your shoes, are missing, they'll know what the answer is. Now it's up to you to get in touch with Bicknell and give him a word of caution. Tell him not to try to get rid of his shoes or his clothes. He must be particularly careful not to send clothes out for cleaning."

"What will happen if there *should* be bloodstains on his shoes?"

I said, "Tell Bicknell to go down and walk on the beach, walk up and down the sand, and occasionally his arthritis will cause him to drag his foot."

"I get you," Bertha said. "What will you be doing?"

"Covering your tracks," I told her.

13

GETTING PINCHED for speeding at that particular time would have been a sure way to purchase a one-way ticket to the penitentiary. I didn't like what I was doing, but it was a job that had to be done.

I made certain I wasn't being followed, then I gave the car all the speed I dared. I knew the way so I didn't have to waste time wandering around finding where Nipanuala Drive was. I swung in there, drove down to about the eight-hundred block, and found the place jammed with automobiles.

Short as the time had been, word had got around about the murder, and officers had put a rope across the street, but the curious were still jammed up against the rope, taking pictures, talking, and staring.

It made things nice for me because there was quite a crowd around the mailboxes. I stood around, waited until I had a chance when most of the people were looking over toward the house, opened the Abney mailbox, and reached inside.

I heaved a sigh of relief. The camera was in there.

I eased the camera out, closed the lid of the box with my shoulder, joined the group that was staring for a while, then got in my car and drove back to the Moana.

I had an hour or so of freedom of action, not much more than that.

I opened the motion-picture camera.

It was the magazine type. There should have been a flat film magazine in it. There wasn't. What it actually held was a small roll of film, receipts for two safety-deposit boxes, one in a San Francisco bank, one in a bank in Salt Lake City, and keys to the safety-deposit boxes, all wrapped up in tissue paper so they wouldn't make noise rattling around the inside of the camera.

I looked at the roll of film.

It was exposed microfilm that had been developed. My pocket magnifying glass showed me the film contained photographs of letters. There must have been hundreds of them.

One of them was a letter in feminine handwriting. I put my magnifying glass on it. Evidently it was a letter Norma had written to some man. It was sultry. The little fool had signed her name.

I didn't have time to do any more looking. I was holding a package of dynamite in my hands. I put the stuff in my pocket.

I drove along until I came to a camera store. I went in and purchased a new magazine of fresh film and slipped it in the camera. Then I drove out King Street to where the spy had left her car parked.

The ignition was the only thing that was locked on the car. The rest of it was wide open.

I took motion pictures of the car parked on King Street, pictures from the front, pictures from the back. Then I spent a couple of long minutes wiping all fingerprints off the camera, put the camera in the glove compartment of the car, went to a drugstore, purchased an alarm clock, took the alarm clock out of the cardboard box, put the microfilm and keys in the box, sealed it up, went to the post office, and sent the package by air mail, special delivery, to Elsie Brand at the agency address on the mainland.

Sergeant Hulamoki had looked like a really competent police officer. I knew that if he was half as competent as he seemed he'd have kept us there at police headquarters until after officers had arranged to search the apartment occupied by Miriam Woodford, but just to make sure, I strolled around past the place. Two police cars were there.

There was no sign of Miriam or Norma.

I waited on the other side of the street, watching the place just to keep posted on developments. The fact that there were two police cars led me to believe that the girls were still there.

It was the right hunch because after about five minutes two officers came out escorting Miriam and Norma. They placed the girls in one of the police cars and whisked them away.

When they had gone I walked across to the apartment and knocked on the door.

Nothing happened for a minute, then the door was suddenly jerked open by a police officer.

"Come in," he said.

I shook my head.

"Come in!" This time it was an order.

I said, "I'm sorry, I'm not coming in. I just wanted to tell you to make a *good* job of searching the apartment."

"Who are you?"

"I'm a friend of the girls. I'm interested in finding out who committed the murder."

"Come in," he said, "I want to find out more about you."

"I tell you I don't want to come—"

He reached out, grabbed the front of my shirt, pulled me through the door, swung me around, pushed me back into a chair.

"Don't get smart," he said. "When I tell you to come in I want you to come in. Now who—"

I said wearily, "My name is Donald Lam. I'm a private detective from the mainland. I am here on business. The business is confidential. I've been up to Sergeant Hula-moki's office, been given a third degree, and released."

"Then what the hell are you doing here?"

"I just came to tell you to make a *good* search."

"You don't have to tell us our business."

"I hope not, but I certainly want you to make a *good* search."

"Why?"

"Because," I said, "I don't want something planted that could be used as evidence against the girls, and then have it appear that you overlooked that hiding-place on your first search."

He thought that over.

"Which one of the girls are you representing?"

"Neither one of them has paid me a dime."

"What's your interest in the matter?"

"I'd like to find out who committed the murder."

"You must suspect that one of the girls did, otherwise you wouldn't have come here."

I yawned and said, "If you'll go about your searching and let me go about my business, we'll all of us be a lot better off. Actually I want you to nab the murderer so the police won't try to blame it on me."

He looked me over. "Why try to blame it on you?"

"So they could close the case."

He said, "I think you came here to plant something yourself."

I stood up and held my arms out. "Go on and frisk me."

He frisked me.

I said, "I'm simply trying to get you to search the place and make a damned good job of it. I knew you were going to be here making a search. I knew that you were going to question the two girls for a while and then have your partners whisk them off to police headquarters to answer more questions so you could stay behind and search the joint. I waited until two officers had left with the girls in the first car, and then came over to tell you that if any evidence is found after you have made your search, I want to be in a position to show that whatever was found was planted here. Now can you make a search that's good enough for that?"

He said, "Don't worry about me. My partner and I are going to take this place to pieces. When we get done if there's anything here we'll know it."

"That's fine," I said. "Would you mind giving me your name?"

"Daley," he said.

"Make a good job of it," I told him, and started for the door.

He hesitated for a moment, then let me walk out.

I went up to my room, put on a pair of swimming-trunks, and went out to lie on the beach. I got a surfboard, paddled along the shore, looking people over.

After ten or fifteen minutes I spotted Bertha Cool sitting under a beach umbrella.

I paddled in, carried up my surfboard, and said, "How's everything coming?"

She glared at me. "You make any crack about my figure and I'll use this umbrella for a lance and chase you all the way back to the hotel. You get that thing fixed up?"

I looked out to sea and said, "I think so. Where's Bicknell?"

"How should I know? I'm no nursemaid."

I said, "What are you doing out here?"

"Looking for an opportunity to see Bicknell and that hussy."

"What girl?"

"Miriam Woodford."

"She's being questioned by the police."

Bertha gave me a withering glance.

"Really," she said sarcastically. "I'd never have suspected it."

She was silent for a moment, then said, "And what are you doing out here, loafing around?"

"Giving the police a chance to search my room," I said. "If you look up on the upper lanai of the Moana Hotel you'll see an officer spotted up there with binoculars watching me down on the beach so he can tip his partner off when I start back to the hotel."

Bertha sighed. "I suppose they're searching *my* room," she said. "I hope they don't paw through my things and get them all out of order."

We sat there for a while in silence.

"Hell of a case," Bertha said. "We're getting some kind of a run-around and we don't know what it's all about."

"What makes you think we're getting a run-around?"

"I can feel it."

I said, "Well, I'd better get on my surfboard and get out where the officer can watch me."

"When are you going back to your room?"

"When the man on the upper lanai quits studying me with binoculars. I'll know they're all finished with their search then."

I carried my surfboard down to the water, eased my stomach into a position of balance, and started paddling out toward the surf.

Half an hour later I rode a wave in. I couldn't see any-one watching me. I turned in the surfboard, went up to my room, took a shower, dressed, and looked things over.

I had the license number of the automobile the maid had been driving. I checked on it and found it was a rented car. I called up the rental agency. The car had been rented by Jerome C. Bastion.

I knew the police would have checked Miriam's apart-ment. I knew they'd have found the tape recorder and the microphone. That would lead to shaking down the maid. What that would lead to was problematical.

I rang police headquarters and asked for Sergeant Hula-moki.

When he came on the line I said, "This is Donald Lam, sergeant."

"Oh, yes." His voice had a great deal of interest. "I wanted to—what's that?—oh, excuse me just a second, Lam. I want to take this call in another office. People are listening here."

I hung on, grinning. I knew what that meant. He was putting in a witness on an extension phone, also probably plugging in a switch so he could have a recording of the telephone conversation.

A moment later his voice came on, friendly and cordial. "That's fine. We can talk now, Lam. I couldn't talk freely before. Some newspaper reporters were there. What's on your mind?"

I said, "I'm interested in that murder."

"I know you are."

"Probably not in the way you think."

"Well, let's not argue about it. You're interested. So what? Why did you call?"

I said, "I did a little checking around at some of the car agencies to see if Jerome C. Bastion had rented a car."

"Yes, yes, go on."

"I found that he had, and have the license number of the automobile. Do you want it?"

"No thanks, Lam. We did that an hour ago."

"I thought perhaps you might find the car some place and it would be a clue."

"One of the cars was in a garage there at the rented house, you know."

"One of the cars. You mean he rented two?"

"That's right," Sergeant Hulamoki said. "One of them he had out at the house. We put out a general call for the other car. It'll be picked up somewhere and we may be able to tell something about it from the place where it's parked."

"Two cars," I said, reflectively.

"That's right. One from one rental agency and another from another agency. If you checked them all by telephone it's strange you didn't find that out."

"I didn't check them all," I said. "I checked some of them, until I struck pay dirt, then I quit."

"Well, of course," Sergeant Hulamoki said, "I wouldn't want to presume to give anyone advice, but in our investigative work we don't stop when we strike one streak of pay dirt."

"Thank you," I said meekly. "I appreciate the tip. I guess I'll conduct my investigations Honolulu-style after this."

"Anything else on your mind?" Sergeant Hulamoki asked.

"I dropped in to see your men over at the Woodford apartment and suggested to them that they make a very thorough search."

"I understand you did. What was the idea?"

"Later on if anybody should plant anything I'd like very much to be certain it was a plant."

"I don't think you need to worry, Lam," he said, and then, after a moment: "Anything else on your mind?"

I said, "There was a man on the ship. His name was Sidney Selma. I thought he might be a blackmailer. If so, he may have had some connection with Bastion."

"Well, well, well! That's interesting. What gave you

the idea he was a blackmailer?"

"Just something about him."

"A hunch?"

"You might call it that."

He said, "Seven hundred and ten passengers, and you look 'em over and get a hunch *one* of them is a blackmailer, so you think we should look him up and accuse him of murder!"

"I didn't say that."

"You intimated it."

"That's right, I did."

That flabbergasted him. "You mean that's the idea?"

"That's it."

"Then you must know something more than you've told me."

"I'd hate to think I could tell you *all* I know in a short phone conversation."

"I mean about the murder," he amended.

"So do I," I said.

He was silent for a few seconds. "Anything else?"

"That's all."

"Feel free to call me any time," he told me, and hung up.

14

I KEPT WATCH on Miriam Woodford's apartment. The police who had been searching the place drove away. About thirty minutes later a police car returned Miriam Woodford and Norma Radcliff to their apartment.

I started over to pay my respects, but before I had even started across the street a car swung around the corner and frail Stephenson Bicknell, despite his arthritis, tried to conform with the idea of masculine strength by helping Bertha Cool out of the car.

It was a strange sight. Bertha, trying to be feminine and dainty, giving him her hand. Big Bertha, who could have picked him up and tossed him clean over the top of the car. But she was playing up to him, and Bicknell was enjoying the role of being the dominant male.

I got a grin out of it, and went back to wait. Evidently Bicknell and Bertha had been watching the place, too, waiting for the girls to get back.

Bertha and Bicknell came out in about an hour. I waited until they had driven away, then went over and punched the doorbell.

Miriam Woodford threw the door open. "All right, who is it *now?*" she asked. "We—oh, hello, Donald! I wondered where you were."

"I'm here."

"So it would seem. Come on in."

I motioned toward the bedroom, and she took me in there. We sat close together on the bed, talking in low voices.

"Tired?" I asked.

"Tired," Mira said. "Those monkeys up there at police headquarters tried to put us through hoops."

"What kind of hoops?"

"All kinds. High jumps, slow jumps, crawls, and just plain hoops."

"What did you tell them?"

"I told them a lot of things," Miriam said savagely.

"Did they interrogate you together or separately?"

"Separately first, then together, then separately."

"Suppose you fill me in on what happened?" I said.

"Well, after you left this morning we went down on the beach."

"Together?" I asked.

She avoided my eyes.

"Together?"

"We were at the start."

"Then what?"

"Then," she said, "Norma met one of the fellows who had been on the *Lurline,* a fellow who had made a couple of passes at her and looked attractive."

I glanced at Norma.

"I thought I'd stop and shoot the breeze with him a

little," Norma said. "He looked lonesome and—"

"Who was he?"

"A man by the name of Ray Geary."

"How long were you with him?"

"I guess a lot longer than I thought," Norma said, laughing nervously. "We went in swimming together, came out and dried off in the sun, and he was handing me a pretty good line. I kept thinking I'd go on down and join Miriam and see if she'd located old pain-in-the-neck Bicknell, but I liked what Ray Geary was saying to me—and—well, I sort of dawdled."

"How long?"

"I can't tell you."

"What happened?"

"Well, I broke away and went down the beach looking for Miriam, and she was gone. I walked all the way up and down that beautiful white beach twice, from one end to the other. Miriam was gone and Bicknell was gone."

"Where were you, Miriam?" I asked.

She said, "I got fed up with parading up and down the beach looking for Bicknell and decided he could come and look for me for a while."

"He wasn't there?"

"Gosh, no, no place in sight."

"So then what did you do?"

"Well," she said, "I went over and got in the shade of one of the outrigger canoes and waited for Norma to show up. I didn't want to go down and bust up her tête-à-tête. I thought she might have a live one."

"And what happened?"

"So," she said, "it was warm in the shade there and comfortable and I could hear the lapping of the water, and the first thing I knew I was sound asleep."

"Then what?"

"I woke up and wondered how long I'd been asleep."

"Did you have a watch?"

"Of course not. I don't wear my wrist watch when I'm swimming."

"So then what?"

"So then I walked down the beach looking for Norma. I went back to where I'd lost her and she was gone."

"Then what?"

"Then I went home, got out of my bathing-suit, took a shower, and just lay around feeling relaxed and good."

"How long?"

"Until the officers came."

"Norma had shown up in the meantime?"

"Oh, yes."

"When?"

"About half an hour before the officers showed up."

"Where had you been, Norma?"

"Looking for Mira. My conscience got to bothering me, and I went around the beach looking for Mira and couldn't see her. Didn't see anyone I knew, got mad at myself for having lost a good opportunity to enjoy a few forward passes, went back looking for my boy friend and he'd gone, so finally I called it a day, went out and took a good long swim in the surf, came home, showered, and joined Miriam in a mutual recrimination bout."

"Each one blaming the other for getting separated?"

She nodded.

"You told the officers all this?"

"Yes."

"How long did you tell them you were with Ray Geary?"

"I don't know. I didn't wear a watch and he didn't, either."

"Some little time?"

"Some."

I said, "I suppose you know that either one of you girls could have gone out to that rented house and killed Jerome Bastion?"

"Don't be silly," Norma said. "I'm not that kind of a girl."

Miriam giggled.

Norma said, "The police have pointed that out repeatedly. Don't be boring, Donald."

"Well, I'm sorry if it bores you."

"It does."

I tried to keep my voice casual. "How about the maid? She can give you an alibi, Miriam. She'll know you came home, showered, and lay around resting."

"No. Mitsui wasn't here. She was out shopping."

"When did she get back?"

"Just before Norma did."

"Have the police questioned her?"

"No. They haven't had a chance. When the officers came in the front door, she went out the back door."

"You're sure?"

"As soon as she heard them announce they were officers I heard steps and the slam of the back door."

"She never came back?"

"Apparently not. We couldn't find her anywhere when we left. We wanted to tell her to stay on and keep things in order. She was gone."

"You don't think the officers spirited her out of the back door and took her up to headquarters for questioning?"

"I don't think so. They were trying to locate her, too."

"You gave them her name?"

"That's right."

"Address?"

"We didn't have any. She came in by the day and went home. We didn't know where she lived."

"They'll find her," I said, "if they want to badly enough."

"I think they want to."

I said to Miriam, "On a hunch, ring up Sergeant Hula-moki and tell him that you've simply got to have your maid released, that you're giving a dinner this evening and you need her."

"Suppose he releases her? What will we do about the dinner?"

I said, "I'll be your guest. I don't care about restaurant eats."

"You're *so* good to us," Miriam murmured.

"And I could have Ray Geary over," Norma interposed hurriedly. "We'd make a foursome. Oh, let's, Mira."

Miriam hesitated a moment, then walked over to the telephone, dialed police headquarters, asked for Sergeant Hulamoki, said, "This is Miriam Woodford, sergeant. I've got to have Mitsui this evening. I'm giving a dinner. You'll have to release her."

There was silence for a minute, then Miriam said, "You don't? . . . Well, I can't understand. . . . No, I told you, we *don't* have her address. . . . Oh, I see. . . . Yes, I'll hang on."

We waited in silence while Miriam hung on to the telephone, then she moved her mouth up closer to the mouthpiece, said, "Yes. . . . Oh, I see. . . . Well, thank you very much. You think we can have her for dinner, then?"

Again there was a period of silence.

"I'll call you back," Miriam said and hung up.

"What happened?" I asked.

"He said they didn't know where Mitsui was, but right while I was talking on the telephone a bulletin was flashed in. Mitsui had been picked up driving one of the cars that had been rented by Jerome C. Bastion."

I said, "Wasn't it fortunate that that bulletin came in just at that time?"

"You mean you think it's phony?"

"No," I said. "I think she was picked up driving the car."

She looked at me. "Donald, you know something about this you're not telling me."

"I'm trying to help you, Mira."

"You may be trying to help me but you're not telling me all you know."

I said, "The police found that tape recorder. They know that it must have been serviced. There must have been someone around to change records. Naturally that made them want to question the maid. Now very opportunely they find her driving one of Bastion's automobiles."

She said, "That will furnish a direct link between Mitsui

and Bastion. They'll know then who put the tape recorder in there."

"And," I said, "it furnishes a direct link between you and Bastion."

She bit her lip on that one.

"What did you tell the police about Bastion?"

"Told them I didn't know anything about him, that he was a complete stranger as far as I was concerned."

"Didn't admit that he'd ever tried to blackmail you?"

"Don't be silly. Would I go around pinning a motive for murder around my own neck?"

"If they can prove he'd been trying to blackmail you they'll know you were lying."

"They're going to have a hard time proving anything now, with Bastion out of the way."

I said, "Look here, Mira. Mitsui went shopping this morning. She was away a long time. What did she buy?"

Norma and Miriam exchanged glances.

"We wouldn't know."

I said, "Let's take a look and see if we can find out."

We went out and prowled through the kitchen and the icebox. We couldn't find a thing that Mitsui had purchased.

"All right," I said, "let's remember that one."

"But she wasn't dressed in a bathing-suit," Miriam said.

I led the way back to the bedroom and said, "According to Bicknell, the girl he saw could have been in the nude. A smart babe would have slipped her clothes off. Then if any blood got on her she could go home and wash it off. It wouldn't be like having it on clothes where the blood-stains would stick."

"Well, now," Miriam said, "that's an idea. I wonder if it will occur to the police."

I said, "It doubtless will occur to them, but it might be a very good plan for you to ring up your friend, Sergeant Hulamoki, again, tell him that you want to talk with Mitsui, that it's important and that you have to talk to her as soon as she's brought in for questioning."

"Will he let her call me?"

"Good Lord, no," I said. "He'll ask you what you want to tell her. He'll tell you he'll give the message to her."

"And what's my message?"

"Tell him to ask her where the groceries are she went out to get this morning, that you can't find what she did with the things she brought back from the market."

A slow smile spread over Miriam's face. "I get you," she said. "In other words, I put the idea right in his lap."

I nodded and got up to go.

"Look," Norma said, "you'll be over tonight, won't you, Donald? We'll have a nice little cozy dinner. You'll like Ray Geary."

I said, "Suppose Mitsui doesn't show up. I don't think she will."

"Oh, that's all right. You come anyway. Mira and I can cook—"

"You and who else?" Miriam asked.

"You and me," Norma said.

Miriam shook her head. "You can do what you want to with your boy friend, but I don't like any man well enough to stick my hands in a lot of greasy dishwater and put on all that act about a cozy little candlelit dinner."

Norma's face showed dismay.

"But," Miriam said, turning to me, "you can take us over to Lau Yee Chai's for dinner, Donald."

"A foursome?" I asked.

Norma thought things over. "Oh, all right," she said, somewhat defiantly. "If you feel that way about it, Mira. I guess you're right. You can let Donald take you out and I'll let Ray take me out."

"Does he know it yet?" Miriam asked.

"Of course not," Norma said. "I'll give him a ring, and invite him for dinner, and then at the last minute I'll tell him the police are holding our cook and the whole thing is off. Naturally he'll come through like a gentleman."

I laughed and said, "I'm beginning to learn about women. What chance does a mere man stand against technique like that?"

Miriam looked at me meaningly. "None," she said, "absolutely none, Donald. And that might be a good thing for you to remember."

15

I RANG UP the airlines to see if there was any chance of getting a night plane to the mainland.

Luck was with me. There was a vacant seat on the night plane. I grabbed it.

The ticket clerk wanted my name. "Sidney Selma," I told him, and then went down and picked up the ticket.

If I went on that plane I'd go as Selma. If the police were keeping check on outgoing passengers they'd know that Sidney Selma was planning to leave Honolulu in a hurry.

I wasn't even certain that this vacant seat on the night plane wasn't a trap. The police might have arranged for that vacancy just to see who would be trying to snap it up.

I'd been back at the hotel about an hour when the phone rang.

I answered it and Miriam Woodford's voice said, "Donald, could you come over here, please?"

"When?"

"Right now."

"What's happened?"

She said, "Mitsui came back to work. Sergeant Hulamoki and one of the officers are here."

"Coming over," I said.

I made time over to Miriam's apartment.

Sergeant Hulamoki didn't seem too glad to see me. "You're not an attorney are you, Lam?"

"I'm not appearing as one, no."

"You're not licensed to practice in Honolulu?"

"No."

"What's your interest in this thing?"

"I'm trying to get it unscrambled."

"Are you employed by Miriam Woodford?"

"I told you before, she hasn't given me a dime."

Miriam said, "I want him here."

"Why?"

"Because I think he can get this thing straightened out."

Sergeant Hulamoki said, "I'm going to put the cards on the table with you folks. When we searched this place we discovered a microphone behind that picture and a line leading out to a tape recorder under the service porch. Every six hours someone had to change tape on that recorder.

"Naturally that had to be someone who was conveniently located, who had access to the place, who could come and go without arousing suspicion. We began to think it was Mitsui here."

Mitsui said, "I have nothing to do with tape recorder."

"So," Sergeant Hulamoki said, "we put out a request to pick up Mitsui, and also we had a general call out to pick up the second car which Bastion had rented." He paused to look at me significantly and said, "There were two of them, you know."

I grinned. "Yes, I know."

"We went through the Bastion place with a fine-tooth comb. We were really looking for something."

"Find it?" I asked.

He ignored the question, said, "When we made a check on inventory we found some film magazines, but we couldn't find the motion-picture camera that went with them. That bothered us a little. Everything else seemed to be in place.

"When we searched Bastion's house we found a peculiar hiding-place. A book on a shelf filled with books had been cut so that it would conceal an object the exact size of the camera that took the film we found."

"Indeed?" I muttered politely.

He looked at me. "What would you think of that, Lam?"

"You can search me," I said.

"Don't think we won't," he said grimly. He paused for

a moment, then went on. "When we picked up the second automobile Bastion had been renting, we found it was being driven by Mitsui and in the glove compartment was the motion-picture camera that had been taken from Bastion's place."

"I know nothing," Mitsui said.

"How did it happen you were driving that car?"

"It was loaned to me."

"By whom?"

"By a friend."

"What friend?"

"Boy friend."

Sergeant Hulamoki turned to Daley, the cop who had been searching the place, and said, "You went through this place, Daley?"

"I'll say we did."

"Covered everything in detail?"

"Uh-huh."

Sergeant Hulamoki looked at the maid with thoughtful speculation. "It looks to me," he said, "as though this woman had been mixed up with Bastion in some kind of a deal involving Mrs. Woodford here, and something went sour. Some woman went over to Bastion's place this morning, slipped off her clothes, and went to work with a gun."

He continued to frown thoughtfully at Mitsui. Abruptly he turned to Daley. "Did you search this place thoroughly?"

"I looked everywhere," Daley said.

"Well, I'll take a look around myself," Sergeant Hulamoki said.

"Now that's just the thing I didn't want," I interposed. "I told Daley that I wanted this place searched so that nothing could be found later and—"

"We both told him that."

"And I searched it," Daley said.

Sergeant Hulamoki walked into the bathroom. "I'm going to look around," he said.

I went in there to watch him.

"What's the idea?" he asked.

I said, "You were suspicious of me."

"It's my business to be suspicious of everyone."

"I'm suspicious of you," I told him. "It's my business to be suspicious of everyone."

"What are you afraid of?"

"You might plant something."

"*I* might?"

"That's right."

"What, for instance?"

"A gun."

He said, "You know, Lam, I could shake you until your teeth rattled and teach you some manners."

"You could shake me until my teeth rattled," I said, "and I'd still be suspicious that you might plant a gun."

"All right, come on," he said. "We'll look together."

He opened the medicine cabinet, climbed up on a chair to look at the top of the medicine cabinet. He got down on the floor and shone a flashlight around in the corners. He flushed the toilet. He looked in the hamper for dirty clothes. He pulled open the drawers in a cabinet and carefully took out all the towels and supplies.

He stood in the center of the bathroom looking around.

After a few moments of thoughtful speculation he walked over to the toilet and started taking the things off the porcelain shelf on the top of the water tank.

When he had everything removed he lifted off the top cover, then almost dropped it.

"Good Lord," he said, "look here, Lam."

I went over there to look over his shoulder.

There was a .38-caliber revolver submerged in the water in the tank.

I said, "That's exactly what I was afraid of."

"Hell," he said, "I didn't put it here. I haven't been near the place."

I said, "Who did put it there?"

"You've got three guesses," he said. "Mitsui, Miriam Woodford, and Norma Radcliff."

"More than that," I told him.

"Who?"

I said, "Anybody who could have sneaked in through the back door and planted it there. That's what comes of not making a thorough search."

"Wait a minute," Hulamoki said. He raised his voice. "Daley, come in here."

He replaced the cover on the water box.

Daley opened the door. "Yes, sergeant."

"You looked this place over?"

"I sure did," Daley said.

Sergeant Hulamoki looked at him meaningly, then said, "Come over here. I want to show you something."

"Wait a minute," I said, "I want to ask a question."

"Shut up," Hulamoki said. "I'm doing this. Daley, take a look."

Sergeant Hulamoki lifted the cover off the water box. "See that gun?"

"My God, yes," Daley said, his jaw falling.

"Did you look in there when you searched the place, Daley?" Sergeant Hulamoki asked.

A crestfallen Daley shook his head.

"Why didn't you?" I asked.

"I just never thought of it," he said.

I gave him my opinion of his ability by using one short pungent word and walked out.

Miriam Woodford raised her eyes.

"A frame-up," I told her. "Sit tight, say nothing, answer no questions. The same applies to you, Norma."

Mitsui looked at me with her inscrutable Japanese eyes, her face as placid as a lotus blossom.

"What about me?" she asked.

"Let your conscience be your guide," I told her, "if you've got one." After a moment I added, "All you've got to do is tell a few more lies about Bastion and you'll find yourself with a murder rap draped around your neck."

Sergeant Hulamoki and Daley stayed in the bathroom for darned near five minutes. When they came out they had the gun all fixed up so it could be tested for finger-prints when it got dry. They knew it wouldn't do any good and I knew it wouldn't do any good, but they were going through the motions anyway.

Sergeant Hulamoki said, "I'm sorry about that, Lam."

"You should be."

"You think that gun was planted, don't you?"

"Yes."

"Can you prove it?"

"Prove it wasn't," I told him.

He looked at Daley and said, "That's the hell of it."

Daley said, "It just never occurred to me that that was a hiding-place. It was all so built in as part of the fixture. I looked every place else, sergeant."

"In other words," Hulamoki said, "you looked every place except where the gun was."

"Except where the gun was subsequently planted," I said. "How do you train your men, sergeant?"

"I train them pretty damn well," he said. "I have good men and I train them well."

"It looks like it."

"We all make mistakes."

"Some more than others."

"I think I can get along without any wisecracks, Lam."

"Sure," I said, "you can *now*."

He looked at me with his face darkening.

Daley said, "You say the word and I'll tie him up so he looks like a pretzel."

Sergeant Hulamoki shook his head. "We aren't done with *him* yet," he said. "I think he knows something."

Daley said, "I know damn well he knows something."

"I'm afraid I can't return the compliment," I said, looking directly at Daley.

Daley moved a step toward me.

"Daley!" Sergeant Hulamoki said sharply.

Daley stopped short.

Sergeant Hulamoki looked at Mitsui. "You were sup-posed to go shopping this morning," he said. "You didn't do it. You took a bus up King Street. You had this car parked there. You got off and got in the automobile."

Her face remained wooden, but her eyes started moving around like rats in traps.

"Oh, we do *some* things right," Hulamoki said. "We picked up the drivers of busses that made trips this morning and asked them about you. One of them remembered you. What's more, he says you've been getting off there for the last week and getting into an automobile."

"Is it crime if someone loans me automobile?" she asked.

"It depends on who it is."

"Boy friend."

"Was Bastion your boy friend?"

She thought that over for quite a little while.

"Was he?"

"No," she said.

"Just gave you an automobile because he wanted to protect the downtrodden working class, I suppose," Hulamoki said.

She was silent, in that impassive, utterly Oriental way that seems to constitute a complete barrier to questions.

Sergeant Hulamoki wasn't bothered. He knew the Oriental type and how to handle them. "Unless you tell the truth you will be arrested."

He sat looking at her in silence.

She returned his gaze, and a cloak of heavy silence descended on the room.

Mitsui could have been a carved figure, all except her eyes. They slithered about nervously, trying to avoid the steady searching eyes of Hulamoki.

He kept looking at her, an insistent, steady mental pressure.

No one said anything.

Sergeant Hulamoki looked at his watch, then looked at Mitsui.

He didn't say anything about giving her a certain time limit within which to tell the truth. His actions did that. He sat there, relaxed, not hostile, not friendly, just a cop doing his duty and trying to be courteous about it, but giving the impression he could be very, very tough if he had to.

The strain was too much.

Mitsui said, "I will talk."

"Talk," Hulamoki said.

She said, "A little over one week ago this man came to me."

"Who?"

"He said his name was Bastion."

"What did he want?"

"Some things."

"What did he give you?"

"One hundred dollars each week."

"What were you to do?"

"To let him in the house when Missy go out."

"You did that?"

"I did that."

"What did he do?"

"He bored hole in wall, put in microphone, put in wires. He told me to sweep out all powdered plaster, make it very nice and neat so no one can tell anything happened."

"You did that?"

"I did that."

"Then what?"

"He fixed recording-machine and showed me how to change spools. Every six hours must change spool."

"You did that?"

"I did that."

"What did you do with the spools of tape taken from the machine?"

"I put in my bag."

"Then what?"

"Put in automobile and take them to Mr. Bastion."

"What did he do with them?"

She shrugged her shoulders.

"Bastion furnished you with the automobile?"

"Yes, with automobile, so I can get tape spools to him

very quickly."

"What about that camera?"

"Know nothing about camera."

"Who else knew Bastion gave you an automobile to use?"

"No one knows."

"What else did you do for Bastion?"

"That's all."

"He paid you?"

"Twice."

"Two one-hundred-dollar payments?"

"Yes."

"You listen to things that were said here? You remember names of people that call?"

She nodded.

"You report to Bastion?"

Again she nodded.

"Where did you go this morning?"

"Shopping."

He shook his head. "You intended to, but you got sidetracked. Something happened to make you change your plans. What was it?"

"I went shopping."

"All right, what did you buy?"

She paused to think. "I buy coffee. I buy—"

"You bought the coffee yesterday, Mitsui," Miriam said.

Mitsui again became silent.

"What did you buy today?" Sergeant Hulamoki insisted.

She looked helplessly at Miriam Woodford, than at Sergeant Hulamoki.

"What did you buy?"

"Cannot remember what I bought."

"Where did you go?"

"Market."

"What for?"

"To buy."

"Buy what?"

She was silent.

I said, "Do you know someone named Sidney Selma, Mitsui?"

She whirled to face me, her nostrils widened, her face a mask of deadly hate.

Sergeant Hulamoki's eyes narrowed. "Do you know Sidney Selma, Mitsui?"

Her face suddenly became without expression. "No," she said.

Sergant Hulamoki got to his feet. "All right, Mitsui, you're coming with me. I'm going to hold you until I've checked that gun for fingerprints."

"You might also check the cover of the water box in the bathroom for prints," I said.

"Hers will be on it anyway. So will Mrs. Woodford's and Norma Radcliff's. They won't mean anything. Come on, Mitsui."

16

RAYMOND L. GEARY was staying at one of the cheaper hotels off the water front. It seemed an interminable wait before he came in.

I let him get up to his room so he wouldn't think I'd been waiting, then I went on up and knocked on the door.

He opened the door, probably expecting to see a bell-boy, looked at me, and said, "Hello, I've seen you—you were on the ship with me."

"That's right. I'd like to talk with you for a minute."

"Come on in." He was all cordiality.

There wasn't any time to engage in diplomatic preliminaries, but I plunged through a few perfunctory warming-up questions.

"Having a good time?"

"Swell."

"Been swimming?"

"Sure."

I looked around and, as though inspired by something I'd seen, said, "Just get in?"

"Just got in," he said. "I've been taking a tour of the Island—by bus." And he laughed.

He opened a gadget bag, took out half a dozen rolls of film and a cheap camera.

I said, "I'm interested in finding out something from you that I think may help."

"What is it?"

"Do you know Norma Radcliff, who came over on the ship with us?"

He stopped in midmotion, stood perfectly still, and looked me over. "Yes."

"She was with you for a while this morning."

"That's right."

"I wonder if you have any means of checking the time?"

"Why?"

"I think it would be a help to her."

He looked me over again. "You related to her?"

"No."

"You aren't her husband?"

"No."

"She sent you over here?"

"No."

"What's the idea?"

"I'm just trying to check up."

He said, "You were pretty thick with Norma on the boat. I had an idea you were paying for her ticket."

"It was the wrong idea. I never saw her before she got on the *Lurline*."

"Then what difference does it make to you what time she was with me on the beach this morning?"

"Nothing personally. It may make some difference to her."

"Why?"

"For certain reasons we're trying to check the time."

"Who's we?"

"Some other people who are interested."

He sat down and said, "Well, now, how terribly interesting. Sit down. What's your name?"

"Lam, Donald Lam."

He said, "This is a very, very interesting situation."

I laughed and said, "It's just routine. It happens that for certain personal reasons Norma is trying to check her time and have witnesses."

"Certain personal reasons, eh?"

"That's right."

He thought things over for several seconds, then he said, "You know, I was on a cruise once before with Norma."

"Were you?"

"She didn't notice me," he said.

I said nothing.

"She was with a rich playboy who was paying the expenses and he was certainly monopolizing Norma. I've wondered about her a lot."

I didn't say anything.

"I don't have money to spend on women," he said. "What little money I have to spend I spend on me.

"I like to take trips to various countries. I want to study people. I want to get a background. I want to know something about what's going on. I have just enough money to take carefully budgeted trips."

I still didn't say anything.

"Girls like Norma," he said, "don't notice people who take carefully budgeted trips. And they can tell. Oh, believe me, they can tell."

"How?" I asked.

His laugh was sarcastic.

"From the number of the stateroom that they have down on E deck up to the fact that they don't appear in the cocktail lounge buying drinks for passengers before dinner. Mind you, I don't say she's a gold digger, but she has a predilection for men with money. Norma was on the loose this morning. I like her. I like her a lot. I have an idea she'd like me—if I had money.

"Girls like Norma just can't afford to waste their time. I have certain objectives in life. Norma has certain objectives in life. They don't coincide."

He laughed bitterly.

"You still haven't answered my question," I said.

"That's right, I haven't."

The telephone rang.

He looked at me with half-hostility in his eyes.

"You," he said, "traveling in a single stateroom, by yourself, up on A deck, and yet you aren't the playboy type. You—"

The telephone kept on ringing. He interrupted himself to pick it up.

I could hear his end of the conversation, nothing of what was said on the other side.

"Hello. . . . Yes, this is Raymond Geary. . . . How's that? . . . Who? . . . Oh, yes, sergeant. Yes, I know her. . . . Yes, I was. . . A murder? . . . Well, well, well! . . . I'd like to think it over a bit in a matter of this importance, sergeant. I. . . . Yes. . . . Well, I'd have to reconstruct events. Yes. . . . I will. . . . I have a friend here at the moment. Suppose I call you back in about ten minutes? . . . . Yes, that'll be fine. . . . All right, I have the number. . . . Thanks a lot. Good-by."

He scribbled a number on a pad and then turned to face me, a slow grin spreading over his face.

"Well, well, well!" he said.

I didn't say anything.

He came over and shook hands. "Awfully glad to have met you, Lam, and thanks a lot for dropping in. Now you'll have to excuse me. I have a heavy date for tonight. A very heavy, sugar date."

I said, "Pardon me, I didn't know you were in a hurry to get dressed."

"I'm in a hurry to make arrangements for my date," he said, grinning all over his face. "It looks as though Raymond Geary has struck pay dirt, doesn't it?"

"How come?"

"Key alibi witness in a murder case. You know, Lam, a girl like Norma would never have noticed me until I got too old to care. After I'd acquired jowls and a potbelly and a bank account I could take a cruise, and, of course, by that time Norma would be out of the running, but there'd be some other little girl just like Norma on the ship, some girl who had a good figure and watchful eyes, some girl who would smile at just the right people, some girl who would be available under the proper circumstances.

"It takes money, Lam. It takes money. And now suddenly Raymond finds himself in the position of being a key witness.

"I hold no hard feelings against you, Lam. I don't know what your interest in the matter is. I just don't give a damn. But you were trying to get something for nothing. Now if you'll get the hell out of here I'll telephone Norma and make arrangements for my date tonight—and tomorrow night and the next night. Yes, Lam, I'm right in the gravy."

"And you can't fix the time that Norma was with you?"

"Not now, not now! I've got to call a Sergeant Hulamoki in about ten minutes and try to tell him. It'll be a long ten minutes. I'll get in touch with Norma first. Perhaps by the time we put our heads together we can find out a little more about the time element. Of course, one doesn't carry a wrist watch when one goes swimming down on the beach. It'll take me a little while to reconstruct the time element by putting various events together. I'll tell Sergeant Hulamoki there are several people who can help me. But you aren't one of them, Lam. I'm sorry. You had things all your own way on the ship. I'd look up and see Norma plastered up close to you in a deck chair. They tell me that she bribed the deck steward to change her chair so it would be close to yours. The person who was next to you had to be appeased by having one of the choice locations handed to her for free. Naturally I thought you were a rich playboy. I suppose you are. I suppose your interest in the matter is because you'd like to be the knight in shining armor who rides up to save Norma from a nasty murder rap. Well, well, well!"

He kept grinning.

I smiled back at him. "Remember, Norma's phone may be tapped. Don't press your luck too far," I told him.

"Oh, I won't," he said. "I can assure you I won't, Lam. It just happens that little girl clicks with me, and if I had money I think I'd click with her. I know very well I would. But now I have something even better than money. And I didn't know there was anything even better than money.

"Well, good day, Lam. I'll not be detaining you, and I've got a lot of work to do. Thank you for dropping in."

I got up and opened the door. "I happen to know Norma really does like you personally," I said.

"Thank you. Thanks a lot, Lam. Things keep coming along better and better."

"Have a good time," I told him.

"I will," he said. "Good night, Santa Claus."

He was laughing to himself as I closed the door behind me.

17

I GOT BACK to my hotel to find a peremptory summons from Stephenson D. Bicknell. He had been telephoning every fifteen minutes. In addition to that he had left word for me to get in touch with him as soon as I came in.

I put through a call.

Bicknell's voice was edged with impatience. "It is certainly difficult to get in touch with you."

"I've been out."

"That's the answer you always give," he flared.

"Can you think of a better one?"

"I brought you over here for a purpose, you know," he said.

"I know. That's why I was out."

There was a sticky silence for a minute, then he said in a slightly mollified tone, "You'll pardon me if I get impatient, Lam. My nerves are all on edge. I wonder if you can get over here. I have Bertha with me and we're very,

very anxious to have a conference before things go sour."

"I'll be right over."

I hung up, walked over to the Royal Hawaiian, and took the elevator to Bicknell's room.

I could tell from his eyes that he'd been drinking. I could also tell from the uncordial expression on Bertha's face that Bicknell had just about used up his allowance of Bertha's patience for the afternoon.

"Sit down," Bicknell said.

I drew up a chair.

Bicknell said, "We are going to have to work fast in order to save Mira from some disagreeable publicity."

I didn't say anything. He wanted to talk so I was willing to let him.

"With the finding of that gun," Bicknell said, "the entire situation changes. It means that there are three women who are prime suspects—Mira, Norma, and Mitsui."

"Cross Norma out."

"What?" He looked at me suspiciously.

"Cross her out."

"Now look here, Lam. You are employed to represent the interests of Miriam Woodford. I think you understand the situation, and the minute you cross any one of the others out you do that much to eliminate Mira's chances. You—"

"I told you to cross Norma out," I said. "That's not because of sympathy or sentiment, but because of cold, hard facts. That's what I was out working on. I was trying to get Norma's alibi to talk before he knew what it was all about. Unfortunately Sergeant Hulamoki telephoned in the middle of our conversation and—"

"Norma's alibi?" Bicknell asked.

"Oh, she has one," I told him.

"I didn't know she had one."

"I didn't say she *had* one. I say she *has* one."

Bertha said, "What's his name?"

"Raymond Geary. He was on the ship. He's a budget

vacationer, traveling for information, touring the Island on buses, staying at a hotel off the water front. He was on the beach this morning. Norma came along, sat down, and talked with him."

"How long?" Bicknell demanded.

"That," I said, "is what I was in the process of finding out when Sergeant Hulamoki phoned and spilled the beans."

Bicknell frowned. "Just what difference does that make?"

I said, "Ray Geary suddenly realized that in place of holding only a few low hearts in playing the game for Norma's affection, a game in which he felt diamonds were the only trumps, he's holding every ace in the deck."

"Would Norma capitalize on that?" Bertha asked me.

I laughed. "Don't worry about Norma. She and Mira are great friends, but those girls have been thinking for themselves. You give Norma a chance to have a perfectly good alibi for the exact time the murder was being committed and you can gamble that Norma will have it. She probably has it by this time."

"You mean Ray Geary would work that fast?"

"I mean he would work exactly that fast."

"This complicates the situation," Bicknell said.

"I never claimed it didn't."

"Couldn't you have forestalled that?"

"I don't know. I do know I could have had the truth if Sergeant Hulamoki had held off that call for another five minutes. Whether we're getting the truth now is anyone's guess."

"Hell!" Bertha said fervently.

I asked, "What time was the murder committed?"

"We arrived there right around ten-forty," Bicknell said, "and the murder must have been committed not more than two or three minutes before we got there. The woman who committed the murder was running around looking for something."

I said, "The police know that?"

"Oh, yes. Furthermore they checked. The autopsy surgeon says that the murder was committed within less than an hour of the time he arrived."

"What time did he get there?"

"I'd say it was about eleven-fifteen, something like that," Bicknell said. "That leaves it between Mitsui and Mira. I've been thinking things over. I think I can make a substantial contribution."

"What?"

"The color of the girl's leg," Bicknell said. "I keep reconstructing in my mind what happened, and now I'm satisfied that the bare leg that I saw had a natural brown tinge."

I said, "Miriam has been down on the beach and has a beautiful tan."

"I know, I know," he said impatiently, "but this was different. Miriam wears a swim suit. Her legs are a beautiful tan, but the—upper part—the—"

"Her bottom," Bertha interposed, suddenly interested.

"Exactly," Bicknell went on. "The—er—that part would be white, a dead white. Now I am satisfied the more I think of it that this girl was in the nude and that there was no white area around the—er—upper part of the legs —what Mrs. Cool had referred to as her bottom."

I said, "You didn't tell Sergeant Hulamoki this when you were questioned?"

"No, I didn't."

"Why not?"

"Well, the whole thing came rather suddenly and I hadn't had a chance to co-ordinate my thinking."

"Exactly," I said. "You've had too much chance now to co-ordinate your thinking. You're interested. You're trying to save Miriam Woodford. You've already spent three thousand dollars trying to save her from whatever was bothering her. You're partisan. Your testimony in regard to a matter of that sort isn't going to be worth that much."

I snapped my fingers.

Bicknell said, "I don't like your attitude, Lam."

"I didn't think you would," I told him. "If you want reassurance I can sit here and pat you on the back and give you a good line of malarky, and you'll think things are going fine. You'll give us a bonus. Then you'll run up against the grim realities and take a knockout punch on the chin. What do you want to do, figure out something that will work, or listen to a good line of chatter?"

Bicknell glared at me, but I saw that the point had registered.

I said, "There's one other possibility that I think we should suggest to the police. This fellow, Bastion, was in the blackmail business. He was making a career of it. He probably knew just how to go about getting material that could be used as ammunition, stuff that would make good blackmail material. He must have had quite a bit of it."

"Go on," Bicknell said.

"Every victim he had is a murder suspect," I went on. "We'd have a hell of a time finding his victims, but if we could find the material he was using for his blackmail, then we could figure out who his victims were."

Bicknell licked his lips. "That's very, very clever, Donald."

"Now why was Bastion living out in that rented cottage? I have an idea there was some very good reason. I also have an idea Miriam wasn't the only victim he had in Honolulu. I think he came here to kill several birds with one stone."

Bicknell said, "By George, Donald, you're using your head!"

I went on. "I don't think Miriam killed him. I don't think Norma did. I doubt if Mitsui did, but you can't tell. But Mitsui surely must have been the one who planted the gun.

"Someone gave it to her to plant. If we can find out who that person was we have our murderer."

Bicknell actually got up, came over to me, and shook hands in his delicate way, being careful not to give me a chance to exert any pressure.

Bertha fairly beamed.

"So," I said, "I want to concentrate on Mitsui. We're ahead of the police on this thing. They have to consider Norma, as well as Miriam, as suspect. We can take a short cut. We know Mitsui planted the gun. Perhaps she killed Bastion, perhaps another blackmail victim did it and hired her to plant the murder weapon where it would implicate Miriam.

"That means we must consider another person as suspect, presumably a married woman. Perhaps someone living right out near where Bastion rented his house, perhaps in the group of houses clustered above that little cove. Her husband has a job in town. When he went to work this morning, she picked up a gun, put on her bathing-suit, slipped into Bastion's house, stripped to the skin, and then gave him the only effective treatment that she felt would be permanent under the circumstances and would buy his everlasting silence."

"Then what?" Bertha said.

"Then she put her swim suit on, ran down the stairs to the cove, jumped in the water, took her morning dip, and came back just as demure as you please, walked into her house, showered, changed her clothes, and went uptown to do her shopping."

"And the gun?" Bertha asked.

"The gun," I said, "was given to Mitsui to be taken in and planted in Miriam's apartment where it would be found by the police eventually. It was luck it wasn't located on the first search."

"But how would she know enough to have Mitsui plant the gun in Miriam's apartment?"

"That's the point," I said. "That has to be our key clue. This person was close enough to Bastion to know that there were other victims. She also had to know about Mitsui. Miriam was the big plum at the top of the tree. This woman was a smaller plum, but she was the more desperate."

"You don't believe that," Bicknell, who had been watching me, said.

"I believe it's a possibility," I told him, "but right now I'm thinking up little monkey wrenches to drop in the police machinery to keep them from making Miriam their only suspect."

"But what do *you* think?" Bicknell asked.

"My guess is Sidney Selma. I think he was Bastion's partner. I think he arranged to get something from Norma that cinched the case against Miriam and then saw no reason to split fifty-fifty with Bastion."

"A swell theory," Bicknell said dubiously, "but can you prove it? Can you bolster it with anything except surmise?"

"Not a single thing," I told him. "That's why I want to dig up some other victim and use her as a red herring.

"Personally, I think Selma was a partner of Bastion's. I think Mitsui knew it. That's why she was willing to plant the gun for him."

Bicknell thought things over, then slowly nodded his head. He sat there for several seconds, nodding thoughtfully.

"Therefore," I said, "anything that will give us dope on Bastion's other victims becomes the most important bit of evidence we need."

He looked at Bertha.

"Did you tell him about the papers in the wall?"

She nodded.

"I didn't have a chance to read them, Donald, but I think they're exactly what you want. Go get them."

"It isn't going to be that simple," I told him. "They'll be watching the place for a while. We'll have to let that wait. I was hoping you looked at these papers and saw something."

Bicknell shook his head. "There was one letter. I didn't read it. There was no time."

"Then we'll have to try something else," I said.

Bicknell started stroking the angle of his jaw, his bony fingers showing up prominently, giving the hand a peculiarly abnormal appearance of exaggerated power.

"If I should identify Mitsui absolutely as being the girl I saw," he said, "the only way they could prove that I was mistaken would be by producing the real woman whoever she might be."

"Don't kid yourself on that," I told him. "A good attorney would rip your testimony to pieces."

"I don't agree with you, Donald."

"Want to try?" I asked.

"Are you a good attorney?" There was sarcasm in his voice.

"Good enough to rip your story to shreds."

"Try it," he challenged. "I have just taken the witness stand and testified that I saw the leg of a nude girl. I am now satisfied that she was nude. She was not wearing a suit. She had taken off her clothes in order to keep from getting any bloodstains on the garments. The skin that I saw was definitely that of a brown-skinned woman."

He thought that over for a moment, then nodded, turned to me, and said, "Cross-examine me."

I said, "You understand, do you not, Mr. Bicknell, that with the finding of the murder weapon in the apartment of Miriam Woodford, suspicion naturally points to one of the three girls who had access to that apartment? Miriam Woodford, Norma Radcliff, and Mitsui, the maid."

"Certainly," he said. "I have a reasonable amount of intelligence. I think that is quite obvious."

"Norma Radcliff has eliminated herself by proving her whereabouts at the time," I said.

"It definitely was not Norma Radcliff's leg and hip that I saw."

"You have no interest in Mitsui?"

"Certainly not."

"Nothing against her?"

"Definitely not."

"You are not her friend?"

"Certainly not! After all—"

"But you *are* friendly with Miriam Woodford?"

"She married my partner. I knew her when she was his

wife, and under the terms of my partner's will I am trustee of a portion of her estate."

"You have an interest in her?"

"In the way I mentioned."

"Enough of an interest to hire detectives to come over here to protect her?"

"As the trustee of her estate."

"You're charging these fees to her?"

"Well, not exactly."

"You're paying them?"

"Yes."

"As an individual?"

"Yes."

"Then you are interested in her as an individual?"

"Just what do you mean by that?"

"Have you ever asked her to marry you?"

He turned a dull red, glared at me, and said, "Damn your impertinence, Lam. I don't *have* to hire you. There are other detectives available who—"

"This isn't Mr. Lam you're talking to," I said. "This is the attorney for Mitsui, the one who is defending her, who is cross-examining you. Answer the question."

"I don't have to answer the question," he said, his face still colored, his eyes angry and embarrassed.

I grinned at him and said, "All right, I'll quit being Mitsui's attorney and go back to being the detective you've hired. I trust, however, I've made my point clear. Also you'll remember that your identification came rather late. That, according to a statement you made to Sergeant Hulamoki, which was reduced to writing and which you signed, you couldn't see the girl clearly enough to recognize her. You didn't even know whether she had on a bathing-suit or not."

Bicknell fidgeted in the chair.

Knuckles sounded on the door.

Bertha looked at me.

"Now who the devil is that?" Bicknell said.

The knuckles pounded again, a peremptory summons.

"I think," I told him, "from the tone of the knock it will be the police."

I got up and opened the door.

Sergeant Hulamoki and Officer Daley were standing outside.

"Well, well," the sergeant said, entering the room without waiting to be invited. "How fortunate catching you all together this way. Discussing the weather, I suppose."

"Planning our Island vacation, sergeant," I said. "Just getting together so we could figure when we wanted to tour the Islands and where we wanted to go."

"Yes, yes. I understand," he said, grinning.

Daley closed the door and the two officers found seats, Daley on the bed, Sergeant Hulamoki in a chair.

"Some rather interesting developments," Sergeant Hulamoki said.

"I have some interesting news, too," Bicknell said.

"Well, things are moving right along, aren't they?" the sergeant said. "What's yours, Bicknell?"

"I think we ought to hear yours first, sergeant," I said.

He shook his head and grinned at me.

"No, no, Lam. The taxpayers always have precedence. We always like to get information. What was it, Bicknell?"

Bicknell said, "I've been thinking it over. I—I have cleared my mind a little bit about that woman I saw."

I coughed.

Bicknell looked at me.

I frowned and shook my head.

Daley, on the bed, said, "You aren't in a draft there, are you, Lam? If so, we'll change places. Here on the Island we get accustomed to breezes. We live in the open."

"No," I said, "just something sticking in my throat."

"Go right ahead, Bicknell," Sergeant Hulamoki said.

"I don't think that girl had on a bathing-suit," Bicknell observed, blurting out the statement.

"Well, that might simplify things," the sergeant said, glancing at Daley. "Of course, you couldn't see very clearly."

"I could see pretty plain."

"I know," the sergeant said, "but when you gave me your first statement you said you couldn't tell whether she had a bathing-suit on or was in the nude. After all, Bicknell, there's quite a difference between the feminine figure completely unclad and one that's in a bathing-suit."

Bicknell said nothing.

"But go ahead, Mr. Bicknell, tell us the new development."

Bicknell said, "That was it."

"Nothing more than that?"

"That's all. But you must remember that a white woman in the nude would have tanned legs and white hips. A brown-skinned woman would have a uniform coloring."

"Very interesting."

"I think it's quite significant."

"It may be at that. And I take it you've told us everything you remember now?"

"Yes. This supplementary statement covers all of it."

"Nothing else that you forgot to tell us when we had our little conference?"

"No."

"No further developments?"

"No."

"Well, that's fine," the sergeant said. "You know we always dislike being put in the position of having someone remember vital facts afterward. I'm glad you've taken time to think the thing over in detail. You have, haven't you, Bicknell?"

"Have what?"

"Have thought over everything in detail?"

"Yes."

"You've thought it over a good many times?"

"I suppose so."

"And aside from the fact that you now think the girl you saw probably didn't have on a bathing-suit—and, of course, you're not sure—there isn't any single new development?"

"No."

"Not one?"

"No."

"Well, that's fine," Sergeant Hulamoki said. "Now I'll tell you about *our* new development."

I braced myself to hold my face in a position of expressionless immobility.

"We went through that house pretty carefully," Sergeant Hulamoki said. "We had a very strong suspicion that this fellow was making a living by methods that were not readily apparent. In fact, no one seems to know how he made a living. He didn't have a Social Security card. He hadn't filed income tax returns. And yet he managed to get around. He spent quite a bit of money. It's rather strange the income tax people hadn't gone after him, but, of course, not filing any returns whatever probably caused him to have a certain respite."

"Go ahead," Bicknell said impatiently.

"Well, we came on a few receipted bills. One of them was a receipted bill to Jerome C. Bastion from the Wide-Awake Photostat Company of Denver. The amount was only two dollars, but for some reason Bastion had seen fit to save that receipted bill."

"A Photostat?" Bicknell asked.

"That's right," the sergeant said, beaming. "And you know, we wondered about that. Well, over here we're more or less isolated by distance, so we have to rely on people to help us, you know. I've been in touch with the Denver police by telephone off and on during the day, and I asked them to look up the Wide-Awake Photostat Company and see if they could learn anything about the charge.

"It just happened that the Photostat service keeps rather detailed records, and it turned out that that two-dollar charge was for Photostating certain documents in the files of the Rocky Mountain Pharmaceutical Chemical Supply Company.

"Well, do you know, the Denver police went out to that company and the secretary of the record clerk happened

161

to remember the occurrence and brought out the records that had been Photostated. A most remarkable coincidence."

Sergeant Hulamoki paused, making the pause dramatic, waiting for questions.

I'd have seen him burn before I asked a question, but Bicknell led with his chin. He moistened his lips with the tip of a pale tongue and said, "What was it?"

"It was a signed invoice receipt for a large quantity of arsenic," Sergeant Hulamoki said. "It was billed to Ezra P. Woodford, who, it seems, has an account there, and the invoice receipt showed that it was picked up by Mrs. Ezra P. Woodford, and the date of the invoice was just four days before the death of Ezra P. Woodford.

"Now I think probably at this time I'm in a position to disclose something that has hitherto been kept confidential, but that's the reason that Edgar Larson of the Denver police force is over here. As it happens, police had already become suspicious of certain circumstances surrounding the death of Ezra Woodford and the body had been secretly exhumed. Toxicologists had found enough arsenic in the body to kill a horse."

Sergeant Hulamoki looked at each of the three of us in turn, Stephenson Bicknell, Bertha Cool, and me.

"Who—er—er—who ordered the arsenic preparation?" Bicknell asked.

"Ordered over the telephone by a woman who said she was Mrs. Ezra Woodford. Of course, we can't prove anything by that in a court of law, you understand, because a witness can't testify to a voice over the telephone unless the witness knows that voice. It is, of course, a circumstance to be considered in connection with our investigative work.

"You'll understand, Mr. Bicknell, that police quite frequently consider certain things in connection with their investigative work that they couldn't consider as proof in a court of law. There is, of course, considerable difference. In court you have to be absolutely positive. You have to swear to cold, hard facts. There is no room for conclusions. The jury draws the conclusions. But in investigative work we're entitled to draw certain conclusions."

"Have you—have you talked with Mrs. Woodford about this?" Bicknell asked.

"I believe one of my associates is discussing the matter with Mrs. Woodford right now," Sergeant Hulamoki said. "I thought I'd drop in to talk with you about it."

"With me?"

"Exactly. You are trustee of Miriam Woodford's estate."

"Yes."

"You have authority under that trust to pay portions of the principal in addition to the income, or to make advances against the income if you think it necessary and there is any emergency. Any reason for you to do so?"

"Yes."

"Now, then," Sergeant Hulamoki said, "wouldn't it be an interesting situation if Jerome Bastion, armed with Photostatic copies of that signed invoice, with the date and with Mrs. Woodford's signature, came over here and tried to blackmail her for a substantial sum of money, say twenty or thirty thousand dollars, and Miriam Woodford, in terror, advised you that due to an emergency, the exact nature of which she didn't wish to disclose, it was necessary for her to have a large sum of money, either from the principal or as an advance against income, and—"

Bicknell started to say something.

"No, no. Now just wait a minute. Let me finish," Sergeant Hulamoki said. "I don't want to trap you, Mr. Bicknell. Now wouldn't it be strange if you, feeling that Mrs. Woodford was in some sort of difficulty, went to the firm of Cool and Lam, who are pretty good investigators, with a reputation for being very discreet but getting results, and asked them to come over here and help you protect Miriam Woodford against whatever it was that was bothering her?

"I'm willing to give you the benefit of the doubt in assuming that you didn't know what it was. You probably suspected blackmail, but you didn't know and you didn't have any knowledge of the purchase of arsenic, but you knew something was bothering Mrs. Woodford and you were not at all surprised at the idea that it might be blackmail.

"Our investigations show that Mrs. Woodford has not led exactly a sheltered life. Our investigations also indicate that you made out a check to Cool and Lam for three thousand dollars. Of course, some of that was for traveling-expense money.

"However, when you add all of that together we have a very interesting picture. This picture shows that you didn't bring your two friends over to the Islands just for the vacation, Bicknell."

Bicknell ran his fingers through his hair.

Sergeant Hulamoki turned to me. "There is one other very interesting fact, Lam.

"We found that motion-picture camera in the trunk of the car Mitsui was driving. We developed the films in that camera. They were motion pictures of the car in which the camera was found. Those pictures, apparently taken for no particular reason at all, showed the car parked at the curb on King Street.

"Those pictures showed a little of a street scene. There was a glimpse of traffic. One frame of the pictures showed a car in traffic clearly enough for us to make out its license number.

"So we talked with the owner, a most attractive young woman, by the way, and asked her when she had driven her car on King Street lately, and, do you know, she'd been away. The only time in the past week she'd driven her car on King Street was today about two hours after the murder was committed."

I stifled a yawn with four polite fingers.

Sergeant Hulamoki looked at me.

I'm satisfied that my face was completely without expression.

He looked at Bertha and she glared at him.

"I thought perhaps you could contribute something, Mr. Lam."

I said, "Bastion had been here a month. Those pictures could have been taken any time during that month. Ask your attractive woman driver how many times she'd driven down King Street in the last month."

"Of course," Sergeant Hulamoki said reproachfully, "I wasn't trying to get this in final shape. I was talking in terms of investigative work, not courtroom evidence."

I met his eyes. "I'm talking in terms of courtroom evidence. That's the only evidence you can use."

Bicknell said, "I don't know if you're accusing Miriam Woodford of anything. If you are, or if you intend to, I'll obtain the best lawyer in the Islands for her, and she'll quit talking until she gets on the witness stand."

"No, no, we aren't accusing her of anything."

"What are you doing?" I asked.

"Just trying to enlist your co-operation."

Bertha snorted.

I frowned at her and said to Hulamoki, "We certainly thank you for your consideration. We pledge you our co-operation."

There was a ghost of a smile on the sergeant's lips.

"Thank you, Lam. Thank you very much indeed. We'll call on you. Don't worry about that. We'll be in constant touch with you. In fact, we consider your co-operation so valuable that we wouldn't want any of you to try to leave the Islands without letting us know."

Abruptly Sergeant Hulamoki shook hands with us very solemnly, and he and Daley left the room.

Bicknell looked as though he'd just had two ounces of castor oil.

"She didn't do it," he said. "She wouldn't. I trust her. I—I'm in love with her!"

He put his hands to his face.

Bertha and I sat silent.

Abruptly he looked up at us and said, "Get out of here. I want to be alone. And get on the job. See that Miriam is protected from these hyenas—and I don't care what it costs. The sky's the limit now."

Bertha glanced at me, her greedy little eyes glittering. She said, "Don't worry, Bicknell, we're just about ready to give this Hawaiian police force the surprise of its life."

She opened the door and we walked out, leaving Bicknell there with his head in his hands.

"That's it," Bertha said in the hallway, "he's in love with the girl, Donald. Did you hear what he said?"

"About being in love with her?"

Bertha's face showed a spasm of expression. "No, bird brain, about there being no limit to what we could charge."

"If we get her out of it," I reminded her.

"Well, get busy and get her out of it," she snapped.

"How?"

"I don't give a damn how, but if you let that woman fall in love with you, we're licked. You can see now why he wanted a woman detective. He was afraid of you from the minute he saw you. He realized you were Miriam's type."

"No," I said, "Ezra Woodford was her type."

18

I WAITED by my telephone. It was after dark when it rang.

"Do you know who this is?" Miriam asked.

"Yes."

"Where's your car?"

"In the hotel parking-lot."

"I'll be in it."

"Do you know it when you see it?"

"Yes."

I said, "Okay. Right away?"

"Right away."

I hung up the telephone, switched out the lights, and walked out in the warm Hawaiian night. I turned in at the parking-lot, got in the car, and waited.

A muffled voice from the back said, "Well, start driving."

I knew better than to look around.

Miriam was down on the floor.

I started the motor, drove out of the hotel parking-lot, and after I'd gone half a dozen blocks Miriam got up from the back seat, said, "If you haven't seen legs before I'm going to shock you."

She pulled her skirt up above her knees and came over to the front seat.

"I've seen them before but not that pretty," I said.

"This," she announced, "is no time for blarney."

She snuggled up against me and gripped my arm. I could feel her hand tremble. My rearview mirror showed we weren't being followed.

"What happened?" I asked.

"Keep driving until you come to some place where we can park and talk."

I went past Koko Head, on out around the Island until we came to a place where the road swung up over a beautiful bay. There was a wide parking-place out next to a stone wall which looked down onto the ocean. No other cars were there. There was very little traffic along the road. I parked the car, cut the motor, switched off the lights, turned to Miriam, and said, "Well?"

She swung around on the seat and leaned her back against the steering-wheel so that her face was toward mine and not over eighteen inches away.

"Donald," she said, "do you have confidence in me?"

I slid my arm around the back of her shoulders so as to ease the pressure against the steering-wheel. "That depends."

"On what?"

"On what you're going to say now. What did you tell the police?"

She said, "I laid it on the line."

"With whom did you talk?"

"Donald, you may not believe it, but I talked with the chief of police himself."

"How was he?"

"He was nice, Donald."

"Tell me what you told them."

She said, "I think they know something."

"They didn't tell you what it was?"

"No."

"What did they say?"

"The chief told me that I was in a spot. He said that what happened next was very apt to depend on just how trustful I was; that he wanted me to tell him all about my relations with Ezra Woodford, all about my marriage, all about what I knew of Bastion. He said that if I told him the absolute truth it might help. He said that if I lied it was going to be just too bad."

"So what did you do?"

"I told him."

"Tell me."

"How much of it?"

"All of it."

"All of it except that I didn't go too far back for the police."

"Go that far back for me," I said.

She said, "I always wanted adventure. Suppose I was daring and—well, there was all of life before me ready to be explored and—I got seduced."

"Other girls have," I told her. "Go on from there."

She said, "I was handed a regular package. I gave him my confidence, my love, everything. I was his. And he used a line of malarky, and then went off and left me."

"What happened?"

"I should have been dazed, shocked, hurt, angry. I wasn't. I'd enjoyed it, and to tell you the truth I was getting just a little bit tired of him when he broke off the affair.

"It hurt my vanity when he ditched me for another girl who apparently had something I didn't have. I resolved that wouldn't happen to me again. I made up my mind I'd know more about things and be the one to do the jilting in the future. I don't like to have them walk out on me."

"Go on from there."

She said, "The next time a guy made a pass at me I knew all of the lines. I wrote some lines of my own and I kept him guessing."

"Then what?"

"Then he really and truly fell head over heels in love with me. I thought I was in love with him. He had money and he wanted marriage."

"Then what?"

"Then I tried marriage and it didn't click."

"Why not?"

"Because I really didn't love him. He was a fish I was playing on the line, not anyone I really loved. I just didn't respect the guy.

"After about a year we came to a parting of the ways. What made me so mad was that once again another woman beat my time."

"Who was she?"

"A brunette who would look at him with the most soulful dark eyes, and raise her lids so wide he'd practically fall in, and then she'd lower the lids and sigh tremulously."

"An act?" I asked.

"Donald, don't be silly," she said. "Whenever a woman is good-looking she studies her good points in front of a mirror and she knows how to accentuate them. That little tart had worked out that technique to a fare-you-well. She crawled into my nest and pushed me out. Not that I cared a fig about the nest. I just hated having someone beat my time."

"Then what happened?"

"When I got out," Miriam said, "I had something to take with me."

"How much?"

"Quite a bit. He was eager for the little brunette. The lawyer got a big slice of it, but I had about forty thousand —not all at once, ten thousand in cash and the rest of it coming in in alimony."

"Then what?"

"Well, that was the last time anyone ever beat my time, even if I do say it myself. I had a mirror and I did a little practicing. I made up my mind that if men wanted that soulful, fluttering-eyelid stuff that I'd know all the tricks, all the technique."

"You studied?"

"And practiced."

"And got good?"

She giggled.

"Go on from there," I told her.

"Well," she said, "I couldn't see settling down to work. I decided to go on a cruise, thinking that would give me a wider horizon."

"Did it?"

"It did."

"All right, what happened?"

She said, "There was a playboy on the cruise. He had lots of money. He wanted action. I wanted money."

"Why? You had plenty."

"I wanted more. I had a feeling that money was security, at least for me. I didn't think there'd be any other kind of security."

"You sold yourself?"

"I don't like that expression, Donald. He was generous, and I certainly wasn't going to be a teaser or a piker. We went all around South America, and then we went through the Mediterranean."

"All on one cruise?"

"On several cruises."

"And what happened in between times?"

"I was in an apartment."

I didn't say anything.

"Now don't get shocked," she said. "After all, Donald, there are certain facts of life that you have to recognize. You'll never know how easy it is to slip into—"

"Into what?" I asked.

"I don't know just what it is," she said. "It isn't the moral cesspool that the sob sisters would make out. It's just—well, it's just expediency."

"All right. Go on."

She said, "Somewhere along in there I met Ezra Woodford."

"Did he make passes?"

"Don't be silly. He was a lonely, sick individual. He'd worked too hard, and when it came time for him to play he'd forgotten how to play. If he'd tried to play people would have looked at him askance. They thought he was an old fossil whose proper place in life was walking around the deck with a dour look on his face, and perhaps paying court to some of the old women who wanted to tell about their operation and their sister's grandchildren."

"So what happened?"

"I knew Ezra liked me. I could tell it, but I didn't give him a personal tumble. I did try to cheer him up and I did a pretty swell job."

"What did you do?"

"Oh, I'd let him buy me drinks, and I'd get him laughing, and when he'd make some corny joke I'd laugh fit to be tied, and I'd put my hands on his arm once in a while, look up in his eyes and flatter him by telling him what a marvelous business executive he must be."

"But you were tied up at the time?"

"I was tied up and I wasn't cheating. I'm not that kind, Donald, although I get the name for it. People think I am."

"Then what?"

"Well, Ezra got writing post cards to me, and when I broke up with the playboy Ezra came to New York, and he wanted to try and recapture some of the carefree gay spirit of the cruise."

"Did he?"

"You can't do it on land, Donald."

"Why not?"

"I don't know. There's something about shipboard.

You're thrown together. Everyone has common interests. You dine at the same time. You have cocktails. You meet a group, and everyone is out for pleasure. There isn't anything else to do. There's no hurry, no tension. You start laughing and playing along, and—well, it's different.

"When you're in New York you sleep late, you get up and make yourself beautiful, and then your escort comes and you start out to see the town. There are only a certain number of things you can do. You can go to shows if you are able to get the tickets. You can go to Twenty-One or the Stork Club. You can prowl around in some of the little atmosphere restaurants. You can get good food. You can drink and you can talk. But you're all by yourselves. You haven't got a crowd around. You don't have community interests with a lot of other people."

"So then what?"

"So then," she said, "Ezra became serious. He was terribly, terribly lonely, and he was feeling old."

"And he wanted you to marry him?"

"He wanted—well, he wanted life and action, and he wanted me."

"What did you tell him?"

She said, "Donald, I want you to believe me. I'm telling the truth. I told him that I could be had, and I told him he didn't need to marry me, that he'd be sorry if he did."

"What did he say?"

"Donald, it's almost impossible for me to tell you about Ezra and make you see him the way he was. Ezra had worked hard. He hadn't played. At one time he'd married a woman who developed into one of these suspicious nagging creatures who wanted to know where he was every minute of the time. His home life must have been hell."

"I know," I said. "His wife didn't understand him."

"No, Donald, it wasn't like that. It was different with him. I know it was. I'll tell you what it was. He was one of those men who tried marriage and it didn't work, and he just—well, he just started going to the office and losing himself in business because he didn't *want* to go home.

So he put in his time on business, and he made a lot of money and a lot of success, but—well, he became—how is it they say, 'All work and no play.' "

"He became a dull boy?"

"That's right."

"Then what?"

"He didn't think he had long to live. He had a lot of money. He told me he knew I didn't love him in the romantic sense of the word, and he was frank enough to tell me that he didn't think he loved me, but he was fascinated by me and he was captivated by my spirit of youth. He said he just wanted to watch me. He wanted to have me where he could watch me play, hear me laugh, and have me around. He said he was willing to pay for it."

"How did he want to pay for it?"

"By having me as his wife. He told me that in Denver it couldn't be any other way. He didn't want to have me as a mistress, where he'd sneak around to see me at intervals. He wanted to have me where I could be in his home all the time, where I could know his friends and all of that."

"So what did you do?"

"I said yes."

"And then you regretted your bargain?"

"Not me. When I make a bargain I make it with my eyes open, and I live up to it. I knew Ezra couldn't get his money's worth unless I was happy. I gave him his money's worth. I did everything I could to see that he got everything he paid for."

"He was happy?"

"Like a lark. He blossomed out like a rose, and I enjoyed it. Denver is a nice place. Ezra had a lot of friends. They were perfectly swell to me. I gave him what he had wanted. I kept him laughing. I was always keyed up and joking and—well, Donald, I made him really and truly happy."

"Did you," I asked, "get tired of waiting?"

"Waiting for what?"

"Waiting for him to die?"

She said, "Donald, look me in the eyes. Believe me, I'm on the square. I wasn't waiting for anything. I was carrying out my end of the bargain and I wasn't a bit unhappy doing it."

"All right, what about Bicknell?"

She said, "Bicknell, of course, disapproved when he first heard of it. When Ezra went on to New York, Bicknell knew he was going on to meet me. We'd had correspondence back and forth and—well, I suppose there are leaks in a close partnership of that kind, and probably Ezra's secretary babbled a little bit and—well, anyway, Steve Bicknell knew."

"And he disapproved?"

"You have no idea how he disapproved."

"Then what?"

"Ezra went back and told Steve we were going to get married, and Steve hit the ceiling. He talked with Ezra in a way that almost dissolved the friendship."

"Then what?"

"Oh," she said, "the usual thing. Steve Bicknell hired detectives. They dug into my past. Honestly, Donald, you have no idea how thorough a good detective can be. What am I saying? Of course you have. You're a detective yourself."

"How did you know?"

"The police told me."

"Go ahead."

"Well," she said, "they found out everything about me. They went back from the present to the time of my childhood. I guess to the time I was weaned. Certainly from the time I met my first boy. And, believe me, they had the dope. A nasty, dirty smear of stuff. It looked pretty damning when the romance and glamour and moonlight were deleted, and it was spread out on paper in typewritten lines."

"So what?"

"So Steve Bicknell showed it to Ezra, told him to read it."

"What happened?"

"Ezra read it, tore it up, and threw it in the fireplace, and told Steve if he ever mentioned any of that stuff he'd kill him."

"Then what?"

"Then we got married and went to Denver to live."

"Did the marriage make any financial difference to Bicknell?"

"Yes, in a way it did."

"How?"

"There was a partnership understanding that each partner would leave all of his partnership interests to the surviving partner, if there was no surviving widow. If they married the widow was to get half, the partner half."

"So if Ezra had died before he married you he'd have left everything to Bicknell?"

"Yes."

"So Bicknell lost a good-sized fortune because of Ezra's marriage?"

"Of course, he didn't expect Ezra to die."

"But it was a possibility you both thought of."

"I suppose so."

"And Bicknell naturally didn't like you."

"No."

"Then how did it happen Ezra made Bicknell trustee of your holdings?"

"You have to go back to when I first came to Denver to understand that."

"Tell me about it."

"Well, Bicknell treated me like dirt under his feet."

"What did you do? Try to win him over?"

"I did not. I ignored him. I told Ezra he'd have to keep Steve out of the house. That was one thing that I insisted on."

"Then what?"

"Then after a while, when Steve saw I was playing the game, he became sorry he'd taken that attitude. Ezra wanted to bring him up to the house, and finally I let

175

him."

"Then what?"

She said, "I was cheering Ezra up, and Ezra was laughing all the time. He'd become conscious of his personal appearance. He was going to the barbershop and the manicurist. He was wearing fine tailor-made clothes. He was hurrying home from business and relaxing and enjoying life, and entertaining and—well, he was showing me off, and you'll understand that I'm not just tooting my own horn when I say he was proud as Punch."

"And how did people react?"

"At first they thought I was something he'd bought in the open market, and that I was a piece of merchandise that wouldn't be good for him. I had all that to contend with, but I had known that I was going to have it to contend with and I didn't let it bother me. In a situation like that, being a wife is ten times harder than being a mistress, but I'd figured all that out in advance and knew just what I was up against. I'd made up my mind that I'd lick it and *make* people like me. Not that I gave a nickel for myself, but I knew that Ezra would want to have friends and entertain, not just closet himself in a big mansion with a young wife everyone was snubbing."

"So you made his friends like you?"

"Yes, a few at a time. It wasn't a difficult job. People are human. I like people, and for the most part they like me."

"How did you go about it?"

"Just being frank and natural. The young bucks made passes at me and intimated I must be pretty lonely and all of that stuff."

"And what did you do?"

"I didn't get indignant," she said. "I just laughed in their faces and told them to go roll their hoops."

"And then what?"

"Then word began to get around that I was on the square and—well, all of a sudden, the first thing you know people were nice to me."

176

"It didn't take very long?"

"I don't think it took two months. You'd be surprised how fast things get around. It seemed like an eternity to me, but people liked Ezra and somehow people liked me. I kept them amused, and Ezra liked to entertain and people liked to come to his house for dinner."

"And Bicknell?"

"Bicknell began to be included in the guests."

"Then what?"

"Then," she said, "Ezra was the happiest man you'd ever seen, and his friends liked me because I was making him so happy. They ceased regarding me as a piece of second-hand merchandise and looked on me as a—well, as a tonic for Ezra and an entertaining hostess for them."

"Then what?"

"Then all of a sudden he died. His will left me half of his fortune."

"How much?"

"Gosh, Donald, the estate hasn't been settled yet, but it's worth a lot of money. He had gold mines, oil wells, business ventures. He had everything. I'm rich now. That is, I will be."

"Not if you become involved in anything that would bring a scandal to the name of Woodford," I said.

She said nothing.

"And a murder is a scandal," I went on. "And so was the thing Bastion was blackmailing you on."

She said, "I didn't kill Bastion."

"You feared him?"

"Yes."

"You would have paid him money?"

"Yes."

We were silent for half a minute. "Tell me more about Bicknell," I said.

"Bicknell has fallen in love with the idea of falling in love with me."

"Can you tell me more about that?"

"Well, he—oh, it's hard to put it in words. He had been

rather lonely himself. His wife died years ago and he never remarried. I guess he never had many desires along those lines. He was—well, he was what we call a grouch-face, a drizzle-puss, a wet blanket, a cold turkey."

"I know," I said.

"Well, he knew how Ezra was before I married him and how lonely Ezra was, and then he saw the change that had been made after I came along, and I think he got pretty well converted to the idea that marriage might be a mighty fine thing."

"Marriage to a very young and very good-looking girl," I said. "Nice business if you can get it."

"Well, he's trying to get it."

"Has he asked you to marry him?"

"Do you have to know that, Donald?"

"Yes."

She said, "Yes, he wants me to marry him. He even put it in writing."

"What do you mean?"

"After I came over here he wrote me a letter saying how much he'd misunderstood me and what a square shooter I was, and asked me if, after a few months when things had reached a point that people wouldn't talk, if I'd consider marrying him."

"What did you tell him?"

"I didn't tell him," she said. "I wrote and told him that I had a lot of things I wanted to discuss with him when I saw him, and let it go at that. He'd a middle-aged man in love with the idea of being in love. If you know what happens to men like that—they get goofy, ga-ga."

"How much of this did you tell the police?"

"I told them all of it except about Steve wanting to marry me. I felt that it was not incumbent upon me to tell them anything about Steve's private affairs."

"Well," I said, "I guess you did a good job of it, all right. You evidently talked your way out of it, otherwise you wouldn't be here."

"I didn't talk my way very far out of it. They're making

further investigations all the time."

"The police suggested, of course, the possibility that Bastion was blackmailing you, and that you decided there was only one way to handle the blackmailer?"

"Yes. They didn't exactly accuse me, but they asked me about it."

"And what did you tell them?"

"I told them they were crazy. I wouldn't take a gun and go out and shoot anyone. That's not the way to handle things."

"What is your idea of the way to handle a blackmailer?"

"I don't know," she said.

"But you wanted to pay him?"

"Yes."

"Why?"

"Oh, I don't know. I can't tell you. It was just the fact that I didn't want to be bothered. After all, the money that he wanted wasn't too much and—well, Bastion said that would be all there'd be to it. He just needed some quick money and—"

"Don't you know that blackmail is a quicksand? You can't get yourself out of it. The more you struggle the deeper you get."

"I guess that's true with most blackmailers, and probably would have been true in this case," she said, "but Bastion certainly handed me a good line."

"What?"

"He said that he happened to stumble onto this information, that he hated himself for even thinking about using it, that he wasn't that kind of a person, that he wasn't a blackmailer, that he tried to be a pretty decent sort, but that he found himself in a hell of a position financially. He needed money. He said that he happened to have this information, and he knew that I had more money than I knew what to do with and he thought that I could make him a loan. He said that was all it would be. He swore that he was going to pay it back. He said he was in a position where he needed some money to straighten out

179

some debts and take advantage of a business opportunity that had presented itself and—well, you know how it is."

"And what was this information he'd stumbled on?"

"About me buying arsenic just before Ezra died."

"Ezra wanted you to get it?"

"Yes. It was for his taxidermy. I've told you the entire truth about that, Donald."

"And you told the police all that?"

"Every bit of it."

I said, "Okay, Mira. You've convinced me."

"Of what?"

"That you didn't kill Bastion," I said, "and that you're a good scout."

"Donald," she said in a low voice.

"What?"

"I like you."

"Swell. I want you to."

"You don't like me, do you?"

"Yes."

"You don't show it."

"This is business."

"This is after office hours."

"There aren't any office hours on this job. I'm just really getting warmed up to start work."

"On what?"

"On getting you out of a jam."

She said, "Donald—"

"What?"

She didn't say anything, but lay there on my arm which was across the steering-wheel, looking up at me, her face an oval blur in the moonlight and filtered through the windows of the car.

After a moment she said, "You can't get out of it that way, Donald. If you don't kiss me I'm going to kiss you."

"No you're not," I said. "We can't mix romance with this. We—"

Her arms were around my neck, her lips a flaming circle against mine. She came closer to me, pressing her body against mine.

For a moment we were pretty busy.

I pushed her away and came up for air. "Now, listen, Mira—"

"Don't start preaching sermons, Donald," she said. "I'm going to take a few good long breaths, and then I'm going to have a repeat. I'm going to give you one more round, and then I'm going to sit right back on my side of the seat and let you drive me back to town and—well, from then on my business is in your hands. You can handle it any way you want. But right now I'm lonesome and I'm—I'm having a little spell of yearning and you looked good to me from the minute I saw you."

I said, "If we start necking it's going to mess things all up. You'll be—"

"I know," she said, and put a straight forefinger across my lips gently. "Don't preach, Donald."

I said, "You've probably got me smeared with lipstick from—"

"Don't be silly. I took my lipstick off when I was sitting in back of the car."

"Why?" I asked.

She laughed and said, "Because I planned it that way."

My pulse was hammering away like a machine digging up cement pavement.

"Now look, baby," I said, "this is serious. You're in a first-class jam. I think Norma Radcliff is bailing herself out."

"She would," Miriam said, "and you can't blame her. Norma's been playing the game for years where she had to look after number one. If she didn't no one else was going to."

I said, "All right, suppose *you* look out for *yourself*. Now where were you right around ten-forty in the morning?"

She said, "I tried to figure it out, Donald, and the only way I can account for my time is that I was down there on the beach for about an hour and a half."

"Doing what?"

181

"I started out to look for Steve Bicknell and then I detoured when I couldn't find him and lay around for a while, and—well, like I told you, I was just on the beach, sleeping, getting a tan, and strolling around."

"Did you see anybody you knew when you were strolling around?"

"No. I didn't stay there long after I woke up, and started walking around on the beach. There was a whole shipload of soldiers in port, and I guess a couple of hundred of them went down on the beach at Waikiki. The poor kids, I felt sorry for them. They were trying to be well mannered. I suppose they'd had instructions about whistling and wolf calls and all that, but they couldn't control their eyes. They'd keep their heads straight ahead, but their eyes were certainly looking me over. You could just see that the poor kids were lonely and wanted someone to talk to and probably wanted to make passes. Every one of them had somebody at home and four or five other gals who thought he was pretty nice. Then all of that feminine companionship was suddenly taken out of his life, and he comes into a strange port and starts walking up and down the beach and sees a lot of delectable babes in bathing-suits and—well, you know how you'd feel."

I said, "I know, but that's beside the point. How many friends do you have in Honolulu?"

"Darned few."

"Have you formed friendships on the beach?"

"No. You know what that is. A bunch of tourists who come and go. They start out with milk-white skins, try to get a tan, overdo it, get burned, turn beet-red, stay off the beach for a while, then come out and venture a little more tan. You find them peeling like an orange or some of them just getting tanned like saddle leather. That's all they seem to be intent on. Lying there and getting a tan. I like it myself. I like to have my skin brown and well tanned, but that business of making it your sole goal in life is a little bit out of my line. What I mean is that I don't have anything in common with those people and—"

"And how about wolves?" I asked.

"They don't have many there at the beach at Waikiki. They're pretty well behaved. It's watched and patrolled, and the rough element doesn't get out there. Of course, you find a lot of people who look but—what you're getting at, Donald, is whether or not I've formed any sex friendships, is that it?"

"That's right."

"Well, I haven't."

I said, "We've got to find some way of proving you were on the beach at Waikiki."

"You'll have a hell of a time doing it," she said.

I started the motor. "That's what I'm afraid of."

"You mean we're going back, Donald?"

"We're going back."

"To what?"

"I'm going to work."

She sighed and said, "Darn me, you're sure a determined cuss."

"Damned if I ain't," I told her.

I didn't dare to take Miriam all the way home. I knew that the place was being watched by the police, and right at the moment I didn't want the police tagging along and finding out what I was doing.

I stopped the car about four blocks from her apartment. "This is it," I told her. "You walk from here."

"Where are you going now?" she asked.

"Places."

"Won't you tell me?"

"No."

"Will you be at your hotel?"

"Not for a while."

"Donald, I want to know where you are."

"Why?"

"So I can reach you."

"Why do you want to reach me?"

"I don't know. I feel terribly alone over here. I have a feeling that something's going to happen."

"Sit tight," I told her. "There'll be officers watching your place tonight."

"Yes, I suppose so. Donald, are you going to kiss me good night?"

"I've already done that."

"You're all business, aren't you?"

"About ninety per cent."

She laughed. "I like the ten per cent."

"Some other time."

I reached across her and opened the door. She got out of the car, then started to say something, but I had the car in motion before she could change her mind.

I drove directly to Nipanuala Drive.

Apparently the police guard had been removed. The house where the murder was committed was dark and silent. A few curiosity seekers were wandering around the premises.

I parked my car and got out and looked around.

A man asked me, "Is this where the murder was committed?"

"I believe it is," I told him. "I'm not sure. I have the street address. It was 922 Nipanuala."

"This is the place, then," he said.

"Any particular reason you're interested?" I asked.

"Just curiosity," he said. "Same as you."

I moved around the premises, and my new-found friend stuck to me like a burr on a blanket.

I walked along the lawn next to the brick wall. At the exact spot Bertha had described I saw the rock she had mentioned with the white stain on it. Just below that was a chink in the wall, a little cavity made where a stone had been pulled out.

The stone was lying on the ground at the foot of the wall. The cavity showed dark in the moonlight.

Were there gloves in there, wadded up into a ball, with papers inside of them? I didn't know. I didn't dare to go any closer to try and find out. I couldn't tell whether the loose rock had dropped out of its own accord, or whether somebody had found the loose rock and the gloves.

I acted the part of a casual observer, trying to get nearer to the wall without being observed. It was no dice. The "rubberneck" kept watching me. He might as well have had his badge on the outside of his coat. When I went back to my car, my "friend" went along with me.

I knew by this time he was interested in the license number of my car.

I decided I'd make a good job of it so that Sergeant Hulamoki would know I was acting natural.

I said, "Don't tell anyone, but as a matter of fact I'm interested in this case. My name's Donald Lam, and my partner, Bertha Cool, was the woman who found the body."

"The hell you say!" he exclaimed in surprise.

"That's right. I just wanted to take a look at the place and get the lay of the land," I said.

"Why?"

I shrugged my shoulders. "Did you ever try to get a mental picture of a place from a woman's description?"

He laughed.

I said, "Well, now at least I can make sense out of her story and know what she's talking about. That's all I wanted. Good night."

"Good night," he said.

I got in my rented car and drove off.

19

I WENT up to Bertha's room in the Royal Hawaiian and started to tap on the door.

I paused as I heard the unmistakable strains of Hawaiian music coming from inside the room.

It was the catchy tune of the popular hula song, "Everybody's Going to the Hukilau."

I tapped on the door.

Abruptly the music ceased. I heard Bertha's voice. "Who is it?"

"Donald," I said.

"Just a moment."

She hesitated for a second, then apparently changed her mind and opened the door.

I went in. Bertha was in her Hawaiian dress.

A portable phonograph was on the top of Bertha's steamer trunk. She had shut it off as I entered, and a certain redness of Bertha's face convinced me she had been practicing the hula.

I didn't say anything, but Bertha knew I was just being tactful.

"What *the hell* is it about this damned Island that gets into your blood?" she asked.

"I wouldn't know," I told her. "Climate, friendliness, hospitality, racial tolerance. It might be any one of a dozen things."

"Whatever it is," Bertha said, "I'm acting like a damn fool."

"Why?"

Bertha indicated the mirror and the phonograph. "If you tell Stephenson Bicknell on me I'll cut your heart out."

"Don't worry," I said, "the climate's getting Bicknell, too. If he stays here two more weeks he'll be swinging from the trees like Tarzan of the Apes, beating his chest and giving the call of the bull ape that has made his kill. Now put away the musical accessories and the Hawaiian costume because you're going to work."

Bertha glowered at me.

I said, "This is a job that has to be done by a woman, a woman who has to be levelheaded, sensible, and tactful. They'd laugh at a man who tried to do it."

"What is it?"

"It has to be handled in such a way the police don't know anything about it until we have secured the evidence we want."

"Go on," Bertha said.

I said, "A troopship came into port and the men were

all out on shore leave this morning. A whole flock of them invaded the beach at Waikiki, strolling along with cameras and trying to make their eyes behave."

"So what?"

I said, "Miriam Woodford tells me that she was lying asleep on the beach, all sprawled out, getting the sunlight."

"Well," Bertha said, "*perhaps* she was." She looked at me and said, "And then again perhaps she was down murdering Jerome Bastion."

"She could have been," I admitted.

"That's better," Bertha said.

"Meaning what?"

"Meaning that that snaky little two-timer is making sheep's eyes at you, and she's going to twine herself around you like a piece of string on a Christmas package. She's going to completely hypnotize you so that you'll think she's innocent first, last, and all the time. Everything else will have to be interpreted in the light of your assumption of her innocence."

"Is that bad?" I asked her.

"You're darned right it's bad."

"All right," I told Bertha. "I'm keeping an open mind."

"You may be keeping an open mind," Bertha said, "but I'll bet fifty dollars to five that that girl has already found some opportunity to make a pass at you."

I said, "Do you want to listen to what I have to say or—"

"Fifty dollars to five," Bertha said, "and it's Bertha Cool's money—private and no expense account. I hate to lose money. I wouldn't make a bet like that unless I felt absolutely certain."

"I know you wouldn't."

"Are you going to take it?"

"I'm trying to talk business."

Bertha snorted. "It was a damn-fool bet in the first place," she said. "If she hadn't made a pass after you, you'd have grabbed it. If she had you wouldn't be taking it. You'd be talking about business. All right, talk about business. What do you want?"

I said, "I want you to find one of the young officers in authority on that troopship. Those fellows are lonely, they're impressionable, they glamorize women, and you can—"

"You mean they'd glamorize *me?*" Bertha snorted.

"Certainly they would."

Bertha said, "I'm listening and that's all. I've kept from laughing, and I'm trying to keep from getting mad."

I said, "Go to that officer and tell him to start circulating around among the men, to get a couple of fellows to help him if necessary."

"What do you want?"

"I want him to question everyone who took pictures at the beach at Waikiki. As soon as the films are developed and printed I want to look at them. Each man can sign his name on the back of his pictures. I want pictures showing people on the beach."

"You think they'll show Miriam Woodford?"

"If she was there they will. If what she says is true, and she was sleeping all sprawled out in her bathing-suit, or walking on the beach you can gamble that at least a dozen cameras will have been pointed her way for a more or less surreptitious picture."

"Why?"

I said, "You've probably noted Miriam Woodford's figure."

"Well, yes," Bertha said.

"So would a couple of a hundred soldiers," I told her.

"Suppose the pictures don't show Miriam?"

"That," I said, "is the reason we want to find out about it before the police think of that particular angle, or before the police realize what we're trying to do."

Bertha sighed. "All right, I'll get busy on it tomorrow."

I grinned at her.

"What's wrong with that?"

"Everything."

"My God, Donald, you don't expect me to get started on it tonight."

I nodded.

Bertha heaved a sigh. "Somebody's always taking the joy out of life. I'd tell you to go to hell only I can see the thing is logical. Suppose we find her in the pictures, then what?"

"Then we'll get in touch with the people who took the pictures and try to get them to fix the time they were down on the beach."

"That," Bertha said, "isn't going to be easy, and it isn't going to convince the police."

I said, "You won't be the one who asks those questions."

"Who will?"

"Miriam, provided she's still at liberty."

Bertha snorted. "Send Miriam down to the troopship and ask if the boys recognize her. She'll get a ninety-eight per cent affirmative answer. Every one of them will be willing to swear that—"

"That's just it," I said, "that's what I want to avoid. I want to get pictures first. I want to build up proof."

"Well, it's logical," Bertha said reluctantly. "Okay, I'll stick my neck out."

"How's Bicknell getting along?"

"Okay. He certainly is carrying a torch for Mira. Do you know what happened?"

"What?"

"He came to my room and told me that if it cost him a hundred thousand dollars of his personal fortune he was going to see that Miriam wasn't railroaded. He's going to get attorneys and he's giving us a free hand."

"Good," I said.

"Dammit, Donald," Bertha said, "I wish you wouldn't be so completely indifferent to figures."

"I'm not."

"No," Bertha snapped. "I notice you were looking Miriam over every time she moved. My God, that girl has a gait like a grunion dancing on the sand."

I grinned at Bertha and walked out, leaving her sputtering something about designing women and susceptible men.

I drove to the place where Mitsui had parked her car the night before, went up the steps, and rang the bell.

A Hawaiian-Japanese lad answered the bell.

"Mitsui," I said.

He looked at me with a blank expression.

I put my hand to the lapel of my coat, moved it back a bit, then dropped it back into position.

"Yes, officer," he said.

A moment later Mitsui came to the door. She saw me, then recoiled as though I'd struck her.

I followed her into the house.

The Hawaiian-Japanese lad looked at her questioningly.

She said something to him in Japanese.

I settled down in a chair.

The Japanese lad came over to me and said one word. "Out."

I sat there.

He moved an ominous step toward me, and I slid my right hand under the left lapel of my coat and looked at him with cold hostility.

He didn't like that look.

The bluff worked and he fell back.

"What do you want?" he asked.

I turned to Mitsui. "Who paid you to take the records out of that tape recorder, Mitsui?"

Her face was utterly wooden. I thought for a minute she wouldn't answer, then she said in her low musical voice, "Bastion."

"Anyone else?"

"No one else."

"Do you know Sidney Selma?"

"Sidney Selma," she repeated after me with a sing-song voice.

"Sidney Selma."

"Don't know," she said.

I said, "Last night you went out to Bastion's house."

Her eyes blinked a couple of times, but she neither

nodded her head nor shook it, just stood looking at me.

"Was anyone else in the house?"

"Woman?"

"Perhaps a woman, anyone, man or woman?"

Again she didn't say anything.

"Did you see anyone?" I asked.

Her dark eyes, as inscrutable as though they had been covered with black lacquer, looked steadily into mine.

"Did you see a person who was visiting there with Jerome Bastion?"

She remained silent.

I said, "Sidney Selma was there last night, or else he got in touch with you today. He's about thirty, fairly tall, with blue eyes and broad shoulders. He may have given you some other name, but he saw you either yesterday or today, and he paid you some money to do something. I want to know what it was."

She continued to look at me with perfectly steady features and calm, inscrutable eyes.

It was the Japanese-Hawaiian man who gave me the tip-off. He couldn't control his features. Something was happening.

I whirled around.

Sidney Selma was standing in the doorway, his eyes cold and hard, a blued-steel revolver pointed square at me.

"You're a nosy sonofabitch," he said. "Korioto, take his gun."

The young Japanese came toward me. He was smiling now, a smile of cold triumph. He was moving like a cat.

"Don't get in the line of fire," Selma warned.

I held Korioto with my eyes. "Don't try it, son," I said. "You're going to get killed. Selma can't explain another corpse. I can."

Korioto hesitated.

"Go ahead," Selma said. "Don't let him bluff you. I'll drill him and we'll explain afterward."

It was Mitsui who broke the deadlock. She said something in Japanese, and Korioto suddenly came at me like a cat making a swift striking leap.

I side-stepped and lashed out with my fist.

That was what Korioto wanted. He circled my wrist with fingers of steel. I had a brief glimpse of him pivoting from the hip, and then I saw the room revolving, in a sickening circle. The table was over my head, the ceiling was beneath my feet. Then I made another complete turn and slammed against the wall.

Korioto was on me just as though he'd been a cat and I was the mouse.

I was so shaken I was nauseated, but I tried to make a grab to get some kind of a headlock on him. He twisted me up like a pretzel, and I heard the *slip-slop* of Mitsui's feet as she came shuffling over and stood impassively by my side, handing Korioto a roll of linen bandage.

Selma said, "Get his gun."

Korioto's swift hands tied my wrists, then he darted his hand along my left side, underneath the coat, looking for a gun in a shoulder holster. When he didn't find it he patted my pockets.

"Well," Selma said, "come on, get the gun."

Korioto's voice was thick with self-condemnation.

"No gun."

Selma threw back his head and laughed uproariously.

I caught a glimpse of Korioto's eyes. I thought perhaps Selma was making a bad play with that loud laughter.

"All right," Selma said after a while, pocketing his gun, "look him over."

They unbuttoned my coat and shirt, took off my pants, rolled up my undershirt. They had me completely bare on the floor. Selma searched the clothes. Korioto and Mitsui searched me. And I *mean* searched me.

When they got done Sidney Selma made an inventory of the stuff from my pockets which he piled on the table.

"All right, wise guy," he said, "where is it?"

My head felt as though someone had operated on it with a sledge hammer. Every time my heart beat I experienced a pounding, throbbing ache which ran all the way through my brain.

"Where's what?" I asked wearily, trying to keep the bitterness of defeat out of my voice.

He laughed and walked up to me, drew back his shoe and kicked me hard on the buttocks.

I winced.

Korioto laughed, a nervous Japanese laugh.

"Now, look," Selma said, "we know you've got it. We've been through your room. We've been through your car. We've gone through every inch of everything you've ever touched, and we can't find it. Now, I'll admit you're smart. I'm not going to start playing blindman's bluff all over the Island. I haven't got the time. I want it."

"I don't know what you're talking about," I told him.

I could see his face darken.

I said, "I don't know what you're trying to do with Mitsui and Korioto here, but if you want to hold out on them there's nothing to prevent you. Double-crossing partners seems to be a habit of yours. You killed Bastion because you thought a one-way split would be better than a two-way split. I don't know what your arrangements with Korioto and Mitsui are, but—"

He kicked me again.

Those kicks hurt. They jarred my spine. They rocked my aching brain. I knew that my only chance depended on getting Mitsui and Korioto to lose confidence in him, but I couldn't stand those jarring kicks. I felt I was going to be sick to my stomach if he kicked me again.

I tried to get my nerve to the point where I could continue.

"Come on," Selma said. "Where is it?"

He kicked me again and I wasn't expecting it.

I started to get sick.

"Put his clothes on," Selma said.

Mitsui got down on her knees and put my clothes back on me. She pulled up my pants, buttoned my shirt, even pulled my coat back down from where it had been wadded up behind my tied wrists. After she had my pants back on she tied my ankles.

Selma pulled up a chair and sat down. He said, "Don't think I'm through with you. I like to kick you. I get an awful thrill out of it. If you want to have pain that suits me fine. I'm going to give you lots of it. I'm going to take you to a place where you can just make up your mind what you want to do."

I fought back the pain and said, "You're on the wrong track. If you want to go in for sadism that's all right, but you can't beat something out of me I don't know."

He laughed then, that nasty, coarse, rasping laugh. "I don't know how it got there in the first place," he said, "but you weren't quite smart enough when you took that motion-picture camera out of the mailbox. We found a witness who happened to see it. He didn't think anything of it at the time. And I'm frank to admit that motion-picture camera was a new gag on me. I never thought Bastion would keep the stuff there. Don't make any mistake. *I* didn't kill him, but I sure as hell would have high-graded the stuff if I'd known where to look for it."

I knew then that he had me. There was no use trying to play dumb after that and get beaten up. I think he'd have clubbed me to death and enjoyed doing it.

Selma drew back his foot.

"I'll tell," I said.

He held the kick, being reluctant to cut out the brutalities.

"Well," he said, "where is it?"

"The only place you didn't look," I told him.

"I looked every place."

"Then you've found it."

He couldn't resist that logic. He thought it over for a while, said, "All right, where's the place I didn't look?"

"The Venetian blinds."

He said, "Don't be a damn fool."

"Not on the wooden slats," I said, "but on the inside of the frame that furnishes the decoration at the top."

"On the *inside?*"

"Inside," I said. "I took Scotch tape and taped the stuff to the inside. You can't see it except by pulling up the Venetian blind halfway and then sticking your head out of the window."

"You sonofabitch!" Selma said with half a note of admiration in his voice.

I lay there silent, my eyes closed.

Above me I could feel Selma standing there and thinking.

Suddenly he said, "All right, here's one for good measure, just for cheating me out of the pleasure of kicking you to a pulp."

He kicked me, and then suddenly started a frenzy of jabs with the toe of his shoes, searching for my stomach.

I doubled up to protect myself, and Korioto pulled him off. The Japanese said, "That comes later. Now you beat police to papers."

Despite Selma's fevered desire to kick me to a pulp he couldn't overlook the cold logic of the situation. At any time the police might find the thing he was looking for.

Korioto took his shoulders, turned him toward the door. "Go," he said.

Selma said, "Hold this guy here until I get back. Keep him right like that. Don't let him talk you into anything."

Selma shot out of the door. A moment later I heard the grind of a starting motor and a car raced away from the curb.

I opened my eyes.

Korioto was standing above me, holding a lighted cigarette, looking down at me speculatively.

"Hello, sucker," I said.

"What you mean, sucker?"

"I mean sucker, easy mark, cat's paw."

"You wish more to be kicked?"

"I was just telling you," I said.

"When Selma comes back I think is more kicking. Perhaps I help."

I said, "That's where you're a sucker. You think Selma

195

is coming back."

Korioto looked at me, lowered his lids so the eyes were half closed. He took a deep drag on his cigarette.

I said, "Do you think that when Selma gets what he wants he's going to fool around here to share it with you? Do you think he's going to stay where the Island police can shake him down? Don't be silly."

"What does he do?" Korioto asked at length, as though reluctant to play my game by even asking the question, but unable to control his curiosity.

I said, "He gets aboard the plane for the mainland. He's got a ticket for tonight and a reservation for tomorrow night."

"Plane to mainland?"

"Sure."

"He has reservation?"

"Reservation, hell! He's got a ticket!"

His eyes were mere slits now.

Mitsui rattled something to him in Japanese.

"Don't take my word for it," I said wearily. "Go call up the airline."

There was some more rattling Japanese, then I heard Mitsui's sandaled feet walking with that peculiar slithering *slap-slop-slap* which characterizes the Japanese pigeon-toed walk.

I heard the dial mechanism on the telephone and Mitsui's voice asking very politely, "Please does Mr. Sidney Selma leave on airplane tonight? . . . Is he holding reservation? . . . Ticket already? . . . Thank you, thank you very much."

She hung up the telephone.

Japanese words flew around there like the clacking of hysterical castanets.

I heard running feet. Mitsui stood over me. She bent down; a thick piece of adhesive tape was plastered over my lips.

There was more Japanese, more steps. I heard the sound of a banging door once more, and again the sound of a starting motor and a car pulled away from the curb.

I tried twisting my wrists. They had been bound with deft cunning, the skill of a Japanese whose ancestors had been working with ropes for the past ten thousand years.

I could roll over. That was all.

There was a little table by the window with a red Japanese pigeon-blood vase and a carved statue on it.

I got my feet under the lower rung of the little table, gathered myself, raised and pushed.

The table went through the glass, the pigeon-blood vase clattered out to the porch. I could hear it rolling.

I raised and lowered my feet and more glass clattered to the floor.

I waited.

It seemed an interminable age of silence. I wondered if I could get strength enough to push the table clean through the window.

Then I heard steps outside and a man's voice, in frightened tones, asked, "Is everything all right?"

He sounded as though he'd run at the first intimation things weren't all right.

I made noises in my throat. I jiggled the table some more.

I saw a face looking in the window, then the man turned and ran. I heard his steps running down the porch, then after a moment's silence, the steps came back again, frightened, cautious, tentative steps. The white face once more peered in the window. After a moment a hand tried the knob of the door and the man came in.

He was scared to death. If I'd moved he'd probably have run. He leaned over me and put his finger under the corner of the tape on my mouth and pulled.

It felt as though every bit of skin was coming off my lips, but the tape came off.

"Burglars," I said. "Untie me. Get the police."

"Where are they?"

"They've gone," I reassured him.

That was what he was really waiting for. He set to work

and untied the knots around my wrists, then I sat up, got my knife, and cut through the bandage around my ankles.

I felt like hell.

"They had to go away," I said, "but they expect to be back. That's why they left me tied up so they—"

That was enough. He didn't even wait for thanks. He went out of the place as though somebody had shot him from a catapult.

I figured I had ten minutes at the outside.

I hurt all over. Every time I took a step my bruised muscles raised a protest, but I gave the place a pretty good going-over.

On a nail in the kitchen were two keys. They were keys to expensive locks. I looked them over. They were keys to different locks. They wouldn't fit either the front or the back door of the house where Mitsui was living.

I put them in my pocket.

I could find nothing else worth while.

I was starting for the front door when I heard quick steps on the porch. I stepped behind the front door and stood still.

Sidney Selma jerked the door open and stepped inside.

He was in a wonderful position as he stood there staring stupidly at the empty living-room.

I gave him everything I had.

With the impact of my foot he shot forward to his hands and knees.

I kicked him in the side.

"How does it feel?" I asked, and kicked him in the chest.

He looked up, sheer surprise and incredulity were reflected in his eyes.

He was trying to scramble to his feet when I kicked him in the chin and walked out.

I knew then how easy it would be to become a sadist.

That last kick really felt good.

20

THE AIRLINE COMPANY was courtesy personified. They had a couple of stand-by people waiting by for a last-minute vacancy and they were very glad to let me cancel my ticket. All they wanted was the ticket numbers. I'd taken the precaution of writing those in my notebook so it was all duck soup. They told me I could surrender the ticket at their office the next day or exchange it for other transportation.

I knocked at the door of Bertha Cool's room. She opened the door, glared at me, and said, "Well, you've scared up a pretty kettle of fish. Come in. You're just in time."

I walked in.

Stephenson Bicknell was sitting on the edge of his chair, holding his cane in his hands, looking mad enough to put cream and sugar on ten-penny nails and chew them up for breakfast food.

"What's the matter with you?" Bertha asked. "You walk like you're all crippled up."

She tried to catch the last two words before she spoke them, but it was too late. She hastily tacked a mollifying phrase on the end. "Been in an automobile accident?" and looked out of the corner of her eye at Bicknell to see if he'd taken offense.

I eased myself down into a chair.

"I've been in a fight," I said.

"My God," Bertha said, "you've let yourself get beaten up again. Honestly, I don't know how you do it. You just seem to let them bounce you around like a tennis ball. Can't you lick *anyone?*"

"Apparently not," I said.

"Well, we're in a hell of a mess," Bertha said.

Bicknell glared at me and said, "When a person is working for me I expect his fullest confidence and loyalty. I trust him and I expect him to play square with me."

I tried to ease around in a position where my bruised

muscles pressing against the seat of the chair wouldn't give me torture.

"Now, don't get Donald wrong," Bertha said. "People kick him around, but he's a brainy little bastard, and he'll come through with the right answer."

"Not for my money he won't," Bicknell said. "As far as I'm concerned I don't like being taken for a ride."

"Now, listen," Bertha said. "This thing can be settled and—"

Bicknell shook his head.

Bertha glared at him as though she wanted to kill him.

"What's the beef?" I asked.

Bicknell said, "I have now learned, unfortunately, for the first time that Mrs. Cool discovered something at Bastion's house."

"Just an old motion-picture camera," Bertha snapped. "My God, I'll buy you a dozen motion-picture cameras if you're going to act that way about it."

"It isn't the camera," he said, "it's what was in that camera. Now, then, Lam, what happened to it?"

"The police have it."

"I mean what happened to the stuff that was in the camera?"

"Films were in it. The police developed them."

"I know," he said, "and found pictures of traffic on King Street taken two hours after the murder was committed. My God, I thought I could at least trust you folks. I paid you money and played square with you and certainly didn't look for a double cross."

"Who said you were getting a double cross?"

"I say it."

"Well, you're getting exactly what you paid for."

"I am not. I hired you people to—"

"You hired us," I said, "to protect Miriam Woodford."

"Exactly," he said.

"We're protecting her."

"No, you're not. You should have turned that information over to me, whatever it was."

I shook my head.

"I consider that absolute, utter disloyalty."

I told him, "There are times when it's advisable to give a client all the information you have, and there are other times when it's advisable not to. It happened that this was one of those times."

"I want to know what was in that camera, Lam."

I said, "A roll of microfilm, a couple of receipts for safety-deposit boxes, and some keys to safety-deposit boxes."

He sat bolt upright in his chair. "Now," he said, "we're getting to pay dirt. That's the exact stuff we want. That's the stuff that will make all the difference in the world. Now we can really give Miriam Woodford some protection."

"You're glad we got that?" I asked.

"Need you ask?"

I said, "All right. Bertha got the camera and I got the stuff out of the camera. It's in a safe place where nobody's going to get hold of it, and there's no need to bother about it. That was the stuff you wanted out of the way. It's out of the way now. You can quit worrying. And you should be congratulating us on doing a good job instead of sitting there and crabbing."

"If you'd only told me about that I could have quit worrying."

I shook my head. "You forget that the police found the receipt for the Photostat and know all about the purchase of the poison."

"Yes," he said thoughtfully. "That's so."

I glanced at Bertha Cool and raised my eyebrows.

"Oh, I told him," Bertha said angrily. "I got conscience-stricken and told him in strict confidence, and then he blew up and started raising the roof."

"Well, why shouldn't I?" he asked. "We were supposed to be working together on this thing, and this was the first intimation I had that anything like that had been found."

I said, "You didn't know it when the police were interrogating you, did you?"

"No."

I said, "When you say your prayers tonight, don't forget to include that as something you had to be thankful for."

"Why?"

"Because the police would have found out about it if you'd known about it. Bertha handled it the right way. Now, as I understand it, you had some light gloves and you put some papers in those, rolled them up and hid those papers in the stone wall."

"That's right."

"Did you get them?"

"Do you mean did I get them from the wall?"

"Yes."

"No."

"Where are they?"

"Still in the wall I suppose."

"You didn't get anybody to go out there and pick them up for you?"

"No."

"You didn't tell anybody about what you had done?"

"No. Mrs. Cool was the only one who knew it."

I said, "They aren't there now. They're gone."

"You're sure?"

"Not absolutely sure because I didn't have a chance to stick my hand in the recess in the wall and find out definitely, but I could see that the little stone that closed up the opening in the wall had fallen down, and in the moonlight I couldn't see anything in the recess. I think that if anything had been in there I could have seen it."

He frowned and said, "That could be very serious."

I didn't say anything.

"However," he said, "I want to get back to this thing that I consider a distinct breach of faith on your part."

"I don't so consider it."

"I do."

I said, "You hired us to protect Miriam."

"That's right."

"All right, we're protecting her."

"From what?"

"As I remember it, we were hired to protect her against any danger that might threaten her."

"Exactly," he said, "and the first thing you do is to hold out the first valuable piece of information you have uncovered."

"That's right. We did it for Miriam's protection."

"You mean you couldn't trust *me* with information pertaining to Miriam?"

"Exactly," I said.

"What?" Bicknell shouted.

Bertha said, "Now take it easy, Donald, take it easy. We can get this thing all squared up and—"

"No, we can't," Bicknell said. "You're done. You're finished. Both of you. You're fired, as of now. It's too late for me to stop payment on the check I gave you. You've already cashed that, but, by God, you can pay your own expenses from here on. Try and sue me for your fee if you want to. Try and sue me for expenses. I'll drag you through the courts and expose you for the double-crossers you are. I'll spend fifty thousand dollars if I have to, to keep you from getting one red cent."

Bertha looked at me with exasperation.

I said to Bicknell, "How did it happen that you had those gloves in your pocket this morning?"

"I don't know," he said irritably. "I try to protect my hands. I got a little sunburned and—"

I said, "People don't wear gloves in Honolulu."

"Well, I wore them."

I said, "That was because you knew you were going to search Bastion's house and didn't want to leave any fingerprints."

"What are you talking about? The murder was committed just as we got there."

"By whom?" I asked.

"By some woman."

I shook my head. "Naughty, naughty, Bicknell! You

shouldn't hold out on your detectives that way."

"What are you insinuating?"

I said, "You had the thing pretty carefully planned—"

Bertha interrupted. "No, no, Donald. Now don't get off on the wrong foot here. We can't afford to guess wrong on this thing, you know. Bicknell was on the beach all morning until I told him about Bastion. Then we went down there together. I was with him all the time."

"When was the murder committed?" I asked Bertha.

"Just as we drove up," Bertha said, "or just before."

"When you went to phone the police," I told her.

"What?" Bertha exclaimed, "You're crazy. I phoned the police after—" Abruptly she stopped talking.

"Sure," I told her. "*You* didn't get out of the car. *You* didn't see the body. Bicknell walked up on the porch, looked in the window, came back and told you Bastion had been shot between the eyes and was lying there in bed dead, with a crumpled newspaper on the floor."

Bertha looked at me and blinked her little green eyes.

"But it's true," she said. "I saw the body with my own eyes."

I grinned at her. "After you got back from telephoning the police the body was lying there on the bed. When Bicknell walked up on the porch, Bastion was in bed reading the morning newspaper.

"Bastion started blackmailing Miriam. But Selma, who was the mastermind in the business, realized that there was bigger and richer game than Miriam Woodford, a victim, moreover, who had a guilty conscience and so was doubly vulnerable."

"What do you think you're talking about?" Bicknell said.

"Bastion's murder."

"Talk about it, then."

I turned to Bertha. "Bicknell told you to go and telephone for the police, that he'd wait right there. You started climbing stairs to a neighboring house intent only on calling the police. Bicknell walked in, took the gun out of his pocket, shot Bastion squarely between the eyes, and then was back on the porch by the time you had explained what you wanted to the neighbor and had gotten to where you could see him from the window of the neighboring house.

"He'd been hoping he'd have time to kill Bastion and find the documents he wanted before you got back from phoning the police, but he couldn't find what he was looking for in the time he had available, so then he had to talk you into going in there with him and searching the place."

"You double-crossing liar!" Bicknell exclaimed. "I'll have your license for this!"

I didn't pay attention but went on speaking to Bertha.

"Bicknell doesn't care a snap of his fingers about Miriam Woodford. That's all an act. Miriam Woodford got the arsenic, all right, but that wasn't the arsenic that killed Ezra Woodford. That was just a blind. Ezra asked her to get the arsenic. He did that because Bicknell asked Ezra to get some arsenic for him because *he* wanted to experiment in the taxidermy business."

Bicknell, in a cold rage, said, "I don't know just what I can do to put you two people out of business, but whatever time, money, effort, and patience can do is going to be done. You are the lowest type of investigators. You are the scum of the profession. You are the dregs, the people who double-cross their own clients!"

I grinned at him.

Bertha glared at me and said, "I'm damned if I can figure you out, Donald. Here is one case where we have Santa Claus for a client and *you* go around tying knots in our stockings."

"Now then, I'll tell you something else," Bicknell told me. "There's a little thing called proof. I don't know whether you've ever heard of it or not, but in case you haven't, this might be a good time to learn about it. You've been reading too many of these detective stories where the brainy detective points a finger at someone who immediately breaks down and confesses, or pulls a gun and tries to commit suicide, or starts running.

"Now I'm going to reverse that process. You've made a false, slanderous accusation in front of a witness. I'm going to sue you for libel. I'm going to let you try to prove some of these wild accusations you've made, young man. By the time I get done I'll show you up for what you are."

Bertha said, "Well, if you're going to talk that way, you little insignificant, creaky sonofabitch, we'll show you something about fighting you never knew before. As a matter of fact I think—"

Knuckles sounded on the door.

We all broke off talking.

Bicknell said significantly to me, "We don't want any interruptions now. Perhaps, after all, we've been losing our tempers, and perhaps if we come down to earth we might work out a sane basis of understanding and—"

The knuckles sounded again, this time the knock was more peremptory.

I went over and opened the door. Sergeant Hulamoki stood out in the corridor, bowing and smiling.

"May I come in?" he asked.

"No!" Bicknell yelled.

"No!" Bertha screamed.

I stood to one side. Sergeant Hulamoki came in and said, "Thank you, thank you very much."

I closed the door.

Sergeant Hulamoki said, "You were commenting about proof, Mr. Bicknell. It was a very, very interesting discussion, and I thought I might be able to contribute something to it, which is why I decided to pop in for a minute."

"You mean you've heard this discussion?" Bertha asked.

"Oh, certainly," Sergeant Hulamoki said. "We have the room wired, you know. We're monitoring the conversation in an adjoining room."

"It's all recorded?" Bertha asked.

"Oh, of course. Witnessed and recorded. Think nothing of it. Just a matter of police routine, Mrs. Cool."

Bicknell said, "Well, that gives me the witnesses I need

to make a perfect slander suit against Donald Lam for defamation of character."

Sergeant Hulamoki said, "About the proof, Mr. Lam. You have some very interesting conclusions, perhaps I should say deductions."

"Call them suspicions," Bicknell snapped.

"Now we're probably in a position to supply the proof."

"Yes?" I asked.

"The gun in the water box of the toilet," Sergeant Hulamoki said. "That's the murder weapon, and there's no doubt as to who put it there and no question as to exactly when it was put there."

Bicknell started to say something, then changed his mind.

"It became apparent, of course," Sergeant Hulamoki said, "that if anyone had taken advantage of a peculiar combination of circumstances to kill a blackmailer and intended to blame the crime on Mrs. Woodford, that in some way the gun would be planted on the premises.

"I think you had that thought in mind, Mr. Lam, when you kept suggesting that the persons who were searching the premises make a *good* job of it."

I nodded.

"Well, of course, I had the same idea," Sergeant Hulamoki said.

Bicknell snorted sarcastically. "Then why didn't you monkeys look in the water box in the toilet when you made your search? That would have simplified the whole thing."

"But, of course," Sergeant Hulamoki said, "that's a mere matter of police routine. We did."

"You did?" Bicknell asked, his jaw sagging.

"But, of course," Sergeant Hulamoki said deprecatingly. "Good heavens, do you think we'd have a man on the Honolulu police force who would be charged with the responsibility of investigating a crime of this importance who would neglect so obvious a hiding-place?"

"Obvious?" Bicknell asked.

"Well, of course," Sergeant Hulamoki said, his manner ingratiatingly placating, "perhaps not to you, Mr. Bicknell. The amateur who enters a bathroom hastily seeking some place where he may hide an incriminating piece of evidence will look the place over, find the water box over the toilet, and come to the conclusion he has found the ideal hiding-place, that it is a stroke of genius on his part. But you see, Mr. Bicknell, we are professionals. We encounter these things every day.

"With you perhaps it's once in a lifetime. I doubt if you ever before had any object that you had to hide in a hurry in a room where the hiding-places were, by the very nature of the room, limited, so the water box on the toilet impressed *you* as being an ideal place.

"*Our* men have to deal with these problems many times a year, and I can assure you you aren't the first person who has concluded that the water box was an ideal hiding-place, a place where the police would never look.

"Of course, you see," Sergeant Hulamoki went on, "we felt certain that any evidence that was to be planted would be placed in the bathroom unless Mitsui, the Japanese maid, was the one who had planted the object, in which event it would presumably have been placed around the kitchen. She would have thought the flour box or the sugar container would be an ideal place.

"You'd be surprised how many, many times maids and cooks think they can put things down inside the canister containing the flour, or the can containing the sugar, and sometimes even the coffee. They feel that's an inspired idea for a hiding-place. And so, of course, in dealing with searches in a kitchen we look there almost the first thing, just as we invariably look in the water box when we're making a search in the bathroom.

"Now in your case, Mr. Bicknell, you went to call on Miriam Woodford with Mrs. Cool. You wanted to assure Miriam that you were going to stand back of her, that you would retain attorneys who would look after her interests, that you would put up any amount of money that was necessary for her protection and all of that.

"The advantage of that, as far as you were concerned, was that it would leave you in complete charge of her defense. As the person who was paying her attorney, you would be in a position to map out the strategy. That would, of course, give you an excellent opportunity to see that she was convicted of the murder while at the same time you apparently were trying to extricate her."

"Oh, yes," Bicknell said sarcastically, "and perhaps you'd like to tell us *why* I'd go to all that trouble to double-cross the woman whom I admire so much?"

"Oh, but certainly," Sergeant Hulamoki said. "You knew that Ezra Woodford had asked his wife to buy arsenic. So you very conveniently poisoned Ezra with arsenic. Doubtless an examination of the partnership books will disclose the reason.

"This blackmailer, Bastion, he *is* very clever. But he gets the wrong evidence. He is trying to blackmail Miriam, when it is you who are the guilty one.

"Sidney Selma, the mastermind of the blackmailing ring, comes over to set Bastion straight. You knew he was coming so you arranged passage on the same ship—and brought detectives along to 'protect' Miriam. Very clever, very, very clever, but not quite clever enough."

Sergeant Hulamoki beamed and bowed at Bicknell.

"Do you know what you're saying?" Bicknell yelled.

Sergeant Hulamoki looked surprised. "Why, of course," he said. "Of course I know what I'm saying. I am not only formulating the words in my brain, but I can hear them with my ears. Why, certainly."

"You're making a direct accusation," Bicknell said.

"But, of course," Sergeant Hulamoki retorted.

There was a moment's silence.

Sergeant Hulamoki went on. "I trust I'm not being misunderstood. You see, Mr. Bicknell, you had an excellent opportunity to go to the bathroom and that probably was the only room that you could have entered where you'd have been alone and unobserved, and where nothing would have seemed particularly unusual. So, as a friend of long standing, you casually entered the bathroom. You were in there for several minutes with the door closed and presumably locked. You had the murder gun in your hand and you were trying to find a hiding-place. You knew that you must find some hiding-place in the bathroom.

"The only thing that you didn't know was that Mr. Lam had particularly requested the persons making the search to make such a thorough search that a weapon couldn't be planted afterward, and, of course, you didn't realize that *I* had given my men exactly the same instructions.

"So it happened, Mr. Bicknell, that when you entered the bathroom you were walking into an elaborate trap. I can assure you that every inch of that bathroom had been searched. Not only did we search everything in the bathroom, but we were careful even to test the tiles to make certain that there was no loose tile which would lead to a concealed hiding-place. And, as it happens, Mr. Bicknell, you were the only one who entered the bathroom during the visit you and Mrs. Cool made to the Woodford apartment.

"So, of course, later on, when I entered the bathroom, which was the place I started searching first, I went almost at once to the water box above the toilet, and sure enough, there was the gun. I may now disclose, Mr. Bicknell, that tests have proven absolutely that this was the murder weapon."

Bicknell said, "You can't frame anything like that on me. I'm going to fight this thing through to a finish. I've got money to spend on lawyers, and I'm going to get the best."

Sergeant Hulamoki fairly beamed. "Oh, I'm *so* glad to hear you say that, Mr. Bicknell! I'm *so* glad. I was afraid that you might lose your nerve and simply enter a plea of guilty and throw yourself on the mercy of the court. This way it will be better, much better."

"Why?" Bertha Cool asked.

Sergeant Hulamoki looked at her in surprise as though

she should have seen the answer without interpolating the question.

But he explained courteously. "You see, Mrs. Cool, we are dependent upon the taxpayers for our salaries, our expenses, all of our maintenance, and naturally we like the taxpayers to know what we are doing to protect them.

"So many, many times when we have a case that has involved good solid detective work the culprit pleads guilty and throws himself on the mercy of the court. Then the taxpayers have no way of knowing what we have done.

"On the other hand, when there is perhaps a weak point in the evidence, the culprit comes into court with a lot of lawyers and makes the police look somewhat less than infallible.

"People have a habit of failing to appreciate that police do not *make* the proof. They only try to *gather the evidence*. And when some clever attorney keeps hammering away at the police department, saying to the jury, 'Why didn't they bring in this evidence? Why didn't they get that evidence? Why didn't they do so-and-so?,' quite frequently the jurors start nodding their heads in agreement and the next thing we know a culprit is acquitted and the police are subject to censure.

"Now in this case the exact opposite is true. You see, we have such a beautiful case that even the best attorney could—"

"Oh, cut out the chatter," Bicknell interpolated angrily. "I'm a businessman. I know something about what can be done and what can't be done. You're bluffing. Suppose I did go into the bathroom. The only way you could have proved I planted the gun was to have followed me right in there and then picked up the gun. As it was, too many people had an opportunity to go in there. There was Miriam, there was Norma, there was this pint-sized detective here, there was—"

"Oh, but of course," Sergeant Hulamoki said, conceding the point at once. "You are so right, Mr. Bicknell. It is not even open to argument."

211

"Well?" Bicknell said.

"But," Sergeant Hulamoki went on, "*you* had the opportunity. Of course, you must admit that."

"I and several other people."

"But certainly, Mr. Bicknell. Do you take us for children?"

"Then you haven't got a perfect case," Bicknell said. "My lawyer is going to make a monkey out of you on the witness stand."

"But how are you going to account for the fact that when we took the numbers of this gun and inquired back as to the purchase of the gun and the ownership, we found that—"

"You can't trace that gun to me," Bicknell said. "I'll promise you one thing, that gun wasn't purchased by me."

"Why, no, of course not," Sergeant Hulamoki said. "You would not have been *that* stupid! The gun was sold some fifteen years ago to a man who is, unfortunately, no longer available. He is dead."

"Well, there you are," Bicknell said.

"But," Sergeant Hulamoki went on, "the police of Denver are rather careful about persons who carry guns. Any reputable citizen is permitted to carry a weapon if there is any particular reason why he should, but the police like to have a record of it, and so it happened that ten years ago you made application to carry a weapon and the application was promptly granted by the police. At that time, however, you listed the make, model, and number of the weapon you wished to carry."

Bicknell's face showed sudden, complete dismay.

"And," Sergeant Hulamoki went on, "the number of the weapon was exactly the same as the weapon that was found in the water box of the toilet, the weapon that killed Jerome C. Bastion.

"You see, Mr. Bicknell, it is necessary for the police to work swiftly in certain matters and try to cover the ground thoroughly. Here in the Islands we are somewhat isolated, so we use the telephone a great deal and this adds somewhat to the cost of operating the police department. So it is going to be *very* advantageous to have an opportunity to show the taxpayers that these expenses are justified.

"Now I dislike to bother you, Mr. Bicknell, and I know that you are troubled somewhat with arthritis. I am afraid that handcuffs on your wrists might perhaps furnish an element of cruelty which we would not like to have. And, of course, there is the humiliation of crossing the lobby.

"You will, of course, have to check out of your room because unfortunately, Mr. Bicknell, Honolulu is very, very crowded at the moment. There is a long waiting-list at the hotel, and the hotel becomes quite obdurate about such matters. I will have two detectives who will help you in your packing.

"You see, there are many people who would like to move into the suite of rooms which you now have, but at the place where you are going to finish out your visit in Honolulu there are not many people who wish to remain there. You'll forgive me a little joke, Mr. Bicknell, because it sometimes relieves the tension of the situation.

"Now I'll help you to your feet. Take the cane by all means, but remember, please, that it is only to assist you in walking and is not to be used as a weapon. Any attempt to resort to violence would be most unfortunate, particularly to a man in your condition.

"Now, if you're *quite* ready."

Sergeant Hulamoki walked over and put his hand under Bicknell's arm, helped him up out of the chair, handed him his cane, bowed to us, and said, "You will forgive my intrusion, but when we heard the conversation taking the turn it did, we felt that it was perhaps time to intervene. There was some possibility that voices might be raised and, of course, the Royal Hawaiian is a very high-class hotel. It would not care to have a quarrel take place in the rooms—that is, an audible quarrel. And as for the alarm clock which you purchased, Mr. Lam, you are, of course, at liberty to keep it, but as to the box in which you placed certain articles, the box which you mailed to a

Miss Elsie Brand at your office address on the mainland, we are, of course, very much interested.

"I have wired the mainland police so that when the box is delivered tomorrow morning a police officer and a postal inspector will accompany the man who makes the delivery. We will, of course, expect Miss Brand to co-operate."

"She will," I said, "but we in turn expect you to co-operate."

"In what way?"

"Heaven knows how much blackmail stuff is on that microfilm," I said, "and we would like to have our clients protected."

"Your clients? Oh, you refer to Mrs. Woodford and the Radcliff girl. I had for the moment overlooked the situation there, Mr. Lam. I realize now that a man as astute as you would hardly have convicted your erstwhile employer of murder without having made some reasonably advantageous financial arrangements with the two women who would naturally benefit by that action.

"Of course, of course, Mr. Lam. You will find us most co-operative in such matters. We dislike blackmail as much as you do, and I'm quite certain you can trust our discretion.

"And one other matter, Mrs. Cool, the errand that took you to the transport—I am referring to your attempt to get pictures of Miriam Woodford on the beach—that has already been taken care of.

"It was clever of you to think of it, Mr. Lam. Our men went to work on it immediately. Already we have several pictures showing Mrs. Woodford on the beach—what a charming figure that girl has!

"Two of the photographs show her quite plainly against the background of the Outrigger Club, and as you will recall, Mr. Lam, the Outrigger Club has a big clock mounted facing the ocean, so swimmers may see the time.

"Those photographs completely clear Mrs. Woodford. She was on the beach at the moment the crime was being committed.

"Now, Mr. Bicknell, if you'll come with me, please. I can assure you that in crossing the lobby and checking out at the desk we will try to make it seem that you are our honored guest, a prominent, wealthy tourist being given a police escort on a sight-seeing tour about the Island.

"Thank you, Mrs. Cool, and thank *you*, Mr. Lam! In fact, Mr. Lam, we appreciate your co-operation in this matter enormously. Mrs. Cool, I'm afraid has been guilty of an indiscretion about which the chief will wish to communicate with her, but that can wait until tomorrow or perhaps the next day. The chief is, at the moment, very busy.

"We don't like to embarrass mainland visitors, particularly when their efforts ultimately lead to beneficial results, but sometime within the next few days, Mrs. Cool, at your convenience, the chief has a few questions about removing evidence from the scene of a crime.

"There remains one other matter. The blackmailer, Selma, whom you have been so anxious to call to our attention, Mr. Lam. He is being taken care of. For a while we thought he might even have committed the murder, but it seems he did not. Perhaps the idea occurred to him. But he was desperate at the thought of losing the evidence Bastion had secreted. With hundreds of thousands at stake, who can blame him?

"But we have taken care of him very nicely, Mr. Lam. He will, by one of those coincidences of fate, spend the night in a cell adjoining the one which will be occupied by Mr. Bicknell.

"However, I am detaining you. You doubtless have business matters to discuss, so I will escort Mr. Bicknell to his new lodgings.

"And now good night to you both."

Sergeant Hulamoki took Bicknell out into the hallway, where I glimpsed two men waiting just outside the door.

The door was gently closed.

"Fry me for an oyster," Bertha said. "Roll me in batter and cracker crumbs and fry me in deep grease for an oyster."

A finger on my lips reminded her that the room was wired.

21

BERTHA FOLLOWED ME downstairs, out on the lanai, and down to the beach, where palms jutted out over the water, the fronds silhouetted against the night sky. The coral sand loomed silvery-white. The warm, gentle waves on the beach at Waikiki glided to a stop some twenty-five yards out from the beach. They came the rest of the distance in gentle ripples.

Bertha said, "The way those police do things gives me the willies. I'll be searching myself to see that they haven't planted a microphone in my bra."

"It might not be a bad idea," I told her.

"That smooth chief of police," she said. "If he thinks I'm going up there to be third-degreed he's crazy."

"He isn't crazy."

"What do you mean?"

"He doesn't think you're coming up there."

"But he sent word for me to come up."

"But he's busy right at the moment," I said. "If you showed your credentials and explained that it was an emergency matter, I feel quite certain you could get on one of the airplanes and get out of here before the chief got over being busy."

Bertha looked me over carefully and said, "You're the brainy one. Do you suppose that's what that sergeant meant?"

I said, "I wouldn't be too surprised. You went in and purloined evidence, and you suppressed it. That's unprofessional conduct. We could be put on the carpet for that and charges could be made in California, and things would be pretty serious."

"I was only trying to protect a client from a blackmailer," Bertha said.

"Exactly," I told her. "That's why the chief of police let you know that if you stuck around he was going to have to put you on the carpet, but that he was going to be too busy to see you for a few days, and if you aren't here when he gets around to it, I feel quite certain he'll be too busy to relay the charges over to the mainland."

"Fry me for an oyster!" Bertha said. "I believe you're right."

I didn't say anything.

She said, "Donald, I think there's a plane out of here in the morning, and Bertha's going to go see what she can do about reservations. Bertha is awful busy these days and there should be sombody at home in the office. Donald, you're going to have to break the news to that Woodford girl."

"Okay, I will."

Bertha looked at me suspiciously. "Remember, lover," she said, "we're in business for cash. Don't let her pay you off in gratitude and lipstick."

"We've already been paid by Bicknell."

"We received a retainer from Bicknell," Bertha said.

"There's an interesting angle," I told Bertha.

"What's that?"

"Under the laws of most states a man can't inherit from the estate of a person whom he has murdered."

"You mean if Bicknell was the one who murdered Ezra Woodford he couldn't keep the money, not even if he got it under a will?"

"That's right."

"What would happen to it?"

"It would go to his estate."

"You mean his widow?"

"I mean his widow."

Bertha said, "Donald, get the hell over there. Get diplomatic with her. See if we can't line up some sort of a deal to protect her interests, and—good Lord, what are you standing here for? Get over and see the girl. She liked you. Cuddle up to her. Let her smooch around. Let's get going on this thing."

"Well, if you insist," I said.

"Insist!" Bertha screamed at me. "With oil wells, gold mines, income property, she's—and you're willing to go see her if I *insist!* Oh, my good Lord! Mash me for a potato and garnish me with that goddam parsley. Donald, you get over there right now."

I left Bertha and went over to Miriam's place.

Miriam was sitting home with the radio on. She had on a negligee. "Hello, Donald," she said.

"I'm surprised you're home."

"I thought you might come," she told me. "Come on in."

I followed her into the living-room. The lights were turned low. Miriam sat on the davenport.

"Where's Norma?" I asked.

"Out with her alibi."

"Geary?"

"That's right."

"How good an alibi is it, Mira?"

Miriam looked at her wrist watch. "Pretty good by this time," she said. "It'll be an ironclad, copper-riveted, air-tight alibi by midnight. By one o'clock in the morning you couldn't shake it with a ton of dynamite."

"That's swell," I told her and started to sit down in a chair.

She made a little grimace and said, "Over here on the davenport, Donald. It's more cozy and intimate."

I said, "I have some things to tell you first. Business."

"They can wait."

I went over and sat down on the davenport beside her.

I took the two keys from my pocket that I'd picked up at Mitsui's place. "I think one of these," I said, "is the key to this apartment."

"Well," she said, "you *have* got brains." And then, with a little laugh, she twisted a bare arm around my neck and pulled me close to her.

>>> If you've enjoyed this book and would like to discover more great vintage crime and thriller titles, as well as the most exciting crime and thriller authors writing today, visit: >>>

The Murder Room
Where Criminal Minds Meet

themurderroom.com

www.ingramcontent.com/pod-product-compliance
Ingram Content Group UK Ltd.
Pitfield, Milton Keynes, MK11 3LW, UK
UKHW022316280225
455674UK00004B/322

9 781471 908989